PASSPORT TO PERIL

James Leasor

James Leasor Publishing

Copyright © 2020 Estate of James Leasor

Published by
James Leasor Publishing, a division of Woodstock Leasor Limited
81 Dovercourt Road, London SE22 8UW

www.jamesleasor.com

This ebook is copyright material and must not be copied, reproduced, transferred, distributed, leased, licensed or publicly performed or used in any way except as specifically permitted by the publishers, as allowed under the terms and conditions under which it was purchased or as strictly permitted by applicable copyright law. Any unauthorised distribution or use of this text may be a direct infringement of the publisher's rights and those responsible may be liable in law accordingly.

ISBN 9781530814961

First published 1966
This edition published 2020

For Joan

Of the Basilisk . . . Nor is onely the existency of this animal considerable, but many things delivered thereof, particularly its poison and its generation. Concerning the first, according to the doctrine of the Ancients; men still affirm that it killeth at a distance, that it poisoneth by the eye and by priority of vision ...
That this venenation shooteth from the eye ... is not a thing impossible. For eyes' receive offensive impressions from their objects, and may have influences destructive to each other.
For the visible species of things . . . streaming in corporal raies, do carry with them the qualities of the object from whence, they flow ... What is affirmed of this animal, the visible rayes of their eyes carrying forth the subtilest portion of their poison, which (is) received by the eye of man or beast...

SIR THOMAS BROWNE, PSEUDODOXIA EPIDEMICA, 1646

CHAPTER ONE: VILLARS, JANUARY 3 – 4

Among the dark boles of the fir-trees, beneath their wide, outstretched branches, feathered with snow, the man seemed only a darker shadow.

He was short, with a sad, spaniel face, the skin luminous and slack, as though originally intended for a far larger skull - a bigger man altogether. As he waited, he chewed gum, his jaws moving ceaselessly.

This was the third afternoon in succession that he had stood just inside the forest, on the slopes by the Col de Soud, overlooking Villars. Like a dozen others that day, he wore a black anorak and ski. pants, a tight black wool cap. But no-one who had seen him coming up on the lift from Les Chaux would have recognized him now; they had seen a man in a yellow cap, a bright red anorak, a man who wore dark glasses. He had skied to the far side of the trees, then removed his skis and tied them to the inside of two fir-trunks, so that they would not be noticed. Then he had turned his anorak and cap inside out, and, as someone else altogether, had walked slowly through the tongue of forest until he came within sight of the ski run from Bretaye down to Villars.

He stood now, three trees in from the edge, sheltered behind a fir's rough, crinkled bark, watching the ski slopes. Under the open zip of his anorak hung a lightweight pair of Zeiss prismatic glasses; every now and then he scanned the empty run.

Also inside his anorak, heavy against his chest, lay a .22 Schultz and Larsen match pistol. Over its barrel was clipped an American Jasco telescopic sight, almost as big as the gun. Around the mechanism he had carefully wrapped a strip of oiled khaki bandage to stop the action freezing. He also had rubbed a little oil into his face to save his skin from cracking in the cold; he suffered from bad circulation and his toes were already in agony.

The Skaters' Waltz' came up metallically from the ice rink far beneath, thinned by distance and the cold afternoon air. It made him wonder briefly what it would have been like to have been born into a world where one could enjoy the sun and the snow miles from home as a right, and as swiftly he dismissed the thought; it had no part of his present task. Nothing must interfere, with that precious trinity of hand, mind and eye that made him a star marksman, selected for a task as difficult as this.

A white, soft mist began to roll up lazily from the Rhone valley towards him, like steam ascending from some immense engine. Soon it would shroud the village beneath, and mute the music from the rink; the last skiers, who had lingered at the wooden café in Bretaye, must be on their way down, before it grew too dark and dangerous to make the journey.

He gripped his pistol, unbound the bandage, and took aim through the cross-hairs etched on the lens, drawing an imaginary bead on a fir-cone fifty feet away. The sight shouldn't be needed, but then it might be. He was a professional; he had never missed before and he would not miss now. It was the waiting that he hated; the waiting and the cold. He put another piece of gum into his mouth and sucked its peppermint sweetness gratefully.

A girl skier swept towards him, trailing long white plumes of snow from her skis, and then was gone. She wore a blue anorak, yellow pants, a red woollen hat with a long tassel that danced up and down.

He'd watched her go up in the ski-train half an hour before, and had counted the passengers through his glasses. So far as he could calculate, only two were left to return.

One of these was the man he had come to kill.

There had been fewer visitors than usual that afternoon in the café at Bretaye at the top of the mountain; the season was still young, and the weather was poor. The little ski-train waited with its red carriages outside the terrace.

Dr Jason Love sipped his Bacardi rum and lime juice and almost wished he had delayed his own holiday by a month, but the unexpected opportunity of a locum for three weeks had meant escape and relief from a round of influenza calls in his Somerset practice. And, anyway, at his hotel they had assured him that this was the first misty day Villars had known since Christmas. Maybe the weather would improve; it couldn't very well grow worse.

As he lit a Gitane, the train driver blew his air horns to announce the departure of the last train that afternoon. The ski instructors, who had been sitting in one corner, stood up, big men in their red anoraks, and clumped out; never keep the driver waiting. Love liked the discord of those tuned horns; they would make a fine addition to his Cord; he must ask the driver what make they were; probably Marchals.

When the train had gone, his only way of returning to Villars would be on skis. This was the first day of his holiday, and Love relished the prospect of the long run down between the fir forests and the white mountains, towards the lights that twinkled like fallen stars in the mist, growing brighter, more warm with welcome, as he drew nearer.

A chair scraped on the tiled floor. Love glanced up, irritated that the sequence of his thoughts was broken. A tallish, dark-skinned man in his mid-thirties stood beside him.

'Excuse me,' he said in English, 'but are you Dr Jason Love?'

Love nodded. He hoped that this was not the prologue to some demand on his professional services. Why was it that a doctor could so rarely escape from his calling? Why didn't people approach booksellers or carpenters on holiday and ask them for free advice? And how the devil did this character know his name?

'Forgive me asking, but I take it you are a doctor of medicine?'
'You take it correctly.'
'Then I wonder if I could have a word with you?'

'If you wish,' said Love, without enthusiasm. 'A drink?' Love didn't want to be bored by this fellow, and yet he felt he should appear hospitable. At present, he was barely being civil.

'No, thank you. I'm a Moslem, and it's against my religious principles to take alcohol.'

The man sat down and looked at Love for a moment as though not quite sure how to continue.

'My name is Ibrahim Khan,' he went on. 'I'm over here with the Nawab of Shahnagar.'

He paused again. Love threw a reply into the silence.

'Isn't that up in the Himalayas, near Hunza? The place where you live to be a hundred as of right?'

'The same. And since illness is so rare, you will think it odd. Doctor, that I wish to ask you whether I could have your advice on something.'

Here it comes, thought Love, recognizing the familiar cautious approach; he probably thinks he's got a dose, or there's a girl friend two months gone, and he's worried.

'You mean you want medical advice?' he asked him bluntly.

'Yes. But not for me.'

Ibrahim Khan paused again, dredging for the right words. At the next table a waiter started clearing away the empty chocolate cups, the plates that had held the sickly cream cakes.

'Who for, then?

'For the son of my employer.'

'What sort of advice does he want? Why can't he ask me himself?'

'He is only twelve years old,' Ibrahim Khan explained. 'It's rather confidential, Doctor. But if you could spare me ten minutes after dinner?'

'I'd rather spare you five minutes now - which is about all we've left before this café closes.'

Ibrahim Khan glanced around the almost deserted room.

'I can tell you a little now,' he said uneasily, 'but the rest must wait. In brief. Doctor, the Nawab arrived here with his only son, Iqbal, the day before yesterday. We had an appointment for the boy with Dr Grussman.'

'You must have had some pull to see him,' said Love conversationally. 'He's a waiting list six weeks long. He's one of the top eye men in the world.'

'Exactly,' agreed Ibrahim Khan. 'So what I cannot understand, Doctor, is that after our great good fortune in being able to see him, the Nawab suddenly cancels the appointment. He has announced that we return to Pakistan in the morning.'

'Well, if you can't understand why, how can I help you?' asked Love. 'I know nothing about it.'

'Agreed, Doctor,' said Ibrahim Khan patiently. 'But I would be grateful if I could have a word with you about the boy's symptoms. They seem to me to be very strange and possibly beyond the scope of our local doctors back home.'

'Of course you can have a word, but I can't cut in on someone else's case. And anyway, I'm just a local doctor who happens to be here on holiday.'

'I would still value your opinion. Maybe I could introduce you to the Nawab, and you might be able to persuade him to have second thoughts about Dr Grussman?'

Love stubbed out his cigarette. He hated becoming involved at second hand in other people's problems. You either had the case yourself, or you hadn't. This seemed already to be so involved, so fraught with possible complications, and was so clearly not the whole story, that all signals stood at danger. Even so, he should at least spare the man a few minutes of his time; the boy was the one who mattered, who might suffer if he didn't.

'What's wrong with the boy?' Love asked.

'He has lost the sight of his right eye. I don't know whether it's temporary or not. He says he was dazzled by a bright light shining in the hills near his home in Shahnagar.'

'What does his father say?'

'He's very worried, of course. But perhaps we could meet this evening after dinner, Doctor? There is a little more to it than I have told you here.'

'I can imagine,' said Love dryly.
'Let's meet outside the Palace Skihaus at nine, then?'
'If you wish.'

Love's lack of enthusiasm sounded in his voice; he had envisaged a different way of spending his evening. Ibrahim Khan picked up his cap and white-backed mittens, shook hands and went out to the veranda. Love watched him fasten his skis; he'd better be on his way himself.

The train driver blew his horns for the second time; the engine began to whir, the red, almost empty carriages slid away down the mountain. Love paid his bill and walked out on the veranda. It seemed far colder than he remembered when he came in, and his skis were the only pair left in the rack. He carried them out to the flat, trodden snow, clipped them on; then he-flexed his muscles, took a few easy paces. Although he had conscientiously performed his ski exercises every morning for the past few weeks; he was still not as supple as he would have liked. Perhaps he was being a bit ambitious in tackling such a long run on his first day? Perhaps he was, but now there was nothing whatever he could do about it; the train was probably well beyond Bouquetins. Behind him, in the empty room, waiters were already closing the unpainted wooden shutters. Ah, well, once more unto the breach, dear friends.

He bent forward on his skis, gave two jabs with his sticks, and, was off. The man at the edge of the trees had also heard the fanfare of horns that announced the departure of the train. He drew farther behind his sheltering tree, raised his left wrist under the heavy barrel of his pistol to steady it and took aim at a snowdrift beyond the ski-run. Then he slowly turned his sights to the right of the drift, and waited, controlling his breathing.

A skier was entering his field of fire; a tall, dark-skinned man who wore black slacks, who had white fur on the back of his, mittens. He skied easily, switching his weight almost imperceptibly from one ski to the other as he entered the fast turn, his body leaning into the bend.

The marksman moved with him, seeing the brown, concentrated face immensely magnified in the sight, keeping the man's left temple level with the top of his ear in the crosshairs of the sight

Then he squeezed the trigger.

The pistol gave its tiny cough. A tiny round black hole appeared on the flesh and he knew he need not fire again. He lowered the pistol, thrust it back beneath his anorak, zipped up the front.

For a second, the skier kept on his way, and then, as his skis bit into the right-hand corner, he rolled heavily to the left and doubled up and fell, scoring the smooth whiteness in a flurry of dry, powdery snow. He slid on slowly until he lost momentum and came to rest, his skis in the air.

The man beneath the trees turned and began to run back into the centre of the wood. By his calculations, one more skier should be passing at any moment, and it could be fatal for him to be seen. He snapped the string from his skis, slipped them on, and was away, driving his sticks into the crisp snow with a controlled ferocity of haste.

Behind him, among the tall trees, the quietness was broken only by the occasional groan of a bough as a little snow fell from it, or the tiny drop of a fir-cone; it was as though he had never been there at all.

*

Love took the corner wide because he was still not quite sure of himself, and to have an accident alone, and so late might mean spending a night on the mountainside. Thus he was halfway round before he saw the two almost vertical skis, and the hump of a fallen body.

He stopped sharply, with a crunching of hard, icy snow, a few inches from the fallen man.

'Vous etes bien?' he asked.

The skis did not move.

'Are you all right?'

An absurd question; obviously the poor fellow was not. He'd

be lucky if he hadn't broken a leg, the way he'd fallen. Love hoped desperately that he wasn't injured at all. He didn't want to become involved, but as a doctor he could not help himself; he had no possible excuse for non-involvement.

The man's face and neck were buried in the snow. Love scraped enough away to give him air. Then he unclipped his own skis, dug the sticks on end in the soft snow at the side of the piste and bent over the man, searching for his pulse. He could feel no heart-beats. What the hell was the matter? It was only when he was close to him that he could see the tiny round hole in his left temple, the freezing, congealed bead of blood on the black hair. He rolled back the man's right eyelid, brushed the snow off the face, and knelt, looking into the dead, empty eyes of Ibrahim Khan.

What had happened? How could he be shot up here on a ski-run? Who would have a gun? Was it even a bullet-hole? Questions raced through Love's mind in search of answers. He glanced uneasily towards the dark edge of the forest, seconds before a friendly, painted backdrop to a winter holiday, now somehow sinister and menacing in the failing afternoon light.

In the distance he heard a faint brush of approaching skis; someone was coming down fast behind him, an expert, to judge from the speed. Love stood up, cupped both hands to his mouth, and shouted: 'Attention! Achtung! *Stop!*'

A man slithered in a racing finish beside him, and pushed up a pair of mica goggles.

'What's wrong?' he asked in English.

Love recognized the waiter who had been clearing the next table in the cafe.

'There's been an accident. I'm a doctor. How can we get him down quickly?'

Alarm touched the man's face.

'The train's gone,' he said uncertainly, looking from Love to Ibrahim Khan and back to Love again. There's a telephone lower down, but it should have passed there, too. I'll ski on down and fetch the blood wagon. Is he very badly hurt?'

'Very,' said Love.

'You stay here, Doctor. I'll be back.'

Love nodded. He stood; watching him whisk away into the gathering mist.

He had not told him that Ibrahim Khan was dead, because then he'd think there was no need for haste. Love lit a Gitane while he waited. The mist thickened and the darkness seemed to rise from the valley,' seeping up to the peaks, bringing a chill that was all its own. It was fifteen minutes before he heard the welcome sound of returning voices speaking French. Three men, an official rescue team, their distinctive orange anoraks just visible in the gloom, were pulling a sledge painted bright red; the blood wagon. The waiter hovered in the background, anxious to see what was 'happening, grateful for any experience outside the ordinary run of fetching meals.

'You are a doctor?' one of the men asked Love.

'I am.'

'Can we move him without morphia then Doctor?'

'Yes. You can move him. He's dead.'

'Dead?'

The man's voice sharpened with surprise. 'We thought he was injured.'

He was broad-shouldered, heavy breathing; probably a farmer in the summer, Love thought inconsequentially. Death to him must seem a relatively remote contingency; to a doctor, it was something he dealt with every day, the final victor who always won the last battle.

'What happened? Did he break his neck Doctor?'

'No. He was shot.'

'Shot? You must have made a mistake, Doctor,' he said sharply. 'There's no one up here with a gun.'

'Maybe not now, but there was then. Look at the bullet-hole.'

'Oh, my God! What a terrible thing.'

Together they lifted Ibrahim Khan's stiffening body on to the sledge, and strapped it down firmly, under wide webbing bands, his skis by his side. One man slithered a canvas cover over the sledge, tied it with a nylon rope. Then, with two men pulling in front, and the third behind holding a rope to act as a brake, they were off. The waiter stayed behind with Love:

'I expect the police will be involved,' he said conversationally, two strangers brought together by a shared experience, another man's dying, 'but naturally they'll want to keep it all as quiet as possible.'

'Naturally,' agreed Love. It would be bad for the tourist trade; death was always best unadvertised unless you happened to be an undertaker.

'The season hasn't been all that good as it is,' said the waiter gloomily. 'You should see the tronc. We only wanted this.'

They skied down together. The man knew the slopes perfectly, even in the dusk. Without him, Love would have suffered a dozen falls in unseen drifts; with him, he kept upright all the way.

'Where will they take the body?' he asked.

'There's a room at the station we use when there's an accident and the ambulance is delayed.'

They unclipped their skis, propped them against the wall. Love stamped his feet to shake the snow from his heavy boots, and followed the waiter into what was usually a second-class waiting-room. Dark-stained benches were bolted to the wooden floor on either side of the table; travellers could either stand at the table or sit on the benches away from it. Someone had lit a stove, but the air still felt chill and damp; there was a shortage of second-class passengers in a first-class world. Death was more democratic.

On a white rubber sheet spread over the table, the body of Ibrahim Khan still wore anorak, trousers and boots. A man in a khaki anorak, possibly a policeman, was going through his pockets. He had already made a little pile on the sheet: his watch, his wallet, a diary, a gold ring, a Parker 61 fountain-pen, a small pile of francs.

A doctor, in a white coat unzipped Ibrahim Khan's anorak, pulled off his sweater, his shirt: A third man, who might almost have been a tourist but for his cold, hard policeman's eyes, sharp as silver fish, approached Love.

'I understand you found the body. Doctor?' he began in English.

Love nodded.

'Yes. I was skiing down from Bretaye some way behind him.'

'You knew this man?'

'No, I didn't know him.'

'But you were speaking to him at the restaurant at Bretaye?' The waiter had already been communicative.

'That is so.'

'So you must have known him.'

'What is this?' asked Love, 'Cross-examination?'

'Not so,' Doctor. 'We're simply trying to establish how he died.'

'He spoke to me in the cafe because he had seen my name in the hotel register. I'd never, seen him before.'

'You saw nobody else up on the slopes with a gun or air pistol?'

'No one at all.'

The doctor rolled up Ibrahim Khan's eyelids, examined his teeth as though he expected to find a clue in his mouth. Then he began to remove his boots. There was no dignity remaining in death. It was the ultimate, infinite democracy, possibly the only one. The words of Love's favourite author, the seventeenth-century Norwich physician. Sir Thomas Browne, came suddenly, ironically, to mind: 'We all labour against our own cure, for death is the cure for all diseases.' But to the sufferers almost any disease was better than the final remedy.

'I understand that this man was a secretary to an Eastern prince, or someone of that kind?' said the detective.

'Yes,' agreed the waiter. 'The Nawab of Shahnagar.'

'We've sent a message to the hotel,' said the man in the khaki anorak. 'He should be on his way here now.'

'You're a doctor of medicine, of course?' the detective asked Love.

'I am.'

'He was quite dead when you saw him?'

'He was.'

'Extraordinary thing,' remarked the Swiss doctor conversationally to Love, one professional to another, speaking over the heads of laymen. 'We're used to broken arms, legs, smashed pelvises, fractured skulls, heart attacks. But we've never had a man shot here on holiday. Got to be a first time, I suppose.'

'I suppose so. How do you think it happened?'

The doctor shrugged; the matter was out of his reach. His problems lay with the living; the dead had solved all theirs.

'Maybe some kid had an air pistol, and was fooling around. It looks like a .22 bullet, which isn't usually chosen for a lethal purpose. The police will check the hotels to see if anyone has been seen with any kind of firearm, of course. Occasionally we do get visitors who carry arms. South Americans, Egyptians, sheikhs. People like that. But it's not usual.'

The detective turned to Love again.

'If we need a statement, Doctor —' he began tentatively.

'Certainly. Any time. I'm at the Palace.'

The detective opened the door for him. Outside the station two sledges waited, their drivers talking together in cloaks and Tyrolean hats, like actors in an. Edwardian musical. Their horses, humped under grey, monogrammed rugs, ate from nosebags, blowing and snorting in the steamy air. Love was reminded of funeral horses; only the purple plumes were missing.

Behind them, a figure turned away. Love only noticed him because he moved. He had been standing near one of the waiting-room windows, and a wedge of light from between the curtains lit up his face briefly. The skin was pallid, the eyes dull and tired; Love noted professionally that he had suffered some wound on his right cheek. It must have taken at least twenty stitches, and whoever had sewn him up had not been too expert.

As the man turned away, he bumped into one of the sledge drivers.

'Excusez moi, s'il vous plaît,' he lisped apologetically, and then was gone.

Love walked up to the Palace, his skis over his shoulder. A dark-skinned, bearded man, tall, his head down in case he slipped on the icy steps, came hurrying through the dusk towards the waiting-room. Love guessed he must be the Nawab. Ah well, there'd be an opening for a new secretary. Death for one man means opportunity for another; one wheel stops and another begins to turn.

Love collected his key from the desk, and once inside his room, removed his heavy boots, slipped the loops at the feet of his trousers from under his heels, and lay back on his bed, hands clasped under his head, as he always did when he had time to pass, when he hoped something interesting might happen. He lit a Gitane. As he blew out the match, the telephone rang by his bed. He picked it up; a girl was speaking on the line.

'Is that Dr Love?' she asked.

'Who wants him?'

'You don't know me,' the girl went on, 'but I'm with the Nawab of Shahnagar. The governess to his son, Iqbal. I have just heard of the accident to Mr Khan. I wonder if I could come and see you?'

'Certainly. Come now.'

He swung his legs off the bed, smoothed down the coverlet, put on a pair of rubber-soled suede shoes, and waited for her to arrive. She was dark-haired, in a deep blue sweater, and honey-coloured *apres-ski* slacks, her mouth a splash of colour in a pale, shocked face. She was not really pretty, but vivacious, cheerful, extrovert; a girl who would laugh easily, but possibly not a virgin. But then what girl over seventeen was nowadays? His ideals were out-of-date.

'Would you like a drink?' he asked her.

'No, thank you. I'd better introduce myself. I'm Mercedes Ryan.'

'Mercedes? Like the car?'

'Yes. Everyone says that. But tell me about Ibrahim, Doctor. I can't believe he's dead. I knew him so well.'

Love wondered how well. He could imagine Ibrahim's dark muscular body against her fair one, thigh on thigh, her firm breasts flattened against his broad chest. It was not hard to visualize, yet somehow the thought saddened him, unreasonably and irrationally. He must be growing old. Why else should the imagined love of others make him feel like this?

He poured himself a Bacardi rum, added lime juice, four cubes of ice, drank to her, to all pretty girls everywhere.

'What was his job, exactly?' he asked.

'Secretary plus. Someone who'd see people the Nawab couldn't be bothered with. Who'd stand in for him at public functions, and so on.'

She paused. Her long silver-lacquered fingernails drummed uneasily on the glass top of the dressing-table. Had she also come to ask a favour?

'Tell me,' Mercedes went on hesitantly, 'were you with him when he died?'

'Just after.'

'I heard he was shot?'

Love shrugged, offered her a Gitane, lit it for her.

'You didn't see anyone near him who could have shot him, though?' she went on. 'Anyone fooling about with a gun?'

'No one at all,' said Love.

'Do you think Ibrahim suffered any pain?'

'As a doctor, I'd say he died instantly, without feeling a thing.'

'That's something,' she said softly. 'You knew him, Doctor?'

'No, but he'd seen my name in the register.'

How many more times would he have to give this explanation?

'Well.'

She paused, obviously wanting to stay, but yet not knowing how to prolong the interview. 'I'd better be going, I suppose.'

'There's no hurry,' said Love; 'Beautiful women don't call on me every day.'

The way he spoke, he made it sound as though it only happened every other day. Under the soft stuff of her sweater her breasts were pointed and round; her pants clung to her legs like a second, darker skin. He suddenly found himself wondering about her. What strange unknown quality was it that one woman possessed so that he could want her without even knowing her, while he could examine a dozen others naked in his surgery and feel no more than a faint revulsion at so much pale flesh, such globular breasts?

'Tell me about Iqbal,' he said, putting these thoughts to the back of his mind and hoping they'd stay there.

'He's the Nawab's only child. Twelve last month, bright, intelligent. I think he's going to Sandhurst as soon as he's old enough. If we can get him through the entrance exam, that is.'

'I'm sure you will. I heard he'd got something the matter with his sight.'

'Who told you that?' She looked at him sharply.

'Does it matter?'

'No, I suppose not. It's simply that the Nawab doesn't like this to be generally known.'

'Why not? What's actually wrong with the boy?'

'I can't say, Doctor. I'm sorry.'

'I see. Well...'

The spark between them both died, but it had been there, it could be there again; and next time it could take flame.

He moved towards the door. They shook hands. Love listened to her footsteps die away up the corridor, and then turned the key on the inside of the door. He sat down on the bed, thought for a moment, and then he picked up the telephone, rang down to the bar for another bottle of Bacardi and half a dozen fresh limes.

Love replaced the receiver and stood looking out of the window that framed the indigo sky. Under the huge, arched flood lamps of the skating-rink a handful of couples twirled and spun to music he could not hear. They seemed oddly remote, impersonal, like figures on a frieze. Behind them, the town blazed with lights, each wearing a golden halo of mist; there would be more snow tomorrow.

Love awoke late next morning to find the Austrian maid pulling back the curtains and opening the shutters. The snowy peaks lay framed and white within the window like some panorama from the lid of a chocolate box. Already, in the streets of Villars outside, the early-morning coaches were arriving full of skiers. The air tinkled with laughter and young voices.

Love stretched under the blankets, luxuriating in the fact that he had no calls to make, no patients to see, no morning surgery to take. But in the background of his mind a cloud lingered. Then he remembered Ibrahim Khan, and some of the brightness went out of the day. He telephoned down for coffee, for hot rolls and honey, took a shower, shaved, and dressed in his ski clothes. By then it was ten, and too late to join any ski class. He'd lose no sleep over that, for after his doubts at the downhill run on the previous afternoon he'd almost decided to spend a day watching the others before he began to ski seriously himself. Maybe he was growing old - or growing up. Time was when he'd have been the first man on the ski-lift. Time was when he would not have let Mercedes get away so easily. Ah, well. He walked downstairs to the hall.

'We have some letters for you, Doctor,' the receptionist told him at the desk.

He turned to a pigeon-hole and pulled out a collection of large, buff envelopes. Love knew from their appearance that they contained circulars from pharmaceutical manufacturers and drug houses, which his housekeeper had diligently forwarded on to him. And then he saw one more interesting, with an American stamp; the familiar brown envelope, bearing the oval crest of the Auburn-Cord-Duesenberg Car Club, that contained its monthly newsletter.

'Anything for me?'

Love turned at the voice. The man he had seen hurrying down the steps to the station waiting-room on the previous evening was standing next but one to him. The receptionist bowed.

'Nothing, Your Highness,' he intoned, as though the words were a religious response; and, so far as he was concerned, they were. He worshipped money.

The Nawab turned away from the counter.

'Excuse me,' he said to Love, and prepared to pass him. Then their eyes met, and he paused. For both men, it was like looking through a camera viewfinder to see a misty impersonal scene suddenly shoot into sharp focus.

'My God,' Love said in surprise, finding his voice first. 'It *can't* be, and yet it is! Old Shagger himself.'

The Nawab grinned delightedly as he held out his hand.

'And you must be Jason Love as ever is - you old golden fleecing bastard!'

'None other,' replied Love, equally pleased to see him.

They pushed through the crowd of guests waiting to collect letters, to buy stamps, who regarded this reunion with disfavour. Really, the sort of people one met in these hotels these days!

'It must be twenty years at the very least since I last saw you,' said the Nawab, as they crossed the tessellated floor of the lounge. 'Remember Bawli?'

'I do indeed,' said Love.'

But he hadn't until then. Now, like a key turning in a forgotten lock, it instantly opened the door on a cohort of hidden memories. A cluster of bamboo bashas in a clearing ringed in by scrubby hills; weapon pits dug in the sand, crawling with earwigs; the taste of tea flavoured with rancid margarine; soya links, hard biscuits and mepacrine tablets. The immense blue emptiness of the Burma sky at stand-to, one hour before dawn. The sadness of roll-call after a battle.

Love had been a lieutenant then in the Lincolns, and this man had been in the Gunners with a battery of 25-pounders. He had been Lieutenant Jem Shahgar Ali then. The nickname had been partly due to his name, partly to his beard that seemed shaggier in retrospect than it looked now.

'What brings you here now, Shagger?' Love asked. 'I thought

you'd have enough snow back in the Himalayas.'

'You think correctly. I'm over here with my son, Iqbal.'

'Oh, so you must now be the Nawab of Shahnagar. I wasn't sure.'

'You're certainly with it today, Jason. Keen. Razor sharp. Also, right. I inherited the title three years ago. Hell, then you must be the Dr Love who was up at Bretaye with poor Ibrahim Khan. I didn't even know you'd qualified.'

'Some of my patients say the same thing when they don't like my treatment.'

'I'm damn glad I ran into you,' said the Nawab, 'for I was going to ring this Dr Love. You've saved me the trouble. I wanted to hear what had happened. I believe you were also the first to find him after he was shot?'

They sat down in two arm-chairs in the lounge near a wide window overlooking the town. A waiter hovered near, a silent ghost in crepe-soled shoes.

'Two coffees,' the Nawab told him, then turned to Love. 'Now, about Ibrahim?'

'He asked if I was a doctor of medicine. I said I was. He wanted to see me last night.'

'Was he ill then?'

'No, Shagger. It was about your son. He wanted my advice about some trouble your boy was having with his eyes.'

'And you said?'

The Nawab's face was as empty of expression as the snow slopes outside.

'Frankly, Shagger, I wasn't very keen. I can't butt into another doctor's case, but he was persistent. And I agreed to meet him. You know what happened then.'

'Quite. Did he say what was wrong with Iqbal's eyes?'

'Not really. Only that he had been dazzled by some light and that you'd decided against seeing Dr Gussman over here.'

'Oh, yes. Grussman.' The Nawab repeated the name as though he had not heard it before. The waiter returned with a silver tray. The Nawab said nothing until the man had left the room.

He poured out two black coffees.

'What kind of medicine do you specialize in?' he asked Love.

'None,' said Love. 'I'm a country GP. A couple of thousand patients around Bishop's Combe in Somerset. I've got an old vicarage down there which I converted, with about ten acres of ground, and also my Cord.'

The Nawab smiled.

'Oh, yes, I remember now; your Cord. Have you brought it over here with you?'

'Surely. In the hotel garage. Want to see it?'

'Well, some time. I'm not a motor enthusiast, though. Shooting's my thing. But I expect you'd be surprised to hear I've got a Cord myself. In Shahnagar.'

'You?' repeated Love, incredulously.

'Yes. It belonged to my father. He was a great car enthusiast, like you. Had the first Rolls, apart from the Governor's, to be imported into Bombay, all brass headlamps and Stauffer grease caps that had to be filled every day or every week, I forget which. When the Cord 812 was announced in the mid-thirties, he had to have one. It was sent up to Shahnagar, got as far as Gilgit under its own steam, and then was dismantled and the pieces carried on the heads of coolies all the rest of the way.

'When he finally got it up to Shahnagar, he couldn't drive it, for the roads then were only mule tracks - and not much better now. But he had his pleasure simply from owning it, like other people find pleasure in antiques and pictures and so on.

'The Cord stayed in a room he had specially built for it. I still have the old fellow my father appointed as Keeper of the Cord. His job was to clean it and run the engine for so long every day. He still does, too.'

'Well, I'm damned,' said Love. 'This would make an item for the ACD Club newsletter.'

'Why don't you come and see it?' suggested the Nawab.

'Hell,' said Love. 'It's about five thousand miles, isn't it?'

'Distance is relative.'

'Maybe, but expense isn't.'

'Look, Jason,' said the Nawab, smiling, 'I don't want to talk about money, but I'm not pushed for the odd bob. Why don't you come and be my guest at Shahnagar? I'll pay the fare gladly. And apart from the car, I'd like you to come to see my son.'

'I thought he was here with you?'

'He left this morning for Geneva with his governess, Miss Ryan. They're catching the afternoon plane to Karachi. They'll be home tomorrow night.'

So Mercedes had already gone; Love felt a sudden, sharp stab of desolation.

'But you must have excellent doctors in 'Pindi and Karachi and probably in Gilgit, too,' he said. 'Anyhow, the expense would be fantastic. I'm used to British Health Service charges where two bob was considered too much for a patient to pay for a bottle of medicine.'

'To hell with that rubbish,' said the Nawab. 'I want you to see the boy.'

'I'm sorry, Shagger. It's very good of you, but I'm on holiday here. I'm booked in for another two weeks. I'm sure you can get far better advice, and much nearer home, at less cost. Anyhow, why choose me when you've turned down Dr Grussman who's about eighty-five times better at this sort of job than I am?'

'Listen, Jason,' said the Nawab, his face suddenly serious. 'There's another reason why I want you to come to Shahnagar. It's because I can trust you. Because you don't know the place or the people in it, I can tell you something I can't tell anyone else. I had to drop Grussman. I was ordered. I'm being blackmailed.'

'Blackmailed?'

Against the rich background of the lounge, the heavily draped curtains, the distant music from a string orchestra playing, for morning coffee, the word jarred like a flat note at the Proms.

The Nawab glanced round the room. A man had come in and was sitting three tables away, his back to them, reading the *Daily Express*.

'How?' asked Love curiously. 'You've not been hanging round the public lavatory in Piccadilly Circus, surely? It's hardly safe to pee anywhere these days.'

'I wish it were as simple. But it's not. I'm being touched for £2,000,000.'

'What have you been doing that can be worth £2,000,000?'

'Nothing. Yet it seems as though I'll have to pay. Look. To be as brief as possible, I was in New York six weeks ago when a stranger telephoned me. He said he wanted £2,000,000 paid over to some charity known as The International Committee for the Preservation of Big Game. I told him to go to hell.

'He said that if I didn't pay, my son would get injured. I put the phone down on him. I'm used to calls from cranks. Every rich man is. But I wasn't prepared for what happened next.

'I came on to London, on my way home, and he got through to me at the Connaught. He repeated his request and this time he was a bit more specific in his threat. If I didn't pay, Iqbal would be injured within a few days. I tried to hold him on the line while Ibrahim contacted the police, but he rang off.

'I cabled my staff in Shahnagar to keep Iqbal under constant watch, without giving them any specific reason, of course, and when I returned, all seemed as it had always been - peaceful.

'Then, ten days ago, I was out preparing for a shoot - the President of Pakistan is coming for a few days' hunting - and Iqbal walked out to meet me. On the way he says a bright light suddenly shone in the hills. It dazzled him - rather like the light St Paul saw on the road to Damascus in the Bible. The poor boy was in great pain and the local doctor didn't seem able to help him much.

'That night the phone rang. The man who'd rung before - I always recognize his voice, for he's some slurring in his speech - was on the line. He said that now I would see he meant business. I had to pay £500,000 to this account within a week, or the boy would be blinded permanently in that eye.'

'This is bloody ridiculous,' said Love. 'Didn't you go to the police or something?'

'No. He said that if I confided in anyone they would blind Iqbal permanently in both eyes. At present, there is some hope that he will regain the sight of his eye. They would know if I told anyone - so they said. I didn't feel I could take the risk.'

'But you've told me.'

'You're different. We were together in the old days. Yet you're a stranger. I can trust you, but I don't know who else I can trust of those around me. Someone must be feeding them information.'

'I'd never pay blackmail,' said Love. 'It's another name for being bled to death. They never give up.'

The Nawab shrugged.

'No doubt you're right. I wouldn't argue with the principle. But how easy it is for you to sit here in this hotel and hold forth in this way. You live in a tight little country, Jason, with law and order at the end of a telephone. Security. Safety.

'Put yourself in my place. Shahnagar is up in the back of nowhere, right bang on the roof of the world. I've got Russia on one frontier, and China on another. If either of them invaded Shahnagar, no-one else would do a damn thing. They didn't do much in Tibet or Hungary, now, did they?'

Love nodded uneasily. 'But why should they invade you?'

'I hope they won't. I only say that to stop you having any quixotic ideas that anyone will do anything positive to help me. They might talk and tut-tut, but no-one would get off his arse to help if it meant becoming involved. Why should they? Shahnagar's a long way off. No influence. No oil. Nothing to make us worth defending. So if my boy *is* blinded it would only rate a paragraph in Hickey or some sob-stuff, somewhere about money not being able to buy everything.

'I'd like you there, Jason, for a week or two. You can treat the boy. And maybe together we could sort out these big-game bastards. Apart from everything else, it's so damned silly imagining me - the best shot in West Pakistan - subscribing to such an aim.'

'I agree, but let's not get carried away on the wings of words. If I came out, what could I *do?*'

'How do either of us know until you're there? I'm putting all my cards on the deck, Doctor. I'm desperately worried about my son's sight. I don't know anyone I can turn to. And if you won't come, well, I guess I'll have to pay - and go on paying.'

'It's good of you to ask me,' said Love slowly. 'But I think you'll have to include me out. Although, if I can give you any medical advice now about your boy...'

He looked away as he spoke, notable to bear the pain in the Nawab's eyes. But what else could he do? He remembered too clearly the last time he' had been persuaded to help someone against his will, against his own plans. (For an account of Dr Love's adventures then, see *Passport to Oblivion.*) He had been on the eve of leaving for a holiday in France, his bags already packed, when Colonel Douglas MacGillivray, the deputy head of M.I.6, Britain's overseas Intelligence organization, had quite unexpectedly called to see him at his house in Bishop's Combe.

They had met before briefly in Chittagong in 1943 barely twenty years before. Love had been a newly commissioned second lieutenant, conducting a draft of men from the reinforcement camp in Comilla to the Arakan in Burma. The commandant of the transit camp in Chittagong, where they were spending a few nights on their way, had sent for him unexpectedly. In his office Love had been surprised to see a civilian in a crumpled tropical suit - Colonel MacGillivray.

Because Love was passing through and would be miles away on the following morning, where he would not be able to talk about this request, MacGillivray wanted him to search one of the buildings in the compound for a concealed radio. They had learned that someone was transmitting information about the indifferent morale of the British and Indian troops to a listening post that relayed the news back to a radio transmitter controlled by the Japanese-sponsored Indian National Army.

It had been a simple enough task, and Love had almost forgotten about it; almost, but not quite. MacGillivray had remembered; he was trained to remember. And when the defection of George Blake had laid bare virtually the entire framework of the British Intelligence services in the Middle East, he had gone through the lists of others who had carried out assignments for him before Blake was involved. He needed to find one man who could fly to Teheran for three days to discover why an apparently unblown agent, due for retirement, had failed to send a routine message. But to find someone able and ready and fit to go had not been easy. Of the men with whom he had worked during the war and just after, some had died, others had been unwilling, others impossible; and then he had turned up the name of Jason Love.

A carefully slanted appeal to Love's patriotism, to his love of cars (a rare Cord Le Baron had been discovered in Teheran), to his pocket, with an offer of a free holiday for his pains, and MacGillivray had persuaded him to fly to Persia instead of France. He was to go as a delegate to an International Medical Conference; no risk, no strain at all. And then everything had gone wrong; complication grew on complication like skins on an onion. The routine task had unexpectedly become thick with dangers, confusions, near disasters.

Love remembered the fearful, almost fatal, consequences without enthusiasm. That was what came from dabbling in problems out of his depth, beyond his experience. He had only become involved because he had wanted to help. If the same reason applied now, why should the results be any different? The only answer was to decline with thanks, to pass by on the other side, to offer sympathy but nothing more.

His last experience had begun in the heat of Teheran and ended in the frozen snows of the North-West Territories in Canada. Looking out now through the double windows at the little red ski-trains, at the cars packed like brightly coloured beads along the edge of the road, at the infinity of snow behind them, Love remembered that cold. Despite the warmth of the room, he shivered. He turned back to the Nawab.

'I'm sorry, Shagger,' he said simply. 'But, well, count me out.'

'As you wish,' said the Nawab, his voice tired and flat, the voice of loneliness, of rejection. 'Well, Doctor, I'm leaving for home this evening. It's been good meeting you, even so briefly. Perhaps it won't take another twenty odd years before we meet again?'

'I hope not,' said Love, but why should, he mean it? He felt embarrassed; worse, a coward. There was no reason why he should become involved, no reason at all, he told himself. But if he didn't help his friend, who would? What was a friend for if he could not ask and receive; he knew now how Peter must have felt when the cock crowed for the third time.

He went up to his room, put on his anorak and went out into Villars. The air felt cold, but not nearly so cold as it had been in Canada; he wondered whether it would be as cold in the Himalayas.

He walked through the little town, past a garage and a cluster of shops, until there was nothing but rutted snow on either side of the road, and the occasional hoot of a car as it swished past him, skis strapped on the roof, the people inside laughing. There was a lot of laughter; perhaps they had much to be happy about; he hoped so. The thought led back to the lonely man in the hotel lounge.

There was absolutely no reason at all, of course, why he should go. None. He was due for a holiday; it had all been arranged, the locum engaged, the room booked. Why had this man come so inconsiderately out of the past to ask his help on a matter with which he could not possibly assist him?

But then another side answered this argument. Why *couldn't* he help him? If no-one else could, surely this was a challenge to him, a challenge he could not ignore and live with himself in peace? It took him half an hour and another mile on up the road before he had made up his mind. Then he turned back towards the hotel, walked back into the lounge. The Nawab was sitting where he had left him, leaning back in his chair, eyes closed, his hands crossed on his lap. Love sat down beside him.

'Shagger,' he said gently.

The Nawab sat up suddenly, as though disturbed in sleep.

'Oh, it's you.'

'I've been thinking,' said Love. 'About your set-up in Shahnagar. I don't know what good I can do, probably no good at all. But at least I might be able to help your son if you can't get anyone else. You must be pretty well scraping the barrel to ask me. But I'll come.'

'Marvellous,' said the Nawab. His face creased into a grin. 'I thought you might. I'm bloody glad you are.'

'I hope you will be when I'm finished, because I'm damn sure I can't do anything to help the blackmail business. But look, I haven't even a thermometer with me here, so first I've got to cancel my room and go back to London to collect some gear.'

'Right,' said the Nawab. 'Now what about expenses? What do Royal doctors get when they fly abroad?'

'That's out of my parish altogether. But I read somewhere that they claimed a pound a mile.'

'Well, if you've read that, that's good enough for me. Why should Dr Love travel for less? I'll give you a cheque for £500 now, which will cover your fare. We can work out the rest when you arrive. Book to 'Pindi then fly on to Gilgit, and from there hire a jeep to Shahnagar.'

'Will I stay with you up there?' asked Love.

'Of course. We have no hotels, and I think it might be best if you stayed at the guest house I run for visitors, rather than the Palace. It doesn't make your visit seem so personal then. And, of course, if anyone asks why you are there, you've come as a tourist.'

'Of course,' echoed Love.

He felt already that the web of deception was gathering, round him as on his previous expedition for MacGillivray. He was becoming involved in something more complicated than he imagined; but then was anything as simple as it seemed? Was anything simple and uncomplicated left in all the world

As they walked through the lounge, the man in the corner lowered his newspaper and pulled out his handkerchief to blow his nose. But even with the lower part of his face concealed beneath the square of blue silk, Love recognized him.

He was the man he had seen on the previous evening, outside the station waiting-room.

For some time after they had gone, the man sat on, still holding his newspaper in front of him, but not reading a word. He knew well enough what he had to do, but earlier and forgotten experiences had suddenly and inexplicably begun to cloud his mind.

First, there had been that record in the Alp Fleurie, where he had gone on the previous evening for a cognac and a coffee, and then for more cognac and coffee, and finally no coffee at all.

'South of-the Border.' He could hum the tune quite well; but somehow it meant more to him than just another song, and he could find no reason why it should. It was like an echo of childhood, one of the secrets of a summer long ago. Or perhaps someone else had told him about that summer? Perhaps it was in a film he had seen, a book he had read? He remembered a boy and a girl on a beach where sunshades were spread like huge flowers, and green wooden breakwaters pushed long fingers into the sea. Two older people (perhaps a mother and a father, perhaps not) sat in striped canvas deck-chairs with newspapers over their faces against the sunshine. How hot it had been then; when all since then seemed cold and pinched and frozen. He was sure he had heard the tune on a portable wireless, the size of a suitcase, which was how they built portables in those days. Odd how he could remember that so clearly - even the cheap imitation crocodile skin that covered it. Otherwise the picture was misty, as though he were looking at it all from a great distance, through a diminishing lens, the wrong end of a spyglass.

He shifted in his seat and lowered his paper; a waiter asked him whether he would like a drink. He ordered a cognac and gulped it down in a single swallow. The raw spirit hurt his throat and then ran like fire through his veins. 'South of the Border'; but what border, what forgotten frontier? The past was losing the struggle for recognition in his mind, but still fought on against the shadowy barriers of forgetfulness.

There had been something else that had also rung a faint, half-forgotten bell in the long aisles of memory: that little Ford Eight, possibly thirty years old, with a bird mascot on the bonnet, he had seen parked outside the station. Some students had driven it from England, so he had been told; but he remembered driving in one like that himself years ago, but where, or when?

Only that morning he had held his face under the cold tap in his bedroom to try to force the memories to the front of his mind. But he could not; .at least, not quite. All he could remember clearly were his instructions, his new name on the new passport, when he had to call, what he had to say should the wrong person answer the telephone, and nothing else, nothing else at all.

He finished his drink, pushed a note under the ash-tray and stood up. He glanced at his watch; he had only four minutes left before he had to make the next call. He walked out to the telephone booth in the hall, repeating the number to himself. Now why should he remember the telephone number of a dentist in Lucerne, a man he had never met, when he could remember so very little about himself? He was still brooding on this conundrum when the call came through.

As Love and the Nawab walked up the red-carpeted stairs to the Nawab's suite, talking together two other men were also talking 80 odd miles away over the snow and the mountains and the ski-lifts.

They were in a stuffy overheated room on the second floor of an. office block near the Old Town Hall in Lucerne. Beneath them, shoppers and cars coagulated the shining streets; rain threw silver spears on the pavements.

The office block was old arid unfashionable and due to be demolished. The room was old, too, sparsely furnished with leather arm-chairs, a table littered with magazines, thumbed and earmarked, the corners of their covers rolled back. An electric fire glowed redly under the brown-veined marble of the dusty mantelpiece.

On the edge of a dingy saddle-back chair, too near the fire for comfort, sat a heavy, thick-set man with the pallid skin and high cheekbones of a Slav. Facing him, his back to the table, stood another younger man wearing the high-buttoned white coat of a dentist.

In his right hand he held a small nickel rod with a tiny mouth mirror on the end. He kept twirling it, and the round mirror, the size of a sixpence, caught the light from the centre bulb in the ceiling, and scattered it across the walls, like Tinkerbell. The dentist was talking, not in the soothing tones he used to his patients, but as a man accustomed to command.

'Are you certain you were unobserved?' he asked in German. He had a slightly oriental appearance, with the edges of his eyes turned up, a hairless, sallow face. Under the hard light his forehead shone slightly. He was excitable beneath the outward calm; the strain of such interviews always made him irritable.

He was not too happy about his own position; the trouble with these Swiss; so heavy and lard-faced, so bound up with their own ludicrous affairs, was that one never knew whether they suspected anyone or anything. They never gave anything away, not even a hint. He'd been in practice there for nearly ten months, and if this fool had done his job well he could be out before the week-end. That thought alone made his heart leap; Bangkok would be a delight after all this snow and cold and tinsel enjoyment.

'No-one saw me,' replied the other man, cutting into his thoughts.

'This Nawab might have had some other coloured people with him,' pointed out the dentist. 'You might have shot the wrong man.'

This had happened once before in Saigon; he still remembered the shame and humiliation of this unthinkable error. It was one of the reasons why he had been posted so far from base, to redeem himself in an alien, friendless climate.

'No, sir. I'd memorized the photographs you provided of my

target. I also had binoculars. There was no mistake. None at all.'

'Good.'

The dentist sounded relieved; odd, how these professional assassins invariably referred to their victim as their target. Perhaps it didn't sound so much like murder that way. It was the jargon of their calling, of course, just as he never spoke of a tooth with a hole in it, but always of a cavity.

'You've already been paid half the sum agreed,' he said; 'Here's the other half.'

He pulled a thick brown envelope out of his coat pocket and handed it to the man in the chair, who put it away in an inner pocket without opening it.

'I need hardly remind you, of course, not to say anything about what has taken place.'

The dentist smiled at his own absurd request. The other man laughed uneasily, taking it as a joke, moving restlessly on the hard cushions, anxious to be away. He didn't like talk; it was a maze where he could lose himself too easily.

The dentist turned towards a glass-fronted cabinet and, opening one of the doors, took out a camera in a soft pigskin case.

'This is by way of a bonus,' he said gently, handing it to him. 'You may never be in Switzerland again. And as they sell the best cameras in the world here, we thought that you might like this souvenir. On top of your fee, of course.'

The other man's lined face flushed with sudden pleasure and surprise; it had been a long time since anyone had given him a gift. He felt absurdly touched; the icicles around his heart began to thaw. Loyalty to the cause swelled so much that it became an almost physical pain.

'Thank you, sir,' he said, dredging for adequate words to clothe the warmth of his thoughts. 'Thank you.'

He opened the zip and the huge, blue-clouded lens looked up at him like an enormous eye. He ran his thick, stubby fingers with their bitten hails over the viewfinder, the automatic focusing device, the little anodized buttons and knobs and triggers.

'Don't use it here,' said the dentist, holding up one hand in mock warning. 'The last thing I want is for you to photograph *me* before you go!'

Again the man laughed dutifully. The dentist glanced at the gold Rolex on his wrist.

'Now I must get back. I've left a patient in the chair. Please go out this way and not through the surgery. Use this in case anyone sees you.'

He handed him a square of lint two feet across. The man stood up and held it up to his face as though he had just had a tooth drawn; in that position and with his hat pulled down over his eyes, virtually all his face was covered. He went down the uncarpeted stairs, and out into the cold street.

He was booked on the afternoon express to Zurich. By midnight he would be over the border to Milan, and then on to Trieste and there he would be met; the organization was good; no, perfect. Even unexpected details had been covered, such as issuing him with a .22 match pistol instead of the more usual heavier gun, so that if the pistol were found, it would all point to some foolish prank that had misfired. His gloves and cap and anorak all bore different names, taken at random from hotel registers in Villars and St Moritz; invaluable false clues if he should lose any of them, for while these people were being traced and their denials that they owned these clothes receiving little sympathy, he would be over the frontier.

But of course, as a professional, he did not make mistakes; he did not lose things. He had the craftsman's pride in his job. Within two days he would be back in his workers' tenement in Tirana, with his neighbours the crane-drivers and the road-menders who thought his frequent trips away were in connection with the Albanian Customs Service which paid his wages.

Now he had an hour in which to take some photographs to show his family. How his wife Magda would envy these women in their red leather boots, their tight ski-pants and what they wore underneath. He paused outside the brilliant window of a clothes shop; it was filled with brassieres, white suspender belts, dusted with flowers; black nylon briefs. Desire pricked him; he would have gone inside and ordered some for Magda but he was afraid. His orders were always adamant that on these assignments he must never visit any shop or cafe because he might be noticed and remembered. He dared not disobey; he walked oh slowly, regretfully, to the Schwanen Platz.

The lake looked misty; rain was still blowing in from the mountains. It would be a shame to waste a photograph on such a scene. He walked on, farther and farther away from the railway station, until finally he stopped. He would have to return; it would be unforgivable (and unforgiven) if he missed his train.

He was in the Schweizerhofquai, and the rain was falling even more heavily now. His clothes felt impregnated with rain and mist, sodden to the touch, steaming from the heat of his body. The lake was a huge pewter plate, pocked with rain; even the peaks were weeping. He paused and turned. One of the lake steamers was approaching out of the grey fog, the horn blowing sadly. He'd have to take this, rain or not, for there was nothing else, and he had no more time.

He unclipped the front of the camera case and held the camera up awkwardly to his left eye. In the tiny rectangular viewfinder, as he adjusted the aperture, the two red focusing needles trembled and then were still. He turned slightly to make sure all the steamer was in the frame. Then gently, lovingly, he pressed the shutter farther.

The explosion blew off his head and both his hands.

The road had been deserted because of the rain, but, with the unexpected thunder of the charge, men came running to the unidentifiable faceless trunk that sank down slowly, spouting blood across the streaming pavement.

Of the camera, with its anodized aluminium fittings in its beautiful pigskin case, only the lens remained. Somehow it had been blown clear. Unbroken, like an open blue eye torn from its socket, it stared sightlessly, reflecting the rain that now rah red along the gutter.

CHAPTER TWO: VILLARS — LONDON, JANUARY 5

'You're leaving us so soon, sir?'

The clerk behind the glass reception desk of the Palace Hotel looked suitably sad, as though every departure hurt him personally. Love nodded.

'An unexpected call,' he said, as convincingly as he could.

'Ah, yes, Doctor, of course. We hope to see you again?'

Again Love nodded. But would the smooth, tamed Swiss snows seem too artificial, too civilized, after the higher, colder, fiercer peaks of the Himalayas?

Love followed the porter round to the single row of open-ended garages behind the hotel. They passed two children coming down from the nursery slopes, chatting to their mother; a man in a dark anorak, the hood pulled up over his head. His face was not European, possibly Mongolian, with high cheekbones, that the hood could not completely conceal. Probably one of the Nawab's men - or one of these rich Eastern characters who attract the loveliest girls at every ski resort.

Love waited while the porter stowed away his luggage in the Cord's cavernous boot. Then he zipped up his fur-lined leather jacket, and climbed in behind the wheel.

He turned the key against the Startix, and the old eight-cylinder Lycoming engine rumbled into life. He let it idle, watching the red liquid in the dashboard thermometer go up the scale to 136 degrees before he wound out the car's concealed headlights and was away.

Unless in heavy rain - and sometimes even then - Love drove with the hood down, stowed away behind the seat. He pulled up the collar of his jacket, accelerated past the shops and the Marie Louise and Dent Du Midi hotels, and then down the long valley towards Bex.

By the side of the road, railway lines stretched across the snow, two silver serpents that had died side by side. At first he met a few other cars swinging towards him with dipped headlights, and once a train came up from Bex like a long illuminated centipede, all windows and eyes. Then he had the world to himself. The road unwound silently beneath his wheels, thick with hard-packed snow that muffled the noise of his tyres.

He lit a Gitane and snicked the tiny gear-lever into top. Fifty, sixty, sixty-five came up effortlessly as the huge car surged through the tunnel of golden light that his lamps bored into the darkness. Love always liked to drive alone and at night, but even the West of England had so few roads left where he could safely turn up the wicks without fear of coming upon some dreary family packed thigh to thigh in their minuscule vehicle, windows all but obscured with pennants and dangling dolls with illuminated eyes. Here, he could be alone and savour his aloneness. Milestones to Bex and Evian came and went and came again like red-topped teeth against the snow.

Suddenly, above the swish of his tyres on the frozen, rutted snow, he heard a tick, tick, tick, like a metronome in his mind. Damn, he thought, it must be the petrol pump. He had replaced the original mechanical pump with an electric S.U. It had never given trouble before, but this sounded ominously like an airlock or a cracked pipe. Oh, well, luckily he had an inspection light, and he was in no hurry to reach Geneva.

He switched off the ignition and coasted to a standstill. To his surprise the ticking continued after the dying beat of the engine. So it couldn't be the pump, which was wired through the ignition circuit. It sounded like a watch left on a glass-topped bedside table, like the old Westclox alarm in the kitchen in Bishop's Combe. He sat in the cold empty night, under the stars, listening to its tiny impersonal sound, time and life being measured away; his time, his life. Then the ticking speeded up, racing together as though a spring was running out.

He waited to hear no more, but swung open the driver's door, leapt out into the road and began to run, sliding and slithering on the frozen snow.

He was fifty yards away when the explosion came. The Cord erupted in a blaze of orange flame against the empty whiteness of the hills, the glittering rails by the side of the road.

Then the flames grew greedy tongues that blistered the Cord's paint, devoured the leather, melted the glass. Rubber ran like liquid tar, hissing against the snow.

Doors opened, people ran from houses. A Citroen D.S. stopped behind the Cord. Two men jumped out with fire extinguishers, but there was little left to save. The white foam hissed uselessly on the oily flames.

'Are you hurt?' one of them asked in English.

'No, I'm all right.'

'What happened?' asked the other.

'God knows. I thought it was an air leak in the petrol pump.'

'Ah, maybe that was it,' said the first man. 'You are lucky indeed. Where are you going?'

'Geneva,' said Love, 'catching a plane to London.'

'We'll take you there,' said the driver. 'You'd better stop at the first police station we come to and report this. It will burn for about another hour yet, so there's no danger of anyone else running into it. They'll send a truck out to tow it away - if there's anything left to tow.'

'Thank you,' said Love. 'You're very kind.'

He climbed into the car and sat back thankfully against the leather, now feeling the reaction with a dry mouth, a racing pulse. His Cord was ruined, a complete write-off, but things might have been worse. His passport, his travellers' cheques, his air ticket were still in the pocket of his leather jacket. And he was still alive, and unhurt.

Then, for no reason at all, he remembered the high cheekbones of the man near the garage, and the man with the scar outside the station waiting-room and reading the paper in the lounge of the Villars Palace.

He shut his eyes to force away the: faces, for he knew, and

could not deny the knowledge, try as he might, that the explosion had not been caused by a faulty pump, a leaky pipe. It had been caused by a bomb.

And he had not just survived an unfortunate accident; he had escaped from his own murder.

MacGillivray sat in the outer office in Whitehall, with that week's issue of *Country Life* open on his lap. Occasionally, he glanced up uneasily from the pages of advertisements to the green light above the door; the leather chair that Sir Robert L —, the head of M.I.6, provided for visitors was strictly Ministry of Works issue, without springs, and not designed for comfort.

MacGillivray was a tall man, wearing a greenish Harris tweed suit and highly polished brown brogues from Tricker's. He had a hard face, with reddish hair going grey at the temples. Years of dealing with weaknesses in human nature, with the hidden greeds, lusts and envies that could so easily be inflamed into direct treachery, often under the convenient cloak of idealism, had left deep calipers of cynicism on either side of his mouth. He had learned long ago to accept that the outrageous improbability of truth outran all fiction, that published reports of political intrigues, of murders and international espionage were only pale emasculated shadows of what had really happened; the laws of libel, the fear of retaliation, effectively protected the wicked.

He looked (and he was glad he looked, for that's how he wanted to look) like a country landowner briefly up in town from his estate in Berkshire or Dorset. Instead, as the deputy head of Her Britannic Majesty's Secret Service, still with the rank of colonel to which he had risen in the Gunners, Douglas MacGillivray lived in a flat off the Brompton Road, and nursed a niggling overdraft he could not bring below £1,800. He sought illusory escape from the horrors of reality by reading estate magazines, auctioneers' catalogues, particulars of sales in remote and rural places, searching for the ideal country house he would buy if he could afford it.

Across the room, at the desk with the fold-away Remington, sat a middle-aged woman, dressed in a severely cut tweed suit that might have been taken from the same bolt of cloth as MacGillivray's. Miss Jenkins was Sir Robert's secretary, and so knew as many secrets as MacGillivray. But they were as safe in her keeping as if they'd been pulped and shredded in one of the document-destroying machines that stood, with much else of an electronic nature, in the locked room next door.

She crossed and uncrossed her legs (her chair was not much more comfortable than his), and MacGillivray glanced at the brief flash of nylon - not out of interest for what he might see, but because, for once, he could not concentrate on the Georgian manors, the converted barns and oast-houses that were for sale in such surprising numbers. The England he knew seemed to be almost entirely a rash of new housing estates and motorways; and yet according to these advertisements it was also a country of green fields and lodges, of long gravel drives where peacocks called. Which was true? What was truth? If Pilate had found no answer, how could he?

He looked at Miss Jenkins and wondered vaguely what secret dreams fluttered through her head, whether she wanted to travel in the sun, whether she had ever been in love, whether she was a virgin. He decided that the first two answers would be negative; the third, positive. Then the green light flickered twice above the door, and they both sighed with relief.

'Please go in,' she said. She had also been thinking about MacGillivray, and particularly about his wife. She wondered how any wife could accept a husband's story that he was employed by an export agency that worked almost inhuman hours. But perhaps she didn't; it was when wives didn't, and began to make inquiries, that trouble often started. She sighed. She liked MacGillivray; she hoped that trouble didn't start for him.

MacGillivray knocked on the panelled door out of habit, and went inside. The door shut soundlessly behind him on its vacuum closer, and was instantly and automatically locked. They could not be disturbed until Sir Robert pressed a hidden switch under his own desk; the green light would then flicker again to show that he was free, and the magnetic door locks would open.

'Sorry to keep you,' said Sir Robert, nodding MacGillivray towards a saddle-back chair. 'The PM's been on the blower. Another bloody scientist missing. From a conference in Bonn. He knows the secrets - or some of them - of our new missile-turning gadget. He's got two days' start, and now they wonder whether he's gone over to the other side. Marvellous, isn't it?'

MacGillivray made sympathetic noises.

'Probably shacked up with some girl,' he suggested hopefully.

'I wish he were,' said Sir Robert earnestly. 'That'd be a happy explanation. But I think it's unlikely. They now admit he's got a police record. The usual. Boys. Why they can't vet these bastards more carefully in the beginning, God alone knows. But maybe one of theirs will come over to us to even things up. The other side's got its problems, too.'

'I'm glad someone else has,' said MacGillivray feelingly.

He sat down in the old leather chair opposite the desk. Sir Robert lit a cigar. He was white-haired, rather like the original Man of Distinction in the American advertisements, and he did nothing to diminish the resemblance. He wore a dark grey Hawes and Curtis suit with a careful puff of silk handkerchief in one sleeve; the thin black cord of his monocle showed at his collar.

Like all members of the Service he controlled, Sir Robert appeared to the public to have another job, even another name. Within Six he was known as C because, during the First World War, the officer in charge was a Captain Mansfield Cumming. To preserve anonymity Cumming had signed his reports with his initial C only; this tradition is still maintained. *Who's Who* was almost equally reticent about Sir Robert's Army career; he'd commanded various regiments, and then held deliberately vague staff appointments (Deputy DPR (SD), ALFSEA attached. Military Adviser, Control Commission, Berlin) and so on. Now he farmed a small estate in Wiltshire, where his neighbours thought he also had a part-time job as director of a Service charity.

But when any of these neighbours called at the registered offices in Victoria Street on the off-chance of a lunch with Sir Robert, he never seemed to be there. They did not guess that the charity was simply a convenient front for other activities no less worthwhile, or that the main task of the woman at the reception desk was to discourage personal callers. And had anyone told them this, they wouldn't have believed it; the human mind is only receptive to information that falls within the narrow spectrum of its own experience. Instead, they would joke that Sir Robert must have private chambers in St James's, and he would smile and never contradict the suggestion. As a matter of fact, they weren't far out; he did have a flat in Duke Street, but under another name, and with two entrances.

'What brings you over, Mac?' he asked, when his cigar was drawing properly. 'Anything special?'

'More bad news, sir, I'm sorry to say. Remember the reports we've been having on this cover organization in Geneva?'

'Which one?' Sir Robert was still ruffled. 'I can think of three without even opening a file.'

MacGillivray lifted from his brief-case a folder marked with the small red star for Top Secret.

'The International Committee for the Preservation of Big Game, sir.'

'Oh, that. Well?'

'S.5 was killed yesterday.'

In the British Secret Service agents generally adopt the initial letter of the name of the country in which they are serving; if more than one agent is in that area, they take numbers. Sometimes they take their letter from the last letter of the country's name, or the second or the third, so that a simple code can still be effective. In this case Ibrahim Khan had been agent number five in Switzerland.

Sir Robert raised his white eyebrows in surprise and sorrow.

He'd known Ibrahim's father; they'd served together on the North West Frontier in the Rajputs in the old days. Because M.I.6 was relatively small, he felt far more paternal towards its members than he had ever done to the men in his regiment; their deaths always diminished him personally. The replacements were always one step away from the originals; they took time to know, to evaluate. And time, like so much else, was always working for the other side.

'Where?' he asked quietly.

'Villars. On a ski-run.'

That made a change. Usually, in their business, death would take place in a motor accident; or, to be more accurate, a dead body, unrecognizable from fearful facial injuries, would be found in a wrecked car. In the daily carnage on the roads, the fact that the driver had been dead before the accident was staged was impossible to prove; and who would wish to prove it, anyway? No relatives would come forward; they would not even know he was in that country in the first place, so how could they? The government concerned stayed silent; they had no subject of that name. The dead conveniently buried the dead.

'Accident?' Sir Robert had to ask the question, although he already guessed the answer.

'No, a bullet.'

'Ah. Any witnesses?'

'No. But you remember Dr Jason Love, sir?'

'I do, indeed,' said Sir Robert with feeling. 'The country doctor you unearthed when K was missing in Teheran, and we bloody nearly ended up with a declaration of war.'

'That may be, sir, but at least we came out of it all right in the end.'

'We always come out all right in the end. If we don't, it *is* the end; I like to come out all right just a bit sooner if I can. But go on.'

'Well, apparently he found the body.'

'How do you know this?'

'We used our Notting Hill address as a next-of-kin pillar box. The Swiss police cabled. I called back this morning. Said I was Ibrahim's brother-in-law. They told me.'

'I see. Who do we have out there?'

'No one in Villars. Nearest is S.2 in Lausanne. And he's pretty heavily involved with that business of forged British passports.'

'What was *S.5* doing in Villars, anyway? On leave?'

'No, sir. On this big game thing. Has been since last summer. A few months ago the Nawab of Shahnagar became involved, so I got him on to his staff as a secretary.'

'What's the Nawab's role in all this? He's a millionaire many times over.' Shouldn't think he plays with the other side, eh?'

'No, sir. Unless he was made to.'

'How?' Sir Robert looked interested for the first time.

'Some time ago I ran into a friend in the Treasury who'd been at Cambridge with the Nawab,' MacGillivray went on. 'He told me that, apparently out of the blue, the Nawab had asked the Bank of England to release half a million pounds from his sterling account and transfer it to this Committee in Switzerland. This needed Treasury approval, and my friend thought it odd that the Nawab would, want to give so much to such a society. After all, he's one of the best big game shots in the world.'

'Hmm.'

'Then, the following week, the Nawab said he might need to take out as much as two millions to give to this Committee.'

'That smells to me. Did we find out much?' Sir Robert liked the royal of editorial plural; he felt that it showed his subordinates how he was also personally identified with their problems as well as their success.

'Nothing, sir. But maybe *S.5* discovered something in Villars. Or maybe he wanted Love to bring back a message.'

'Both seem unlikely to me, Mac. What have we got on this Committee, anyway?'

'Nothing sinister, that's the trouble.'

MacGillivray put on his reading glasses, and looked down at the open file.

'It's been going for two years on a pretty good wicket. They've collected about £10 million so far. Maybe much more, but that's the published figure. And you know what Swiss banks are like, sir. We can't get a peep out of them.

'They're supposed to be financing big game reserves in Africa, as the Europeans move out, because otherwise whole species of animals will simply become extinct. Yet we've no record of any reserve that they've actually established. It's all talk so far. But maybe these things take a lot of arranging.'

'Have we anyone in their office?'

'No. We've tried to get someone in twice. Once into their head office in Geneva, and the second time into a branch office in Nairobi; But we've had no success. They have a pretty good vetting system.'

'Wish we could say the same,' said Sir Robert sourly, thinking of the scientist. Was he the third or fourth that year? 'Well, let me know what happens.'

'Will do, sir.'

MacGillivray went out, along the corridor, down the back stone stairs, and through the side door that opened into Little Scotland Yard. He walked up Whitehall, his *Country Life* under his arm, his thoughts miles away.

There was that place near Coupar Angus; four acres, eighteenth-century manor house with seven bedrooms, two bathrooms; usual offices, outbuildings (why not in-buildings?), garage for four cars, stables. Unfortunately, the advertisement had given no price.

But then, as MacGillivray well knew from past and sometimes sad experience, the best things in life were invariably not free; they were priceless.

*

Love climbed the dusty, uncarpeted steps behind the narrow doorway that opened into Covent Garden. On the pavements boxes of green Jaffa oranges burst out of tissue paper. A lorry, heavy with nets of brussels sprouts like some strange sea harvest, was backing into a space three feet too small near a silvered metal bollard. A man stood guiding the driver, shouting: 'Left hand down, Joe. Left hand bleeding well down.' Pigeons examined the stone crest and motto of the Bedford family; *che sera sera* - whatever will be, will be. It was nearly eleven o'clock.

Love paused on the first landing. Three doors faced him. The first wore a padlock and a notice: 'All deliveries for Hennessey and Co. to be sent to Grape Street Office.' The next was marked 'Private'. He remembered from his previous visit to MacGillivray that it simply opened into a lavatory with a leaking cistern. The third was the door he wanted. He glanced at some of the names of the registered companies whose business was apparently carried out behind it. Sensoby and Ransom, Fruit Importers, he knew was one of several cover addresses for M.I.6, the overseas arm of the British Intelligence Service.

Every few months, so MacGillivray had told him, they would move his office to another cover address behind which they could operate; but always choosing a business with frequent foreign calls, with visitors who could arrive at unlikely hours. A travel agency, an import office, an exporter of classic cars. They had already been here for several months, to Love's knowledge; they would soon be on the move again.

The other names might be genuine, or again they might not. The Belvedere Trading Co. Ltd; Ruskin Holdings; Bedonwell Promotions (1958) Ltd. As he pressed the button labelled 'Enquiries. Please Ring', he wondered whether they were also what they seemed, whether anything or anyone was what they seemed. What trade did the Belvedere company conduct, who or what did Ruskin hold - and what did Bedonwell promote in 1958 or now?

The door opened unexpectedly on an electric lock. A middle-aged woman sat typing in front of a frosted glass screen, against which was pinned a three-colour advertisement for Outspan oranges. There seemed a lot of oranges, about. Love thought, and then he remembered that to find MacGillivray he should ask for the Citrus Development Division. There was something too acidic about all this for his liking; bitter lemons, wormwood, the smell and taste of death.

'Have you an appointment with Mr MacGillivray?' the woman asked him when he gave his name.

So he did not always use his rank; perhaps in the fruit business they didn't do that sort of thing.

'No,' said Love. 'Just a social call. But I think he'll see me.' I'm bloody sure he will, he thought, but did not say.

'Please wait a minute.'

She went behind a green door with another frosted glass panel. There was the whisper of voices. From the street outside came a despairing cry: 'I told you, Joe, left hand down. I can't tell you more than that now, can I, fer Chris-sake?'

The woman returned.

'Please come this way, Dr Love.'

He left his suitcase in her office, followed her down the corridor, whitewashed in an impersonal Ministry of Works way, through a door that shut silently behind him. The inside was covered with green baize, like a servants' pantry in a big house. He had forgotten the second inner door that also opened and shut against a rubber seal. MacGillivray was sitting behind his desk, *Country Life* open before him.

'Well, well, Dr Love,' he said. 'I thought you were in Villars.'

'How the hell did you know that?' Love asked as he sat down in the issue arm-chair. Across one of the arms lay a thin leather strap with a metal ash-tray riveted to it. MacGillivray's office looked like the secretary's room in an unfashionable club; furnished with castoffs, other men's leavings.

'I was speaking on the phone to someone there this morning.'

'How did he know about me?'

'Look,' said MacGillivray patiently, 'I can guess what brought you here. And as you have worked with us before - however briefly and unhappily - let me save time by ending this Socratic to-and-fro.

'First we gave Ibrahim Khan a dummy next-of-kin - we invented a brother for him, Murellah Khan - at an address that doesn't exist, in Notting Hill. When the Post Office receive any letters or cables to this address, they are instructed to forward them to another address in Pimlico.

'One of our people calls in there every day - it's above an antique shop. About twenty-four hours ago a cable came from the police in Villars to Murellah Khan. It said that his brother had been killed. We rang Villars and found out what had happened. That's all. Quite simple, really.'

'Maybe to you,' said Love. 'But how did *you* give Ibrahim Khan a dummy next-of-kin? Was he one of your people?'

MacGillivray nodded. 'That's what's brought you here; isn't it?'

'The hell it is,' retorted Love, angrily. 'I had no idea about this at all. And I certainly don't want to get mixed up with your outfit again. The last time you talked me into that we damn nearly ended up with a declaration of war.'

'Don't *you* start,' said MacGillivray wearily, a look of pain crossing his face. 'Sir Robert was telling me the same thing five minutes ago. Well, if that didn't bring you here, what did?'

'Ibrahim Khan told me he was the Nawab of Shahnagar's secretary. He wanted my advice about the Nawab's son. The boy had got something wrong with his eyes. I suppose he didn't know I'd ever been involved with you?'

MacGillivray shook his head.

'No, no. All cards on that case were destroyed, believe me.'

'I wish I could believe you,' retorted Love. 'Well, when I met the Nawab it turned out that we'd served together in Burma twenty-odd years ago, long before he succeeded to the title. To come to the point, he told me he was being blackmailed for £2,000,000. This money was to be paid to some society to preserve big game. His son's sight had been threatened if he didn't pay.

'He says he can't go to the police, for the blackmailers claim that they will blind his son permanently if he does.'

'So how are you involved, Doctor?'

'Simply because I knew him years ago. And since no-one else seems to care a Charlie whether he's bled white or not, I said I'd go out to Shahnagar to try and help his son. He's paying my expenses - I must say very generously - and I felt that I couldn't turn aside from such an appeal.'

'Quite so. And what about the blackmail?'

'That's as far as we got,' said Love. 'I decided to look you up because you're the only person I know who's even remotely concerned with the police, security, intelligence, or whatever this would come under. I thought I'd pick your brains before I left.'

MacGillivray stood up, looked for a moment through the double windows at the soundless traffic outside.

'Listen,' he said slowly. 'Last time we asked you to do a little job, I thought it would only be a small task, or I wouldn't have asked you, for you're not a pro. But these things escalate, to use a fashionable word, and you know what nearly happened.

'If I were you, I'd give this one a miss. Forget the Hippocratic Oath this once, Doctor. Think of yourself. I know a little about the Nawab and the request for money. These big game people may be genuine, they may be cranks. Or they, may be really dangerous. I'm just not sure. But Ibrahim Khan was in a better position to find out than you will be. And look at him now.'

'Perhaps it was an accident,' suggested Love, not even convincing himself.

MacGillivray shrugged.

'Perhaps it was. But it's a damn funny accident to be shot with a .22 just as you're passing the only bit of cover on that particular slope. That's the sort of accident insurance companies don't like. Nor me, either.'

'So you're telling me to lay off?' said Love.

'Frankly, yes. You can't possibly help the Nawab. But you might conceivably help yourself to a longer life if you don't become involved.'

'Balls to that,' said Love, 'I'm not going out there as one of your spies with a swordstick and a couple of thunder-flashes concealed up my jack, in case I run into trouble. I'm going out as a doctor to treat his son. Obviously, if I can help him stop being blackmailed, I will. But surely you must admit that I should try to help this boy?'

'I admit nothing. But I'd heard already that the Nawab was being touched for money. And with sums of that size around, you can buy an awful lot of trouble for people who interfere.'

'You mean —?' Love stopped in mid-sentence, remembering the explosion in his car. Maybe MacGillivray was giving good advice; maybe he was being an idiot not to take it. He opened his mouth to tell him about it, then thought better of the idea and said nothing; he had no proof, no clues, simply a feeling in his mind and marrow that one or both of those men could have been involved.

'You know exactly what I mean,' MacGillivray told him soberly. 'But since you're one of those quixotic, pig-headed people who must always follow their star or their hunch or whatever you care to call your own inclination, I suppose I'd better give you what unofficial help I can. It doesn't add to much, but it's better than a kick in the crotch with a hob-nailed boot. First, a couple of addresses to which you can send cables if you do discover anything. Next, a simple code, and one or two bits and pieces that might just give you a couple of seconds' edge on some other man if you're in a tight place.'

'None of your gadgets,' said Love sourly.

He still remembered without pleasure the transistor built into his watch, the minute transmitter buried in a tooth filling, that MacGillivray had organized for him on his previous trip.

"Well,' allowed MacGillivray, 'you may sneer at them now, but they certainly helped you then. But there'll be nothing like those now. Just a few Government surplus things.'

He opened a drawer in his desk, pulled out a foolscap envelope, slit one end, shook a pair of brown laces out on to his blotter.

'Wartime vintage,' he said proudly. 'Issued to RAF aircrew in case they were shot down. Each lace contained a modified trepanning saw - the sort you surgeons use - with a loop at each end. Cuts into any metal. You'd be amazed how many POW's sawed their way out of the bag with these.'

'I'm sure. But I don't want to saw my way anywhere. I'm a doctor, not an escapologist.'

'Well, you never know. Take them anyhow. They're free. You can always use them to pull yourself up by your boot straps. Remember my old father's motto - never refuse a good offer! Now here's another thing.'

MacGillivray opened a second drawer, took out a small box of Swedish matches, opened it. All the matches except one lay with their black heads together. He removed the odd one.

'Watch this,' he said.

He struck the match, blew out the flame, replaced the match, tossed the box across the room.

The flash almost blinded Love.

He ducked, one hand instinctively thrown up to shield his eyes as the room filled with smoke. MacGillivray pressed a button on his desk; an extractor fan began to hum above the windows. The air cleared slowly.

"What the devil was that?' asked Love, raising his head.

'A not-so-safety match,' explained MacGillivray impishly. 'Always good for a dazzle. Satisfaction guaranteed to all our clients. And here's another little thing.'

He lifted a chocolate box from the open drawer, removed the lid. Inside, a black leather belt lay coiled, with a gold plated horse-shoe buckle. ',

'Put it on,' he told Love.

'What's the snag here?' asked Love suspiciously. 'Electric shock?'

'No, nothing like that at all. These are simply diversionary things. To throw an attacker off balance, to give you a chance to take the initiative. Look. I'll put it on instead.'

He buckled the belt around the outside of his jacket.

'Now,' he told Love, 'take this knife.'

He handed him a Commando knife with a serrated steel handle.

'Jab me in the belt with that."

'Why?' asked Love.

'Because you have to, to make it bloody well work. That's why.'

Love prodded gently at the buckle. Nothing happened: He gave a harder stab, and suddenly the blade whipped to one side; deflected by some unexpected attraction. He released the handle. The knife stayed horizontal, its blade glittering against the black leather.

'Magnets,' explained MacGillivray proudly, delighted at Love's bewilderment. 'A whole mass of thin iron segments wound with coils that are energized immediately the belt gets a hard blow. There's a switch in the buckle, and two batteries in the money pouch at the back.'

'Very nice,' said Love, unconvincingly and unconvinced. 'But what happens if you aren't attacked in the belt - if you're hit below it?'

'That's your bad luck,' said MacGillivray cheerfully. 'But I'm sure that as a psychologist, Doctor, you'll agree that there's something mesmeric about a big belt buckle.

'It offers a target, almost a challenge, to a man threatening you with a knife or a gun. Generally, he won't hold the blade or the muzzle above it, or below it, but right on it, bang against it. I know, because we've done tests and made a survey in two infantry battalions for their reaction.

'Ninety-three per cent of the soldiers reacted in this way. Anyhow, here they are, for what they're worth.'

'Keep them,' said Love. They're worth nothing to me.'

'But thanks for the offer. It's nice to know you care.'

'Ah well,' said MacGillivray philosophically, holding up his hands like an unsuccessful salesman who concedes defeat.

'Don't say we didn't offer you anything. Now, for these two addresses I've told you about.'

The Customs Officer at Karachi Airport was helpful.

'If you run, sir, you will just now catch the plane to Rawalpindi. If you will be doing this thing, I am now giving you immediate clearance for this purpose.'

He scrawled the chalk symbol on Love's suitcase. A coolie wearing a brown numbered disc the size of a saucer on his tunic, seized the case and raced through the crowd of waiting passengers out on to the tarmac as though his life depended on it, and not simply an eight anna tip.

It was six o'clock in the morning; the buildings on the far edge of the airfield stood out in dark, sharp relief against the sudden and unexpectedly bright sunshine.

Within minutes of Love's arrival in Karachi, he was in his seat again, lulled by the inevitable piped music while the pilot ran up his engines; they shall have muzak wherever they go.

He sat back, thinking about different things, different people, but mostly about Mercedes. Why was it that every woman with dark hair and a wide smile always had the same effect on him, stirred up the old, sad alchemy of loneliness and love that he had hoped lay buried forever? Was he really making the journey because he wanted to help an old friend - or because he thought he could do himself a bit of good with a girl? What the hell did it matter, he thought, rationalizing, so long as one or the other alternatives worked out? And wouldn't it be wonderful if they both did?

Two and a half hours later they were circling Chaklala airport outside Rawalpindi. A dusty Commer airport bus trundled a handful of passengers past Victorian barracks where whitewashed stones spelled out the regiment's name and crest. Old cannons stared blindly, muzzles stopped, from Napier and Wavell Lines; black pennants marked the graves of holy men. Flashman's Hotel had grown a modern extra wing since Love was last there; even so, it was still full, just as in the old days.

'I'm sorry,' the clerk at the reception desk told him. 'Not even if Her Majesty came herself, sir, could we give her a room. Perhaps the Tourist Office across the road can help?'

The Tourist official, a young man with an earnest face and gold-rimmed spectacles, made out his permit for Gilgit and Shahnagar, necessary because it bordered on Kashmir, the possession of which both Pakistan and India had claimed since independence. Love asked him whether he could recommend an hotel for the night.

'I know just the place you want, Dr Love, sir. The McDavid Hotel. A taxi will take you.'

The streets of Rawalpindi lay wide and almost empty, fringed with formal gardens; tonga ponies tapped iron shoes on the metalled roads, harness bells jingling, canvas seat-covers pipe-clayed as though for a military inspection. The little Hillman taxi scudded between them to the McDavid Hotel, a shambling colonial-style house with a porch thirty feet high, set in parched lawns and overgrown flower-beds. From a small room across a dusty courtyard behind the hotel, an Anglo-Indian came out to meet them pushing circular steel spectacles up on his forehead. He had a tired, anxious-to-please face, perpetually worried as though he alone still sought an answer that all other men knew.

'You have a single room?' Love asked him.

'The Tourist Office just phoned, sir. You are Dr Love?'

'Yes.'

'We have just now got the best room in the whole hotel for you. All pukkha bathroom, hot water, all just now ready. Every single thing to your liking, sir. My name is Fernandez, sir. At your service.'

He pushed the visitors' book towards Love, plus a Government-issue pen with crossed nib and a bottle of gritty ink. Above their heads a fan turned lazy blades; the office smelled of dust and scented hair oil. Then a bearer led Love to the room. Its walls were washed in flaking cream distemper; from the ancient china rose in a rafter, the electric bulb wore a china shade, like a coolie's hat; wire mesh covered windows against mosquitoes. Love knew instinctively that the drawers would jam; that the table legs, wedged up by folded spills of paper, would still wobble. Ah, well, he could not change now.

The bearer wanted to unpack his suitcase, but Love waved him out of the room. He felt tired with the journey, the change in the hour and temperature. He'd take a bath and then unpack his case himself.

After his bath he wrapped the big, rough Hyderabad towel round himself, and knelt in front of the suitcase. So tightly was it packed that as he slipped the locks the lid sprang open backwards. On top of his suits he saw a large brown envelope that he had not packed. What the hell was this?

He ripped it open and shook put the contents; a pair of brown bootlaces, a box of Swedish matches, a heavy black leather belt, with a single sheet of memo paper on which was written in pencil: 'Thought you might find a use for these after all. Follow my father's motto - Never refuse a good offer! Good luck, Mac'

The lunatic, said Love to himself. Why the hell had he wanted to lumber him with this rubbish? He must have told his adjutant to put them in his suitcase when he had left it in the outer office. If anyone became suspicious of him and looked through his luggage, those items would mark him as a man to watch. Yet he could not give them away or even throw them away; those matches could be dangerous. He had better wear the belt and laces until he could find a place where he could safely dispose of them.

He dressed quickly, buckled on the belt, replaced his own laces with the ones MacGillivray had packed for him, put the box of matches in his jacket pocket. Then he, opened the unpainted wooden door on its dry and rusted hinges and walked, out on the veranda, arched with fretted wood screens in the Mogul pattern.

Outside another room at the far end of the veranda a man squatted on his haunches. When he saw Love he lifted a dirty grey cloth hopefully from a baker's tray; it was packed with polished wood carvings of serpents, birds, monkeys. Love had seen them all before, twenty odd years before. He hadn't liked them then; nothing had happened since to make him change his mind. He shook his head.

'Very cheap, sahib,' called the man persuasively.

'Sorry,' said Love. 'Not this time. Perhaps on my way home.'

'Excuse me, sahib,' another voice said softly.'

Love glanced over his shoulder, surprised that anyone could have crept upon him so silently. A man with a pocked face, pitted with holes, with narrow, almost slanting eyes, was standing barely a yard behind him. He wore the familiar black astrakhan cap and tweed sports jacket, with the rolled-gold watchchain in his lapel buttonhole, grey shirt outside his baggy trousers, but he was not a Pakistani. From Tibet, perhaps or the Chinese border?

Love glanced down at the man's feet; his canvas shoes would explain his quietness. He leaned on a bicycle as though he were tired and had pushed it for a long way. Over the crossbar were folded a number of hand-woven carpets in russet, blue, red: the prodigal colours of autumn were heaped on that bar.

'You are Dr Love, sahib?'

'How did you know?'

The man smiled.

'All the best carpets,' he went on, not answering his question. 'Just for you, Doctor sahib. Every one hand coloured. All from Chinese Turkestan.'

That would explain his face; yet it seemed a long way to bring carpets across the hills to Hunza, then down to Gilgit, on to Rawalpindi, simply to make a few rupees profit. However, that was his concern; Love had no shares in his company.

'I'm sorry' Love said firmly. 'But I'm travelling by air. They'd be too heavy. Perhaps, on the way back.'

How the devil had this character found his name? From the hotel office?

'Please, sahib,' the man pleaded. 'It costs you nothing just to look.'

'You're wrong,' said Love, shaking his head. 'Even a look can prove expensive.'

He went into the room. The man followed him, wheeling his bicycle in over the haircord carpet; the ticking of the free wheel suddenly reminded Love of the ticking in the boot of his Cord. He did not like the memory.

'You got a lucky face, sahib,' the man persisted. 'I give you special price. Just to look, not to buy. I'm not asking you for money. Just to look.'

'I've told you,' said Love sharply. 'I don't want the carpets. You're wasting your time.'

The man stood watching Love in silence, his eyes downcast, almost masked by heavy, tortoise lids. Even so, Love caught the bright flicker of naked hate beneath them, sudden to rise, as swiftly concealed. Distant danger bells rang in his mind; he glanced down briefly at the carpets over the crossbar.

The man's hand moved like a brown, wrinkled snake. There was a flash of blued metal and, the snout of an Army Smith & Wesson .38 was an inch from Love's stomach.

'What the hell is this?' asked Love. 'You can't get away with robbery here.'

'Get your hands up. Higher.'

Love had hoped to keep his elbows close to his sides, so that, if the chance came, he could swing to the left; deflect the revolver and bring up his right knee into the carpet-seller's groin, the first two fingers of his right hand into his eyes. How often had he demonstrated this sequence to the judo class at the British Legion meetings in the local hall at Bishop's Combe? But the carpet-seller might have been in his class. He clearly knew this basic defence.

'Hold your hands straight up, you English filth,' he said, kicking the door shut behind him. 'You may have ruled the world years ago, but you mean nothing now.'

He spat on the carpet to show how little the English meant.

'What do you want then?' Love asked. 'Money?'

'I want to know who you are, and why you're going to see the

Nawab of Shahnagar.'

'How do you know I am?'

'Don't give me that shit. We do know.'

'We?'

Love batted the dialogue to and fro, hoping someone would come into the room; maybe a bearer to see about his clothes, a *bheestie* with some hot water. He moved forward half a pace towards the carpet-seller. He might still have a card to play, or again he might not.

He didn't like rudeness or being bullied, and the loss of his beloved and virtually irreplaceable Cord had done nothing to change his outlook.

'Don't get any ideas, Doctor,' warned the carpet-seller. "No one can help you. Only yourself. Now - talk.'

Love moved forward another half pace. The man jabbed the revolver muzzle into his stomach. It jolted against the heavy metal buckle of his belt. Suddenly, the barrel whipped to the right, away, from Love. In that splintered second, before the carpet-seller could take a second aim, Love's knee came up. The man doubled forward like a hinge closing. Both Love's fists, locked together, smashed on the bridge of his nose. The carpet-seller collapsed untidily on the floor; his bicycle with its carpets fell on top of him. Love picked up his revolver, broke it to check that it was loaded, slipped it into his pocket. One down and two to play; a mark for MacGillivray's gadget after all.'

'Now,' he said, 'you talk for a change. Who sent you?'

The man pushed the bicycle away, and sat up shakily, his back against the wall. Blood began to drip from his left nostril; he did nothing to stop it, said nothing.

'Well, if you won't talk, I'll have to call the police. Maybe they'll make you change your mind.'

The man shook his head.

'No, please,' he said faintly. 'Not the police. I'll talk - if you'll let me have a cigarette.'

Love nodded, watching him, his right hand around the comforting butt of the revolver in his pocket.

The carpet-seller pulled out a packet of Lion cigarettes, offered it to Love with a trembling hand.

'No,' said Love. 'Not for me.'

Sweat glistened on the man's face; the smell of fear and failure was sharp in the room. He pulled out a cigarette, put it in his mouth, felt in his pocket as though for a match.

'Now,' said Love. 'For the second time, who sent you here?'

The carpet-seller swallowed awkwardly, as though he had difficulty in speech.

'I'm here,' he began slowly, 'because. Because. I came to see you. He swallowed again, his face grimaced with distaste and then he began to chew desperately, grinding the cheap tobacco in his cigarette to shreds. Love watched, not realizing the significance of this until a thin rope of stained saliva drooled from the man's mouth. His speech slurred, the words running together like a record played too fast. Arteries stood out in his neck, his whole body shuddered, and the carpet-seller fell across his cycle, face down against the oily chain.

Love pulled the sodden, shredded, still unlit cigarette from his mouth; he sniffed the sweet apricot smell of cyanide. He picked up the opened cigarette-packet from the gritty carpet, broke the filter of another cigarette; the same deadly scent. So. He rolled the carpet-seller over on to his back, felt his pulse automatically, although he knew there would be no beat. The man was dead.

Love stood up, lit a Gitane, wondering what he should do. In any normal circumstances, his duty would be plain; but these were violently abnormal happenings. Here he was, several thousand miles from home, with one possible, one certain attempt on his life. But what did they think he knew that could endanger them? And who were they?

As Love stood looking at the dead carpet-seller around whose bloodied face the flies were already buzzing hungrily, he remembered the good advice of Sir Thomas Browne: 'Quarrel not rashly with Adversaries not yet understood.'

How powerful must these unknown people be if a man would

try to kill him, first with a gun, then with the offer of a poisoned cigarette, and when he failed, take his own life rather than admit his failure. What complicated nightmare was he beginning, and how, if ever, would the night end?

He had possibly only minutes before someone else would come to the door, a bearer, a pedlar, with other rugs, shawls, carvings, tourist bric-a-brac to try and sell. If he told Mr Fernandez he had been threatened with a gun, the admission would only lead to delays, inquiries, statements, it would be safer to conceal his knowledge simply to say that the man had suffered a seizure. As a doctor, his word would be accepted at least long enough to let him reach Shahnagar and try to accomplish what he had come so far to do.

He made up his mind quickly, wiped the cigarette packet with his handkerchief to remove any fingerprints and then replaced it carefully in the man's pocket. He tore off the corner of one of the pages of the *Civil and Military Gazette* that lined the top drawer in the chest, wrapped it round the damp cigarette butt and put that in his pocket. The bathroom had no flush where he could lose this, only an ancient china pot in a wooden stand. He would have to get rid of the butt later.

Love then took a pair of rubber surgical gloves from his medical bag, and emptied the dead man's pockets. He carried no means of identification, no money, only a book of matches, a piece of string, an imitation tortoise-shell comb with four teeth missing. Love went into the bathroom, poured some water from the ewer into an enamel mug, spread a towel on the carpet-seller's chest and washed out his mouth as best he could to clear away the more obvious traces of cyanide. He'd have to risk there being an autopsy, but from his memories of the East he didn't rate it as a very serious task.

He took the man's revolver out of his pocket, wiped it to remove his fingerprints, slipped it into his zipped shaving bag in his suitcase, glanced around the room to make sure he had forgotten nothing. Then he went to the door, shouted: 'Bearer! Idhar ao, jaldi! Come quickly!'

The bearer had been cleaning a pair of shoes; he arrived wearing a brown brogue on his left hand like a claw.

'This man has died suddenly,' Love told him. 'Get Mr Fernandez from the office. Quickly!'

The Anglo-Indian with the steel-rimmed glasses came running.

'What has happened, sir?' he asked, his face contorted with concern in case it should mean trouble for him.

'This carpet wallah's had a seizure,' Love told him. 'He's dead.'

'Dead?'

Mr Fernandez echoed the word in disbelief, as though this was the first time he had ever heard it. A black crow flew in through the open fanlight, hopeful for a few crumbs, screeched in terror and frustration when it found people, flew right out again.

'Dead,' Mr Fernandez repeated. His eyes, as bright arid and sharp as those of the bird, flickered around the room, missing nothing, finding nothing. How he hated the English with their pale skins, their assurance; and yet it was only by the cruellest chance that he was as he was. His father had been Portuguese, from Goa; his mother, so everyone had said, was three-quarters European. How strong must that last dark quarter of pigmentation have been to colour him like this, to put him perpetually between two worlds, belonging to neither, and as he imagined, despised secretly by both. He bent down and looked into the face of the carpet-seller; already glazed with the patina of death

'He's Bahadur,' he said at last, as though the discovery was important.

'You know him?'

'Oh, yes, sir. He's done many years in gaol. Even in the British time.'

'Well, he's starting his longest sentence,' said Love. 'What do we do now?'

'I'll call the police,' said the man. 'It will, only be a formality for you, sir. He's well known around here, this fellow.'

'Any dependants?'

'None here. He's part Chinese. I don't think he's any relations anywhere.'

He padded away to his office. The police, inspector was a cheerful man in his middle forties, wearing the ribbon of the Burma Star. Four policemen in starched KD bush shirts and shorts covered the body with a blanket, carried it into the back of the Morris ambulance, while he wrote down what details Love gave him.

'Quite a villain. Doctor,' he said at last. 'We've known him a long time, as I think Mr Fernandez told you. Robbery with violence. Been threatening with a gun recently, too.'

'I'll be in Gilgit for a couple of days, if you want me,' Love told him. 'Then I'll be here on my way home.'

They shook hands. Love watched the ambulance crawl away down the drive in low gear, then he locked his door, drew the curtains across the glass panes, opened his suitcase, took out Bahadur's revolver. On the barrel was stamped the broad arrow of the War Department and the date, 1943.

He wondered where Bahadur had been then, to whom it had originally been issued; it was strange to think that it might even have been his own.

He broke it, squinted through the barrel. The rifling was clean; so at least it hadn't been fired recently. Love slipped back the six shells, rolled a shirt round the revolver, put it in his shaving bag. Then he locked his suitcase and lay back on his bed, hands clasped behind his head, thinking. He didn't like his thoughts. Who could have been the 'we' Bahadur had mentioned? Someone involved with The International Committee for the Preservation of Big Game, whoever they might be? Was it likely that they were really trying to be rid of him before he could reach the Nawab or were the accident to his Cord and this hold-up completely unrelated? Either way he felt marked, watched; he liked the feeling no more than he liked his other thoughts. He swung his feet down to the floor, and walked across to the hotel office.

'Is there anything you want, sir?' asked Mr Fernandez, anxious to please as ever, ready with his instant-appeasement kit of a look of concern, the motion of washing his hands without water.

'Information,' said Love, and put a folded ten-rupee note on the desk under, a paperweight. 'Did this man Bahadur ask you whether I was in the hotel?'

Mr Fernandez hung his head; the glass top on his desk reflected the gold caps on his teeth. At last, he nodded.

'Yes, sir. He asked for you specially. The way he spoke I thought you wanted him to call. Did I do wrong in telling him, sir?'

'No. I just wondered. Now tell me something else. How many hotels are there in 'Pindi like this? Small ones?'

'Maybe ten like ours, sir. Then there's Flashman's of course.'

'Right. Leave Flashman's out of it as they're fully booked. You ring these others and find out whether Bahadur has been to see them this morning, asking for me. OK?'

'OK, sir.'

Mr Fernandez nodded. His dark brown hand, dry and scaly as a turkey's claw, folded over the note.

Half an hour later he was knocking on Love's door.

'I have found the information;' he said as he came inside. 'He'd been to six of these hotels, sir. This was the seventh. All times asking for you.'

'Thank you,' said Love.

He lay on the bed and lit another Gitane. So Bahadur had been sent to find him and to kill him; if he had hoped for the slightest doubt before, he had none now. Thus the sooner he was on his way, the less chance anyone else would have to succeed where Bahadur had failed. His best chance was to try the airport direct on the off chance of a seat being free, and be out of Rawalpindi as soon as possible. He was still alive and unhurt, but he felt no elation. This was not final victory. He had only won an early skirmish, not the last battle. He merely lived to die another day.

The airport number was engaged. When he rang ten minutes

later, a voice explained that the number was out of order. He telephoned for the third time.

'They are not just now taking messages,' another voice informed him, 'it is a rest day,' and rang off. He remembered telephones in the East; they did not seem to have changed greatly. He must drive out to the airport and try his luck in person.

He paid his bill, hired a bedding roll with brass padlocks on its strap buckles, folded some clothes inside it, pushed Bahadur's revolver in the inside pocket of his jacket, and left his suitcase as a deposit against his return. Then he hired a taxi and drove through the midday, heat of empty streets and clouds of dust that the wind blew listlessly across open compounds and the squares.

The waiting-room at Chaklala was crowded when he arrived; men dozed on benches around the walls; women wore black, like nuns, with eye-holes cut in the cloth. Children with bare feet and running noses played at their mothers' knees; flies buzzed busily and hopefully around their tiered, aluminium cans of food. Love called over their heads at the harassed clerk: 'Any hope of a seat to Gilgit?'

The man looked up from his sheaves of passenger lists. 'There's just one seat that has been cancelled. The plane is on the runway now. Please let me see your ticket.'

A coolie led Love out to a silver Fokker Friendship that glittered in the afternoon sunshine. Inside, the fuselage was green, with the words 'Emergency Freight Drop', 'Signal Alert' stencilled in white on one wall. Love's bedding roll and several drums of ghee were lashed to the floor under a net in the centre of the aircraft. The scent of apricots that had been the cargo brought in from Gilgit hung sweetly on the air. The only other passengers were a group of soldiers in grey mazri shirts and khaki shorts; they all sat on leather tip-up seats in the tail of the plane.

The pilot ran up his engines against the brakes; the smell of the fruit, the metallic-flavoured breeze from the ventilator made Love remember wartime flights in Burma, when everyone, sat on the floor, backs against, the cold-headed rivets on the walls.

When they were airborne, he opened his eyes and looked out of the oval window. They were flying above the Gilgit river. Mountains soared up on either side; behind them stood mile after mile of even higher, snow-tipped peaks, as remote and unreal as the painted backcloth of a play. Flecks of foam whitened the jade-green river where it ran over hidden rocks.

They passed another plane on its way back to 'Pindi, like a silver minnow in the sky; the pilots joked with each other over their radios. Love dozed until they began to lose height. Ahead a mountain brooded, craggy and uncompromising as Gibraltar, over a grey runway. The safety-belt warning lit up, and for a moment Love thought they would actually hit the wrinkled rocks; then the pilot veered sharply away, and came down with a three-point landing.

They stopped beside a flower-bed built around a stone building. Over this, a model airplane with a huge rudder moved like a weathercock, its propeller spinning as a crude wind-speed indicator. Twenty or thirty locals in flat woollen hats and baggy trousers and sweaters loafed around a pyramid of petrol tins and army equipment. Someone wheeled put a set of aluminium steps. Love climbed down into the fading afternoon sunshine.

So this was Gilgit. It might have been almost any wartime airfield; even the Willys Jeep on the perimeter seemed the right vintage. As he waited while his bedding roll was unloaded, a man in sports jacket and sambur-skin shoes strolled up to the pilot. His skin was the colour of polished oak; he wore a military moustache and the look of a soldier in mufti.

'Anything for me?' he asked in English. 'Regional Tourist Officer.'

'Oh, yes. A package: Perhaps you'd sign for it?'

The pilot handed down a large foolscap envelope covered with red official-looking seals; on the front was printed in block letters: 'Regional Tourist Officer - Gilgit. To be collected personally.'

The man turned to Love.

'I'm the Tourist Officer. You're booked in at the Rest House?'

'I'm not booked in anywhere,' said Love.

'Come with me,' said the man. We've no hotels, you know. Only the Rest House. I'll fix you up. Your name, please?'

'Dr Jason Love.'

They climbed into his Jeep. The road ahead was powdered with dust; Love had forgotten about the dust; now, he remembered. On either side, water trickled in deep irrigation ditches; cottonwood trees lent circles of shade to little boys playing their own brand of polo with round stones and peeled sticks.

Gilgit, the centre of a wide area known as the Gilgit Agency, that stretched to the borders of Russia, Afghanistan and China, was virtually only a single street, lined with silverbarked chinar trees that threw shadows across the open-fronted shops. Outside the headquarters of the Gilgit Scouts Regiment, two old cannons pointed fiercely at the road; a couple of hundred yards farther on a wooden archway stretched across a gate. Love saw a sign in English: 'Government Rest House.'

They drove in round the dusty lawn; blue and yellow flowers flamed in a centre bed. The driver stopped outside a single-storeyed, L-shaped building with a veranda. To one side, a cow was tethered: to a tree; a goat made water at the end of a rope; men gathered fallen twigs for firewood.

There was some coming and going and banging of wire mosquito screens across doors by a babu in sports coat and baggy flannels who resented being prized off his bed in the middle of sleep, and then Love was given a room. It had green walls, wooden rafters, a stone floor covered by. blue and red carpets. In the hearth stood a crude stove made out of a five-gallon oil drum with a hole cut in its front. The air felt chill, as though the dying warmth of the sun had not penetrated the thick walls; Love shivered.

'You are a tourist?' asked the Regional Tourist Officer.

'Yes. I'm going to Shahnagar.'

'Then I wish you a pleasant journey. You'll need to see the Political Officer here before you go. It's only a courtesy. You have a pass already, I expect?'

'Yes.'

'Then my driver will take you to his bungalow, and bring you back. Perhaps you could drop me off on the way?'

'Delighted. It's most kind of you. What's my best way of getting to Shahnagar? I didn't get your name, by the way.'

'That's because I didn't give it you, Doctor. Let me introduce myself: Ismail Beg. At your service.'

They shook hands gravely.

'You'll have to hire a Jeep. I know several drivers in Gilgit who'll take you. I'll send one along. You may have to bargain, of course.'

'Of course,' said Love. 'I know that. I was here years ago.'

'In the war?'

'Yes,' said Love. 'Why?'

'Nothing. I was also in the old British-run Indian Army for a time. A lieutenant in the Baluchis. I was captured in the Andaman Islands. You British abandoned us to the Japs. But then, all that belongs to the past. Like so much else.'

Just for a moment Ismail Beg's eyes grew cold with the memory: the little ships sailing away from Port Blair over the strangely dark sea (the local name of the penal settlement was Kala Pani, meaning black water). Beyond the reefs and breakwaters the sharks turned and dived and turned again. The prisoners in the gaol shouted a lunatic chorus to the gloom of imminent surrender. Often since that dreadful day, Ismail Beg had awoken sweating in the night at the memory. But not now; not any longer.

'I'm sorry,' said Love. 'Well, these days, we've no one left to abandon.'

'Quite so,' said Ismail Beg briskly. That is the way of history. Imperialist empires rise and fall. Only the people they have ruled go on. And one day - who knows? Now, if you please, we should go before it is dark.'

Love slipped the key of his room into his pocket and climbed into the Jeep. They set off through the narrow main street; goats stood tethered to posts and trouserless children played in the dust. Ismail Beg spoke to his driver; the Jeep slowed and stopped. He turned to Love.

'I get off here. My man will wait for you at the PA's bungalow and take you back to the Rest House. Goodbye, Doctor. A pleasant stay. And if I can help you in any way, please let me know.'

It was only when he had disappeared into a shop doorway that Love remembered he had no address for him.

For a moment after the Jeep had puttered away through the crowds, dodging the running, clucking chickens, Ismail Beg stood looking after it. He wanted to make sure that Love was not returning, that he did not glance back.

Then he walked up a narrow alleyway between two shops. Their wooden floors were raised to keep the leather bags, the bales of cloth, out of the mud in the rainy season; underneath, dogs slept curled up, and goats rooted optimistically among rubbish. The shopkeepers squatted amid their wares, legs crossed like tailors, smoking, watching him.

Above one shop was a red and yellow sign, 'Himalaya Travel'. Ismail Beg went up the steps. Inside, the floor smelled of new concrete, still rough and dusty. The walls were bright with posters; a Basque girl looked at a Tyrolean castle; a Beefeater stood, pike in hand, outside the Tower of London.

Two barefooted chaprassis wearing faded khaki shirts, and trousers leaned against the counter, watching Ismail Beg without interest, simply because they had nothing else to do: They had no shares in the firm, it was of no concern to them who came or went. An olive-skinned man with an unhealthy face and dark-ringed eyes looked up from a desk behind the counter.

When he saw the Tourist Officer, he pressed a button and spoke rapidly into an intercom. Then he banged a handbell. The nearest chaprassi led Ismail Beg through a back door, into an inner office, came back, leaned against the counter.

The office was plainly furnished, with a. brown Turkestan carpet, three chairs, a desk, a row of filing cabinets along the far wall. The air felt too sweet, almost like a sickroom, heavy with scent, from a bowl of red frangipani on the desk. In the far corner a man stood filing his nails, and then blowing away the parings. Because he was of barely middle height, he appeared even fatter than he was, a gross swollen bladder of flesh in a light-weight brown suit, creased at the buttons, dark stains of sweat under the armpits. His neck was so thick and short that his head merged into his body like the head of a tortoise. His face was completely hairless, his brown Chinese eyes as empty of emotion as peeled arid slanted almonds.

Ismail Beg stood respectfully at attention, as the door shut silently behind him. How often had he stood like this, facing the CO of the Baluchis half a lifetime ago, yet with one inestimable difference: he feared Mr Chin as he had never feared his colonel.

Mr Chin knew this, and enjoyed the knowledge. He let Ismail Beg stand for a full minute before he nodded to him. Then he turned on a pocket transistor radio that stood on the desk. He always did this as a routine precaution when conferring with underlings; it confused anyone who might wish to eavesdrop, and also demonstrated to an inferior that he was of little consequence. Even in a classless China, face remained important.

The wail of Indian music, convoluted arid tortured as a basket of shaken snakes, filled the room. Mr Chin blew on his nails for the last time, put away his file and sat down behind his desk.

'Well?' he asked briefly.

'This sir.'

He handed to Mr Chin the sealed brown envelope that the pilot of the Gilgit airplane had given to him: Mr Chin picked up a silver paper-knife, slipped the package open. Inside was a single piece of plain board and nothing else. He tossed it into the waste-paper basket. Ismail Beg watched him, wondering what this signified.

'No strangers on the plane?' asked Mr Chin casually.

'Yes, sir. An Englishman.'

'Ah, yes. What's his name?'

'Dr Jason Love.'

'Ah,' said Mr Chin pleasantly. 'Well, I have news for you. And you'll have news for him.'

He paused. The plain piece of cardboard was a simple yet unbreakable code from a colleague in Rawalpindi. Blank, and with nothing to give away, no message to crack, it told him that the attempt on this English stranger's life had failed. Action was for him to take.

'What do you mean, sir?' asked Ismail Beg respectfully.

'Exactly what I say. You will deal with him,' replied Mr Chin, picking up the nail file again.

'You mean?' Ismail Beg did not dare to dress his thoughts with words. He never knew whether the hidden wire recorder beneath the Chinaman's desk was working or not. Such evidence might not be admissible in the law courts, but neither would it help his chance of an acquittal.

'Just what I say. We've only a matter of days left. We can't risk any possible setback now, however slight. Where is this doctor?'

'I lent him my Jeep to go to the Political Agent's bungalow. He hopes, to leave tomorrow.'

'Well, let him reach the Nawab. Then deal with him as you think fit and when you think best. Bring back any identification papers he's got. Meanwhile, have a look through his stuff and see if he's armed. But don't get caught. We must have no complications.'

The Chinaman turned off the radio to show that the interview was at an end.

'Is that understood?' he asked.

Ismail Beg's mouth felt dry as rind at the thought of things that could go wrong. He would have to shoot the doctor, probably from a distance. This meant the risk of missing, even with a telescopic sight; the wind could blow strongly in the hills, and he might not have a second chance.

Also, he would have to drive himself in case his driver talked too much. But what if his Jeep broke down? It was so old that this happened frequently, and he knew nothing of the mysteries of mechanics.

'Well?' asked Mr Chin impatiently, breaking into his thoughts.

Ismail Beg nodded; he could not trust himself to speak.

Mr Chin watched him go, and then pulled the curtain that concealed a door to the side of his desk. An Eurasian girl stood framed in the doorway, her skin dark, her mouth a flame in her grave, beautiful face. She wore a red dot, Indian fashion, between her eyes, gold rings in her ears.

'Did you hear that?' he asked.

She nodded. Savitra was technically his secretary; sometimes she would conduct a party of American tourists on a package deal holiday to Hunza. Occasionally she would travel to Karachi as a courier, sometimes even to Europe; she carried passports in several names and nationalities.

She had many duties, but she did not consider it a part of them to tell Mr Chin that she had been ordered to work with him so that she could report on his activities. Every evening she wrote an account of his day; this she posted to a newsagent, in Lahore, who forwarded it in a rolled-up magazine to an address in Dacca; there it was micro-photographed, shrunk to the size of a pinhead, and sent beneath a stamp to a pen-friend in Canton.

She wore a sari of gossamer cloth, the colour of wine, sprayed with gold stars. In one hand she carried a thin, pink taper. Mr Chin flicked on his lighter; the incense hissed slightly and then began to burn steadily with its peculiar musky scent.

'Then?' she said softly, running her long fingers with their lacquered nails down the side of his face.

'We shall see,' he said hoarsely. This was the hour of love, the time to which he looked forward, through the barren hours, every day; nothing must, disturb it, not even the ordered death of a man.

Slowly he began to unwind the sari. The silk was so light, so finely woven, that when he threw it to one side it hung for a moment in the air, and then slowly floated down. She stood close to him, thigh against thigh, in her black brassiere, the black net of her pants; her skin was the colour of beaten bronze. He unclipped the hook at the back of the brassiere, the elastic shortened; he uncupped each breast slowly, savouring the feel of the warm, firm, flesh under his hands. Savitra moved against him, her fingers on his body, seeking out his maleness, caressing him. Her nipples grew under his soft touch, hard as cherries in their dark aureoles. He moved slightly, one hand at the thin elastic of her pants; then her smooth shaved body was arched against his, his mouth sought hers. Their tongues moved like warm swords, speaking with the silent language of all lovers.

Still standing against her, Mr Chin leaned backwards over the desk, opened one drawer, pulled out a thin, bamboo rod tipped with leather.

'Now,' he said urgently.

She began to whip him, gently at first and then more savagely as his delight in the sharpness, of the strokes infected her. His huge, soft body writhed in pleasurable pain, his eyes clouded, his voice moaning with inexpressible need. Then she flung the cane away.

He was half-standing, half flying across the desk now; Savitra moved; lay on top of him. Huskily, stroking him gently with her long fingers, she began to recite the words of his namesake, the Chinese poet, Chin Ping Mei.

'The red lips open wide; the slender fingers
Play their part daintily.
Deep in, deep out. Their hearts are wild with passion;
There are no words to tell the ecstasy that thrills
Their souls.'

(*Wang Shih-chen (The Golden* Lotus), translated by Clement Egerton; 4 vols, London, Routledge & Kegan Paul, 1957)

Then, seeking the capsule that lay in the open drawer, she squeezed the thin glass. The burned-banana smell of amyl nitrite sweetened the evening air.

On the desk, amid the multi-coloured brochures for all-in holidays in Bulgaria, river trips down the Rhine, package deal offers to Sestriere, the joss-stick flamed with its peculiar phosphorescent intensity, arid, then went out.

Mr Chin, lost in the delicious labyrinth of his own lust, locked mouth on mouth, body on body, had no light to see the smile of contempt in Savitra's cold, appraising eyes.

CHAPTER THREE: GILGIT — SHAHNAGAR, JANUARY 9

Love braced his right foot against the cut-away side of the jeep as Ismail Beg's driver turned in at the gateway of the Political Agent's house. The garden might have been transplanted from anywhere in the home counties in the 1930s; the lawn, with its tennis net, the croquet hoops; each rose tree grew in a circular bed of newly watered earth.

A sentry saluted, a diesel engine started, and, as though on cue, lights suddenly glowed among the trees, giving a sudden, theatrical illusion of a magic garden carved from the foothills of the grey and towering mountains. Against the early tropical evening, the flagpost stood out like a long white finger. Love could imagine garden parties when the Union Jack had fluttered from it; the small talk on these lawns, the genteel clink of Royal Doulton china against a background of Ivor Novello ('We'll gather lilacs in the spring') from the garrison band.

But spring had long since gone for all those who had been there then, and for the Empire they had served. For, as Sir Thomas Browne had pointed out, 'The lives, not only of Men but of all Commonwealths and the Whole World, run not upon an Helix that still enlargeth, but on a Circle where, arriving at their Meridian, they decline in obscurity and fall under the Horizon again.'

The Political Agent was in his late thirties, a man with a grave, dedicated face; he offered Love tea and sugary sweetmeats from a silver tray in a big, heavily furnished room, thick with carpets. On one wall hung a photograph of the Aga Khan; on another, the horns of ibexes and antelope. Love read the brass plates beneath the trophies. They had been shot, by His Highness the Nawab of Shahnagar in 1963 and 1964. Evidently old Shagger hadn't much interest in preserving wild life then.

Sitting a yard apart on a vast settee, the pounding of the diesel generator muted by the bungalow's thick walls. Love and the Political Agent threw the ball of polite and unimportant conversation back and forth for a few minutes.

'Was there any special reason why you came to see me?' the Political Agent asked him suddenly.

'Yes,' replied Love. 'I met the Regional Tourist Officer at the airport. He said it was necessary for me to see you before I went on to Shahnagar.'

'Oh, yes. Quite right of him. The Regional Tourist Officer. I don't quite know. There are so many new posts of that kind here now, of course, as I suppose in your country, too.'

His voice trailed away. A servant materialized soundlessly, poured more tea from a silver pot and vanished. Their conversation died painlessly from politeness. Love rose to leave. The Political Agent shook his hand.

'Anything I can do to help you...'

Back in the Rest House, the bearer had drawn the curtains and turned down the bed. There was no sign of his pyjamas, so he hadn't unpacked for him. Odd. Then he remembered that his bedding roll was still padlocked. He knelt down on the floor, opened the locks, unrolled the canvas cover. His clothes lay on the blanket just as he had folded them at the McDavid Hotel.

Or did they?

Some of the shirts were not folded in their original creases. Someone had opened the roll and looked through them and folded them up again too quickly, fearful lest he should be discovered. Love examined the two leather loops through which the straps ran. The threads looked new. So. This unknown person must have slit the old threads and slipped the straps off from each end of the roll. Then he had unwound it, examined the contents and rolled it up again, had slid back the straps and sewn up the loops. But who? And why?

A bearer would never have gone to all that trouble when

he knew, that the roll would soon be unwound and he could examine what it contained at his leisure, and in safety. In any case, nothing seemed to be missing. Luckily he was carrying Bahadur's revolver, and wearing MacGillivray's gadgets. His electric razor, sunglasses, and camera were untouched; yet any of these things could fetch more in the bazaar than a bearer earned in a month.

Whoever had searched the bedding roll had obviously not been an ordinary thief. Well, what had he been seeking? For more details about Love, for the reason behind his visit, to discover whether he was who he claimed to be?

At that moment, Love heard a timid knock on the door. He stood up, tiptoed to the door, peeked through the space between the edge of the curtain and the lintel, but it was too dark to see anything or anyone.

God, what a mass of nerves and suspicion he was becoming. Would he ever be able to answer a knock on the door again without a sudden contraction of the heart, a rush of adrenalin through the blood? And to think that at home in Bishop's Combe he didn't even lock his house at night. He must have been mad; or was he sane then and mad now? He reached out carefully, silently slipped the bolt; whipped open the door and jumped back to the protection of the wall.

A man stood on the threshold. He wore an old army sweater, a grey shirt outside his sloppy trousers, a khaki *pugri* on his head. He resembled all the old Indian servants Love could remember, a ghost from Kipling's pages.

'Salaam, sahib,' said this apparition, raising his right hand solemnly to his forehead.

'Salaam, aleikum.'

Relief at the sight of this homely and harmless visitor poured through Love's body. What an idiot he must appear; it was lucky that the English cherished their reputation for eccentricity.

'I understand from the Government Tourist sahib that you wish to hire a Jeep to go to Shahnagar?'

'That's true.'

'I have a Jeep, sahib. Four hundred rupees going and coming. Including waiting time.'

'That's a lot of money for an old Jeep.'

'Not an old Jeep. Nineteen-sixty Willys, sahib. Very strong motor.'

'No matter how strong,' said Love firmly, 'that's too much.'

His mind was still on the matter of the bedding roll. Maybe he should have heeded MacGillivray's advice and stayed away, but that was too late to think about now. He was where he was and he meant to stay that way.

The old man extended his hands, palms upwards, appealing to Allah to bear witness that he was riot asking too much.

'I am a poor man, sahib,' he began. 'I have one mother, three children, two wives and my mother's mother. They are dependent on me, as I am dependent on you, as we are all dependent upon God. Four hundred rupees, sahib. Last price. Absolutely last, rock-bottom price. Not any less can I take, or I am losing money.'

At that moment another Jeep turned into the drive and stopped at the foot of the veranda steps. A Pakistani officer jumped down; dust billowed out from his thick khaki sweater and trousers. Love noticed a Colt 45 in his thigh holster, and a black leather belt studded with polished bullets. He was young, well built, with high cheekbones, strong bone-structure.

'What's wrong?' he asked in English. 'Is this man having you on?'

'No,' said Love. 'We're trying to fix the price for a trip to Shahnagar.'

'Then it should be two fifty chips.'

'He says four hundred.'

'Then he's a bloody robber. Give him three hundred. Last price.'

Love translated this message.

'No, sahib. It is too little. Four hundred. *Absolutely* last price.'

The officer swung round on the driver and spoke rapidly in a dialect Love could not follow. The driver extended his hands, palms lip again, beseeching Allah to bear witness to the trials to which the faithful were subjected. Then he turned back to Love.

'I will then take three hundred, rupees, sahib,' he said in a sad, resigned voice. 'As a special once-only price. But I will leave myself to your generosity. You are an English gentleman, sahib."

'I've been called some other things,' said Love. 'Now, can you be here at seven o'clock tomorrow morning? We'll be away for two or three days, maybe longer.'

'I will be here. My name is Akbar.'

'I'm Dr Love.' He extended his hand. Akbar's grip was firm, his palm hard and dry. Love liked him.

'Good night, sahib.'

Akbar salaamed again and melted away to his Jeep.

'Feel like a drink?' Love asked the officer. 'You've just saved me a hundred iron men.'

'I always feel like a drink, but you'll get nothing here in the Rest House but *nimbu paid.* It's dry. Been here long?'

'No. Only arrived about an hour ago.'

'What are you going to do in Shahnagar? Tourist?'

Love nodded. There was no need to begin the explanations for strangers; too many people must know already why he was here. . .

'Just wondered. Nawab's my uncle. I've just come down from Hunza. That's about thirty miles this side of Shahnagar. Well, good to meet you. I'm Mogul Ahnsullah, the Gilgit Scouts. And you—?'

'Dr Love. Jason Love.'

'Right, Doctor. Can't stop now. Just called to see if any letters have arrived for the Brigade Major, who was staying here. Perhaps you'd join me in the mess on your return, Doctor? Then we'll both have more time. And we're not dry!'

'Delighted,' replied Love.

Ahnsullah climbed back into his Jeep, and was off in a pale cloud of exhaust smoke. Love watched the two tail lights wink away, then returned to his room, slipped the bolt of the door, and sat down on the edge of the bed.

Now that he had made arrangements for the last lap of his journey, he had to satisfy his curiosity about one thing. Years of practising medicine had taught him to heed what the patient did not tell him often as much as what he did. One piece of information, carefully unrevealed, frequently held the key to a successful diagnosis. And here one thing stood out like silence in a song.

He opened his Diners' Club membership booklet at the centre pages, put on the specially lensed sunglasses MacGillivray had given to him and which made visible the hidden groups of his code. MacGillivray had supplied him with two outwardly innocent addresses to which, as a doctor, he could send messages without arousing any suspicion; a maker of surgical instruments in Darwin, and a wholesale medical factor in Cape Town. He chose the former, wrote out his telegram on the back of an envelope, checked it. Then he unlocked the door, and set out through the gates into the dark and deserted bazaar.

Soft, floury dust muffled his footsteps as he walked under the huge trees towards the airfield; the local post office had shut long ago, but, with luck, the radio officer at the airfield might transmit his message.

Gilgit airfield is built on what was formerly the racecourse; air traffic control and the wireless operators work in the old grandstand. Through flyscreens, wedges of light shone out, rich and yellow, across dry lawns, ringed with marigolds and purple and red flowers that Love didn't recognize. Vines grew with tropic luxuriance along trellises on the veranda; a brass bell to announce the arrivals and departures of aircraft was outlined against the moonlight in the fork of a chinar tree. An open door carried a notice: 'Communications Department: Transmitting Station.'

The background was raucous with the squeal of static. Inside the room, an operator was speaking into a microphone, arguing with someone in Rawalpindi about a ten-gallon drum of ghee that had gone astray. He was a plump man with a face shining with sweat and good humour. He flicked over the switch as Love arrived; the explanation from Rawalpindi died in mid-vowel.

'Oh, yes, and what do you want then? Who are you, please?'

'I'm a doctor staying at the Rest House,' Love explained. 'I wonder if you could send this telegram? The post office is closed.'

'I will just now do what I can to help you,' said the operator courteously. Sit down, please.'

He cleared a mass of telegraph forms and messages from a wooden chair.

'Is it to go full rate or night letter?' he asked.

'Full rate, please,' said Love. 'Urgent as you can.'

'It doesn't make any sense,' the operator said slowly. 'Is it a code?'

'Only a private one,' explained Love easily. 'Competition's so fierce now, codes are pretty well essential.' He did not say what competition, but shrugged to show how much a part of his life such things had become; and then he realized with a shock that they had.

'Of course,' the operator replied quickly, not wishing to appear ignorant of such Western practices. 'I quite understand. That will be seventeen rupees, then.'

The money changed hands.

'May I know your name, please?'

'Dr Jason Love.'

'You have been out here before?'

He was glad of any company, anyone at all.

'Never here, but I was in India during the war.'

'Oh yes. I was in Calcutta then for two years,' he said, his round face beaming with the glow of memories. 'I was single, of course. Ah the girls, man. A new one every night. Now, every time I make my water, I say "Shake hands with the unemployed". Still, I must not complain. This is now the best hill station in Pakistan. All greenery and shrubbery. And not any commotion.'

'I hope you're right,' said Love. 'I'm all for not any commotion. By the way, I'm leaving for Shahnagar early tomorrow. If a reply comes, will you send it on to me there?'

'I will see to it. All telegrams to Shahnagar go to the Nawab's palace. Good night, sir. And God bless you.'

'God bless the Prince of Wales,' replied Love, and began the slow walk back with his torch. Behind him, the blip and peep of Morse began as the operator's fingers flew to his key.

*

Three miles away, in the office of the Himalaya Travel agency, Mr Chin and Ismail Beg were also sending a radio message. On the flat roof of the building they had fitted together the polished copper sections of a portable transmitting aerial. They had weighted the three legs of the aerial frame with stones and then gone down into the office through a trap door, paying put the lead behind them.

Mr Chin opened a metal drawer in a cabinet marked 'European-Holidays; Flight Times and Charges'. Inside, the ebonite controls of a transmitter gleamed under infra-violet lamps; He plugged in the aerial lead, flicked over the switches and began to tune to his Wavelength. Static crackled from the round loudspeaker grille; snatches of Indian music, messages in clear and morse, rose and died again. 'This is Lotus Leaf calling,' he said slowly and clearly in Urdu. 'Lotus Leaf calling all amateurs.'

He pushed over the switch to receive, and still the static jumped and blared. He held the switch down again and repeated the message. The third time, he picked up his reply. Through some trick of altitude and atmospherics, the disembodied voice sounded echoing and metallic; a lost and drifting spirit crying aloud for a medium.

'Calling Lotus Leaf, calling Lotus Leaf. We are receiving in clear. Gurkhali Reverse and four. Reverse and Four.'

'Hold,' said Mr Chin and pushed over another switch. He began to speak in Gurkhali into the microphone of a tape recorder. The instructions, reverse and four, meant that he was to re-transmit his message at four times the speed of normal speed, and backwards. To minimize the risk of monitoring, it was either reversed, or had its speed changed halfway through. This, was a trick copied from the Russians who had used it with some success with their spy Lonsdale in England. His regular, sometimes almost nightly, message to Moscow would be transmitted at varying speeds from the Ruislip bungalow of a friend.

Although such messages could eventually be broken by experts in a listening post, to do so might take hours; and by then they would have been acted upon, and their value and meaning lost.

'A visitor has arrived for our friend' said Mr Chin, enunciating every word, as though he were back in the class at the Regent Street Polytechnic where he had studied elocution on a British Council grant.

(He had posed as a student from Penang, whose parents had been killed by the Communists on a remote rubber plantation near Alor Star. In fact, the student had been killed, too, but Chin had conveniently adopted his passport and his name, until the deception had served its purpose.)

'The visitor's plans are being unexpectedly and permanently, repeat permanently, changed,' he went on. 'Should any further guests arrive, we will advise you. In the meantime, repeat your initial treatment. I say again, repeat your treatment. Over and out.'

He rewound the tape, reversed it, and played it at four times the speed he had spoken.

Then Mr Chin switched off, checked some numbers written on the inside of a travel folder to Mexico. He already knew them, but nervousness always gripped his stomach like an iron hand, always drained his mind of coherent thought when he had to send a message his father would read. Again, he turned the dials; static wailed and sobbed in the circular speaker. He looked at Ismail Beg, for the first time almost treating him as an equal; they checked their watches. Ismail Beg nodded; it was exactly eight-thirty, the time they always made their call.

The atmospherics ebbed; a meaningless jabber of voices

roared hoarsely against the metal screen. Chin pressed the white button on the tape recorder; the reels began to turn.

Then he threw the switches for speech, and began to talk.

The radio room overlooking the New Territories of Hong Kong was in the top of the building; still warm and stuffy from the heat of the afternoon sun. The frame aerial criss-crossed like a wire mattress suspended on. strips of rubber under the flaking ceiling. The huge olive-green US army set acquired during a raid on Binh Dinh in Vietnam only weeks before hummed on its rubber-cushioned feet. The two bare foot operators in white singlets and faded blue trousers sat on bamboo stools, silent until the message ended.

'Hold,' said the taller of the two. 'Hold for our return. Over and hold.'

His companion wound a loop of tape between the bobbins and the spindles and the magnetic head. As this threaded its endless, brown, electronic way, the music it contained would play ceaselessly, blocking the wavelength until they received their instructions.

Anyone who listened in, whether amateur or professional, would assume that some ham was experimenting, and pass on to something more interesting.

There would be little point in any Western listening agency in Hong Kong or Singapore putting a fix on the origin; five other radio stations across Southern China, from Yeungkong to Haimun Island, were transmitting the same music on the same wavelength at the same time.

The operator slipped off the reel that contained the recorded message, took it into a small cubicle, hardly bigger than a telephone box. A Gurkha prisoner, captured in Borneo three weeks before by Chinese operating with an Indonesian patrol across the border, sat on a three-legged stool, loosely manacled at the ankles, half shot with opium.

He was suffering from malaria; sour-smelling sweat shone on

his sallow forehead, on the stubble of hair that matted his chin; he leaned wearily against the wall, eyes closed, the opium and the fever warring in his veins.

'Translate this,' the operator told him, curtly, speaking in English.

He slipped the reel on to a portable recorder, reversed the tape and began to play it at the speed of speech. The Gurkha took the note pad and pencil he was handed, and sullenly began to transcribe the message into English as it came through in Gurkhali. As he did so, the operator copied it into Chinese script on a blackboard.

When it was finished, he carried this down the scrubbed stone steps to the room beneath; behind him, exhausted of effort, the Gurkha prisoner lay back, eyes closed, his heart thundering.

Space was short in the house, for space was short everywhere in a country of so many million people. Only the future loomed large, a future without borders or horizon for the people who would crush the West, and control the world. And in that day and at that time there would be full reward for those who had lived and worked and fought in such cramped, airless surroundings as these.

The officer of the guard took the blackboard without a word, without even glancing down at the chalked characters, knocked on the plain, steel-covered door and entered. His orders were to bring in any message immediately, regardless of the hour it arrived.

The room was empty of furniture, save for a bamboo table, a long cane chair of the type they exported by way of Hong Kong to grace many an American patio.

An old man lay on this chair, eyes closed, his swollen legs stretched put in front of him. He might have been sleeping, and for a second the officer stood regarding him in silence and awe.

He wore the blue padded uniform favoured by Mao Tse-tung; but while his clothes might be the anonymous uniform of a million unknown Chinese peasants, his smooth olive face was a mask of power. His legs, puffed up like soft puddings with the disease that would eventually spread over his whole body; thick with the dropsy that would in the end drown even his fierce spirit, gave a false impression of decay. Behind his bland face; his shuttered eyes, his mind turned, restless as quicksilver, sharp and ruthless as the teeth of the killer fish beyond the harbour.

'Do not stand in silence,' he said suddenly, without opening his eyes. 'You have news?'

The officer bowed.

'A message, sir. You said —'

The old man held up his hand; he had no time to waste his dwindling strength on words.

'I know what I said.'

He opened his eyes, put on a pair of round, gold-rimmed spectacles. The officer held the board near his face so that he could read the message; his eyes moving up and down.

'Go,' he said at last. 'They can say I am pleased.'

He paused for a moment, and the officer asked him nervously, 'Is that all, sir?'

'Isn't that enough?' replied the old man, looking at him coldly through his pebble-lenses.

The officer bowed his apologies and backed from the presence. The old man took off his spectacles, closed his eyes again. When the officer had entered he had been in that state of half-sleep, half-wakefulness all old people know. He was proud of his son, of course, but the boy had been given so many chances, so many opportunities that had not existed when he was a boy. He wondered what turn his own life would have taken had he enjoyed such privileges.

The wheels of his mind turned back thirty odd years to the Long March. He had been older then than his son was now, but of infinitely less experience and sophistication. He and Mao, both wanted men, with prices on their lives by Chiang Kai-shek, had led a band of peasants, across the length of China from the far south to the Russian border to prove their solidarity with the Soviet.

He still winced at the sharp, merciless flints that had scored his bare, suppurating, feet on that journey; he felt them far more keenly than he could remember the fine gold needles, with which the acupuncturists had pierced his flesh earlier that afternoon in their attempt to cure him. But now nothing would cure him; death would be his doctor.

He had only to close his eyes to hear again the shuffle of those thousands in. that marching; column through the clouds of dust. Sixty thousand men had died, but what did so few deaths matter against the unnumbered millions his successors would lead on longer marches to distant countries? And not as peasants, not hungry, tired, desperate but as conquerors, as inheritors of such sacrifice.

He poured himself a glass of rice wine, and with the timelessness that comes with illness and age, his thoughts flowed easily into the future.

He would not be there to lead that great march, but his plans would guide them; from the grave he would be their pilot, charting their course. And what a change of direction he would show!

For centuries the people of China had been dominated by others, pillaged by foreigners, tyrannized by despots and warlords. Now all that was changed - and in less than thirty years - and he had been among the handful who had finally put history into reverse.

Now the people of China, disciplined, organized, stood poised for the next move forward. They had already shown their strength in Vietnam, in Malaysia, in Indonesia. They had plans to infiltrate Borneo, even Australia. They had flexed their muscles on the Indian frontier, and opposition had collapsed; just as the myth of British and American superiority had crumbled before the Japanese in Hong Kong, Singapore, Pearl Harbor. But although China was ready to move, one deficiency still put a brake on the country's planned expansion: their indifferent intelligence system. And they must know their enemy's intentions if attacked; how he would react, what forces he could command, how allies would respond; the time lags, the disagreements, the disputes and rivalries over treaties; concessions, loans that they could turn to their own account. But for all these facts they had to rely on the resources of the Russians, and often differences of ideology and outlook existed between the two countries. Peking frequently disagreed with Moscow on points of policy, timing, infiltration, but Moscow's view inevitably controlled the pipeline of information. All arguments had to end in compromise or compliance, because of the overwhelming superiority of the Soviet espionage system.

They maintained spies, agents, sympathizers, believers, in every Western country; in the fabric of governments, trades unions, industry, religious organizations.

Their cover plans ranged from committees to protect the interests of industrial tenants in Scotland, through organizations in America's Deep South arguing the cause of integration and rights for Negroes, to schemes to limit the power of Catholics in Malta. Day by day, hour by hour, through Russian embassies and trade missions, through cultural and business delegations, through ballet tours and visits of football teams, the minutiae on which intelligence feeds, the plankton of power was poured back to the centre in Lubyanka, ironically both the headquarters of the Soviet espionage system, and also the gaol in which foreign spies were held.

In the Communist Central Register in Moscow were files on every person, every undertaking of importance throughout Europe, Australasia, North and South America. Here were the lists of personal weaknesses, failings, ambitions, guilty secrets that could be exploited; as well as details of foreign commercial, military, financial enterprises that served the West as a shield for their intelligence systems and which could be fed false information to throw the calculators off course, the computers out of gear.

Such knowledge was, essential for any modern Great Power, and this knowledge China lacked. They were allowed grudging access to some of it, but-often the information they needed in haste would take days to arrive, either deliberately or simply through inevitable bureaucratic obstruction. China had already tried to penetrate the agencies of the West, but had failed with every attempt. British and American Communists and sympathizers did not admire their system as they had so blindly admired the Russian model. They would defect to Russia but not to China. Since they could not use Western-born agents as the Soviet did so successfully, they were lost; for the question of their appearance made concealment difficult. There was also the incipient fear of the East; Napoleon's old warning about the sleeping giant, the secret dread of the yellow peril.

Now all this would be changed. His plan would, ensure the establishment of a Chinese or independent listening post in every city in the West.

Although the old man realized that he would not live to see this, his son could claim the credit. Up to now the boy had not lived according to his father's harsh and stringent standards. True, he had helped to organize anti-Western demonstrations in Singapore; he had taken the name of a dead Malay, had studied in London. He could speak half a dozen Indian dialects, French and English with a perfect accent. But these were petty achievements when compared with what others had done, in far more hostile circumstances. Also, he could never be quite sure how his son would stand up to danger and the threat of harsh events. It was for this reason, so that he could have an independent running report of his actions, his reactions to orders, his ability to make (and take) decisions in adversity, that he had put Savitra into his office. She was a pervert, of course, with her liking for the stimulus of amyl nitrite; but then the young were all perverted nowadays. Time and space had shrunk. Distance was no more; to want something was to possess it.

Life had not been like that for him; hardly a day went by without hunger, hardly a night without cold, the fear of arrest, of torture and humiliation. His thoughts turned back again, touching on those themes. These children of the revolution were altogether too smooth, too full of honeyed words, for his taste. But the older ones could still teach them what they thought they knew; and all would acclaim his scheme when it had proved successful. The old Chinese proverb, *yi yi chih yi,* use one barbarian to checkmate another, or as the English said, set a thief to catch a thief, had not become a proverb by chance.

He saw in the eyes of his mind the Englishman standing before him; tall, pale as though he had seen too little sunshine for too long, the long angry scar across his mouth and face pulsing with the nervousness he strained to conceal. But the old man smelled his sweat and knew he was afraid. He watched him with a genuine curiosity; it was strange how such long-nosed barbarians had colonized a third of the world - and then been forced to relinquish their colonies, lands they had built from jungle and swamp, in the space of a few years. But then all life was strange; that was the one lesson the years had to teach.

Under the weight of hypnosis that buried the Englishman's mind, his eyes had been blank as the eyes of a fish. The old man registered this approvingly. Some chance happening, some repetition of an action long before, a snatch of song, a train whistle, a term of endearment that only this man knew could break this trance, as any other. But first he would do as he had been ordered; what happened afterwards was of no account - any more than which side killed him, or how, when his usefulness was at an end. Like the Gurkha who had translated the message, they were instantly expendable; they all lived now, only to die another day when their use was ended.

'And what are your duties?' he had asked him.

'To telephone as agreed. To act upon such orders as I may receive as I have been taught, to forward my reports in letters day by day to the address I have been given in Hong Kong. To kill if I am so ordered.' He spoke as though he-had learned the phrases by rote, as a child learns a catechism, without knowing the meaning of the words.

'And what is the reward for failure?'

'The reward for failure is death. Not only to me but to, to...'

The man's voice had slurred again, a shadow of impatience crossed his face; he still had difficulty in pronunciation. He took a deep breath.

'To others.'

'And for success?'

'The reward for success is life. A chance to take my place in the forward march of the Chinese People's Republic'

The old man chuckled at the memory.

'That is good,' he told, the officer who accompanied the man. 'But remember, my friend, the reward for this man's failure could also be your life.'

The officer bowed. He accepted the situation; he had to. The old man chuckled again in dismissal. Then he sank back thankfully on the chair; his heart was racing as though he had been climbing a long hill. His hands were trembling in a way he could not control. He folded them across his chest to try and hold them still. Suddenly, he felt very old and very weak. Against the vast, dark, uncharted loneliness of the voyage he would soon undertake, his plan did not seem so important. Nothing did.

Presently, he slept.

*

Punctually at seven o'clock in the morning, Akbar knocked on the door of Love's room in the Rest House. With him stood a boss-eyed young man wearing chaplis soled from strips of old tyres, an RAF officer's cast-off jacket complete with brass buttons and pilot's wings, loose cotton pantaloons.

'My helper, sahib,' Akbar explained proudly; together they loaded Love's bedding roll on the back of the Jeep. Wedged in beside it were two jerricans of petrol, a tin of BP engine oil, a sheepskin sewn up around some unidentified luggage to be deposited on the way. He drew a rope tight around these oddments, then looped a *chagal,* a canvas bag full of water, on the windscreen frame. The canvas sweated slightly; the evaporation would keep the water cool. The ignition switch had broken long ago and the key was useless. Akbar lifted the bonnet, twisted together the bare ends of two wires before he could start the engine. Then he pulled down the flaps of his fur hat over his ears, shook out a handkerchief to tie around his nose as a dust mask. Love climbed into the front seat beside him, the helper perched like a crow among the luggage as they drove slowly through Gilgit, between the little shops, and out across the new wooden bridge over the Gilgit river. They headed out along the dusty track between the river and the granite mountains, past an abandoned wartime airfield, still raked and wreathed with coils and curls of early morning mist. Stones, each the size and shape of a dead man's skull, marked both edges of the road. Suddenly the hills on either side moved in closer, the plain and Gilgit fell beneath them and behind them, and they began to climb.

According to the meagre details that MacGillivray had given to Love, he knew that they would not stop climbing until they reached Shahnagar. The road had been originally cut into the mountainside for mules, and was barely wide enough for two Jeeps to pass. At intervals, crude lay-bys had been hacked from the rock face. There was rarely more than a foot between the Jeep and the ravine, often less than the width of a tyre.

At intervals, gangs of road-menders squatted in the dust breaking stones to repair the crumbling track. They stood up to let them pass and watched them out of sight, eyes shaded against the sunshine and the dust, thankful for any break in routine, for any chance to straighten their backs.

Time and again Akbar's smooth tyres skidded on a corner, all wheels solid, and then he whipped over to opposite full lock, and the spinning Jeep sprayed a volley of stones into the valley beneath. Frequently these corners were so sharp that the helper had to leap out and jam small rocks from the roadside under the rear wheels, to stop the Jeep sliding back while Akbar turned and reversed and then went forward again until they were round.

Signposts came and went: Chalt, Hunza, where the Mir's palace stood among the tall slim poplars, and it was late afternoon when they reached the outskirts of Shahnagar; the road surface was so atrocious that the eighty miles had taken them more than six hours. Love realized now why it was so expensive to hire a Jeep for the journey. Poplar trees, still amber with last winter's leaves, marched across the green terrace of a valley, dotted with yellow ochre houses. The golden dome of the Nawab's palace, the largest building in sight, glittered like a fallen sun, surrounded by small stone minarets. Beyond it, barley, fields descended in steps a hundred yards across to meet the river that frothed and roared its way down the central gorge towards Gilgit. To the west lay a defile that Love knew from MacGillivray's briefing led to Afghanistan. To the north and east, two unmade mule tracks ran over the mountains to Russian Turkestan and Chinese Turkestan. The road from Gilgit, up through Hunza, and impassable with snow for most of the year, was the only other way out, and this was often blocked by landslides. MacGillivray had explained that the mountains ringing the two tiny principalities of Hunza and Shahnagar were so thick with iron pyrites that rain reacted with it to make sulphuric acid. Year by year this acid gnawed the hills; a hungry sheep tearing at a tuft of grass, a Jeep going too fast, even a change in the wind, could precipitate a landslide. Despite permanent gangs of road repairers, the Gilgit road was blocked almost as often as it was open. And during the freezing winter weather the two states often existed in a virtual stage of siege; helicopters could not be used because of treacherous air currents. Thus, cut off by nature from outside influences, remote from germs and carriers of disease, the inhabitants lived to surprising ages.

Akbar drove to the Nawab's rest house, a single-storeyed building of whitewashed mud with a grey slate roof and a green painted veranda. An old man, his face wrinkled as a tortoise's neck, sat outside it, reading a vernacular newspaper, his lips mouthing every word.

'This is the chowkidar,' Akbar explained to Love. 'He'll look after you. When will you want me again, sahib?'

'Come tomorrow at ten,' said Love. 'I'll have more news then.' At least, he hoped he would have; this place looked a bit rugged for a prolonged stay.

The chowkidar carried his bedding roll into a room, little more than a whitewashed cell, with a glass-fronted cupboard, a carpet in heavy blue weave. Beyond was a bathroom with a floor that sloped to a hole in the wall where the bath water could be poured away. An enamel jug stood on a varnished table; a china chamber-pot lurked discreetly beneath a hinged wooden cover.

The old man unrolled Love's bedding, hung up his few clothes, lit a hurricane lamp which he placed on the mantelpiece. There was no sound but his heavy breathing, the distant, muted bellow of the river. The air felt sharp and cold and damp; Love was glad of his extra sweaters.

'Where is the Nawab?' he asked. 'Can you let him know I'm here?'

He wanted to begin whatever he had to do as soon as possible, before the timeless inertia of the East clogged all impetus.

'His secretary will just now come,' replied the old man, frowning at this Western attempt to circumnavigate traditions and etiquette. 'Will you please to wait until he is here?'

Love sat down in a wooden chair on the veranda and looked out over the little garden of English irises and cabbages, towards the mountains. They stood in rows, wreathed in cloud. As he watched, the setting sun turned the snow to blood. He shivered.

A cough in the dusk made him turn. A man who had approached silently in soft leather chaplis was standing behind him.

'The Nawab is expecting you, Doctor,' he said. 'I'm his secretary. Please come with me.'

Love collected his medical bag, followed him along a path. On either side, water from melting glaciers high up in the snowy hills thundered down through wide irrigation ditches; spray hung over the falls like steam. They walked through a walled courtyard where two chained guard dogs growled half heartedly at them, lip a flight of wooden stairs to the palace door. So this was the end of his journey; or was it only the beginning?

The Nawab's palace was a large wooden house built upon stilts. Underneath ran a warren of servants' quarters, with rooms where clothes could be dried and drums of kerosene and sacks of maize stored.

The floor of the entrance hall was covered with priceless Turkestan carpets, one thrown casually on the other. Rifles, shotguns, the horns of ibex and antelopes hung on every wall, with photographs of the Nawab as a young man; his father, his father's father; a yellowed likeness shaking hands with the Duke of Windsor, as Prince of Wales; a Victorian daguerreotype of all the flags of the British Empire as at 1877. Then the double, glass-fronted doors closed silently behind them, and the Nawab came towards Love, his hand outstretched.

'Damn good to see you, Jason,' he announced breezily, when the secretary had left. 'The Rest House at Gilgit rang to say you were on your way.'

'Did they now?' said Love. 'Not much secret about this operation.'

'Well, it's a small country, and most people are friendly here.'

'Except those who want £2,000,000 off you.'

'They can't have it immediately, anyway. The British Treasury has cabled to say that while they are putting the money, through there's been some delay. Something to do with exchange control.'

'Has there, now?' said Love innocently.

So MacGillivray had been able to hold up the payment for

a short time; it was better than nothing. Love felt suddenly cheered; at least he was not entirely on his own.

'Care for a drink?' the Nawab asked him.

'After I've seen the patient.'

'Oh, you doctors are all the same. Do you remember those days in Moulmein when we used to knock back Carew's gin with juice from mangoes we picked from the tree? You must be a changed man since then.'

'It's a changed world since then,' replied Love. 'But I'll join you when I've seen the boy.'

He followed the Nawab up a flight of unpainted wooden stairs, along a corridor lit by a flickering fluorescent tube, into a bedroom with varnished wooden walls, like a room in a Swiss chalet.

'Wired the palace myself,' the Nawab explained proudly, seeing Love's glance. 'Bought a mail-order kit from the States. The Mir of Hunza and I are the only two up here with electric light.'

He crossed the room and stood by his son's bedside.

'Iqbal,' he said gently, 'this is Dr Love, who's come from England to make your eye better. I'll leave you now, Doctor. Be downstairs in my study.'

On a chest of drawers next to the bed stood some of Iqbal's toys; an Airfix model of U.S.S. *Saratoga,* a plastic airplane with a tiny diesel engine, a pile of books. Iqbal wore a thick white bandage over a pink square of lint above his right eye; his other eye watched Love with grave intensity.

Love waited until the Nawab's footsteps died away, and then sat down on the red, army-style blankets, and felt the boy's pulse. It was a little fast, but then he was probably nervous. He put his stethoscope Over him, tested his knee reflexes.

'Now what's all this?' Love asked-with a smile.

'I don't really know, sir,' replied the boy frankly. Love's smile broadened.

'If you don't, I can't either, can I?' he said. 'Let's start from the beginning. Tell me what happened.'

'There's nothing much to tell, really, sir. My father was out hunting and I went out to meet him on his way home. I often do that. It's fun.

'I'd crossed the river, and was about two hours on from the far bank - about five miles away from here, I suppose, when I saw a light wink high up in the hills.'

'On this side or the far side?'

'On the far side, sir. It's territory that technically belongs to my father for, oh, a long way - about five hundred miles. But no one lives up there as far as we know, because it's simply snow and ice and so on.'

'Any roads?'

'Only a camel track from Chinese Turkestan. Caravans come over with their carpets and take back our apricots and apples, sir.'

'I see. Now, what exactly did this light seem like?'

'It looked a bit like a mirror that was reflecting the sun, but all magnified. You know what I mean?'

'I do.'

'Well, I thought someone was signalling to me, and I looked again, and then the light flashed directly into my right eye, so bright that it felt as though I'd been burned. I couldn't open it for the pain.'

'Your left eye wasn't affected?'

'No, sir, not at all. I held my hand over my bad eye and then scooped, up some snow on the lid. I felt a bit sick with the pain, and frightened. I ran back here, and Mercedes put something on it. But I still can't see properly out of it, though it's not sore now.'

'What happened about the specialist in Switzerland?'

The boy shrugged.

'I don't know, sir. My father cancelled the appointment. He didn't say why. Our local doctor in Gilgit saw me.'

'What did he say?' -

'Nothing to me, sir.'

'I see. Well, let's have a look.'

Love unwound the bandage and gently raised the boy's right eyelid.

'This may hurt a little,' he said, 'but I'll be as quick as I can.'

The eyeball was diffused with enlarged blood vessels; the eye was obviously still very tender and painful. Love examined it with his ophthalmoscope. The iris was contracted, with a pin-point pupil. To do this that light must have been extraordinarily bright, but so far as he could discover, the damage would not be permanent.

The boy should regain the full use of his eye, but it would take time; and another experience like this might mean a different ending. He patted Iqbal on his shoulder.

'You were on your own when you saw this?' he asked, as he replaced the bandage.

'Yes, sir. It was about noon.'

'Have you seen this light since?'

'No, sir.'

'Has anyone you know ever seen this light? Or one like it?'

'No, sir. Mercedes couldn't understand what it was. Nor my father. So far as we know, no one has been so high up in those mountains before.'

'Well, someone or, something must have made the climb. It couldn't be a reflection up there from somewhere down in the valley?'

'I don't think so. And even if it had been, *someone* would have had to be up there to move the mirror, wouldn't they?'

'Quite right, Iqbal. They would. Well, I'll put out the light now, and you go to sleep. We'll have another chat tomorrow. Good night, Iqbal.'

He tucked the blankets in around the boy's shoulders, flicked off the switch. Through the half-open shutters of the window, snow on the mountains glowed beneath the moon with a strange luminosity. Behind the nearer peaks stood other summits, like rows of giant teeth. By some trick of altitude and moonlight, each row seemed whiter than the one in front. When Love blinked his eyes and looked again they seemed to have moved slightly nearer, but that, of course, was another illusion. Could anyone be up there, possibly watching the palace now through night glasses?

Love closed the shutters and went along the corridor, down the stairs, into the hall. A bare-footed servant wearing a long white tunic with a red sash, a gold head-dress, bowed to him, opened the door.

The Nawab was standing in front of a fire of scented apple logs, hands clasped behind his back.

'Well, what do you make of him?'

'It's a bit early to say yet, Shagger, but I'm damn sure he'll get his sight back unimpaired so long as he's not dazzled in the same way again.'

'What do you think could have dazzled him, Jason?'

'It must have been a concentrated ray of some kind that could be aimed with a good, deal of accuracy.'

'Do you know anything that could?'

'The only thing I can think of would be a laser.'

'What exactly is that? I've read about it vaguely.'

'It's basically a beam of light reflected and reflected on itself until it's as thin as a needle. The name laser came from the initial letters of its description: Light Amplification by Stimulated Emission of Radiation.

'I've seen demonstrations of its capabilities. Some hospitals are using these lasers in eye operations. You can step up its intensity and cut a diamond with it, or even a chunk of metal. Or you can send messages along it - bounce it off the moon.

'It's about the biggest scientific breakthrough since the transistor - and with as many different uses.'

'And you think we're seeing one of these uses now - to blind a boy from a distance?'

'It seems likely. It would be quite possible to aim the ray with a good telescopic sight. No strain at all.'

'Hmm. So if you're right, I must have enemies up in the hills, Jason?'

Love nodded.

'Well, let's drink to their downfall. What will it be?'

'A Bacardi and lime, if you've got it.'

'We've got it,' said the Nawab. He poured out two large measures.

'I thought you didn't drink because of religious principles,' said Love quizzically.

'I don't usually, but this drink is medicinal. I've had a shock, a bad shock.'

'What?'

The Nawab glanced around the room.

'We can't talk here,' he said in a low tone. 'Follow me.'

He led the way down a corridor with its floor covered from wall to wall in leopard skins, sewn together to make a giant carpet. At the end was a door of unpainted wood with a large, old-fashioned brass key in the lock. The Nawab turned the key, stood to one side to let Love pass.

They were in a square room, with whitewashed walls. From the ceiling hung two fluorescent tubes. The floor was carpeted, like the corridor, in leopard skins sewn together, but against the far wall was fixed a vertical sheet of brown, perforated hardboard with all the special Cord tools; spanners, wheel braces, grease guns, wrenches.

But all this only provided the frame for the picture. In the centre of the room, its rich royal blue paint glittering under the flickering lights, stood an 812 Supercharged Cord Roadster, identical with Love's, own except for two things; the colour, and the fact that it bore no sign whatever of any wear or use. It might have been delivered from the factory that morning.

An old Pakistani in a turban and khaki jacket shuffled in from a side door. He salaamed to the Nawab and glanced at Love to see his reaction to the car.

'This is the Keeper of the Cord,' the Nawab explained. 'He was working here when my father brought the car up and he has looked after it ever since. I think I told you in Villars.'

'I have the same model back in England,' Love said to the Keeper. 'But not in this condition. This is almost better than new.'

The old man's face glowed with, pleasure.

'Every morning, sahib, I clean this car,' he said. 'Every day, I run the engine for half an hour and turn the wheels to preserve the tyres. They are even the original Goodyear six hundreds. I drive it a few yards forward and back several times each day to keep the gears turning and the brakes free.

'We have an extractor pipe to take the exhaust out of the building. Please to look under the bonnet, sahib.'

He raised the heavy blue alligator mouth. Love saw the familiar glitter of the aluminium supercharger, flat as an inverted frying-pan; the polished alloy cylinder heads; the neat harness of multi-coloured wires to the gear-box solenoids; the long-throated horns. He might be back in his own garage at Bishop's Combe.

And then he remembered that his own garage there was empty, except for the Mini kept as a reserve car for his: practice; that he owned a Cord no longer, only the remains of one. He turned to the Nawab.

'I didn't tell you what happened to me on the way back from Villars, did I?' he said.

'No. What?' asked the Nawab.

'I was a few miles out of town on my way to Geneva when I heard a ticking. I thought it was an air leak in the petrol pump. I switched off the engine, but instead of stopping it grew worse. It was a bomb.'

'A *bomb?*' the Nawab repeated incredulously.

'Well, something explosive, with a time fuse that had been set to go off, after I'd left Villars. And off it went. I'd got eighteen gallons of petrol in the tank, and it blew the whole lot sky high.'

'You mean your Cord's finished?'

'Unfortunately, yes. A total loss. It was lucky I heard the ticking or I'd be a total loss with it.'

'My God!' said the Nawab slowly. Then he looked at Love, motioned him to silence.

Love read the message. He ran one hand under the black four-branch exhaust manifold, where dust collected; his fingers came away clean. He looked beneath the tear-drop front wings on their smoothly contoured pontoons; under the clutch housing, but he could not find a drop of surplus oil, or a speck-of dust anywhere; even the brass grease nipples had been polished.

'What a car,' he said admiringly. 'I've not seen a better one anywhere - and I once went to one of the Club meets in the States where, they spend fortunes on their vehicles.'

The Nawab smiled.

'You are like my father, a true Cord lover, I see.'

'I think you can say that,' allowed Love.

The Nawab nodded to the Keeper of the Cord. He climbed in behind the wheel, turned the ignition key against the Startix. The eight-cylinder Lycoming grumbled awake. Love lowered the bonnet and stood back admiringly. Even with the exhaust boom being taken through the wall, the growl of these 170 imprisoned horses excited him.

Indeed, it was impossible for him to look at the horizontal radiator louvres, the four chrome-steel outside exhausts, the faked V-windscreen fitted with faintly tinted glass against the tropical sun, without feeling the same absurd, irrational thrill of pleasure that the sight of his own Cord always aroused in him. Some day he must write the paper he had promised himself, about the strange psychological association cars possessed for men of all ages; but always different cars for different ages. Some day...

The Nawab nodded to the Keeper; the old man went out of the room. The Nawab locked the door behind him and brought Love back to the present and reality.

'I asked you out here,' he said, 'because someone must be feeding this Committee or whoever else is blackmailing me with information; out here with this engine running we can't be overheard. Bloody marvellous state of affairs, isn't it? If my old father were still alive, he'd think we were both crazy. But then the whole world's mad. You'd hardly gone up to see Iqbal when the phone rang. It was the man with the lisping voice.'

'Where could he be ringing from?'

'It must be Gilgit or somewhere on the way, for the line

doesn't go beyond there.'

'Well, that narrows the field a bit. What did he say?'

'Variation of the other themes. Money. They're getting restive. Someone's coming here at noon on Friday for the money.'

'But you haven't got it?'

'That's what I told them. However, they'll take a letter of intention to the bank. Have you anything else in mind?'

'Nothing, really. Just turning over possibilities.'

'I can't see any possibilities,' retorted the Nawab. 'I pay or I don't. These characters certainly mean business. They killed Ibrahim Khan and they've tried to blind Iqbal. And it seems pretty certain to me that they must have realized why I wanted you out here - that's why they tried to kill you in Villars. It would seem like an accident - an old car - a high altitude. I'd have thought it was an accident myself.'

'Well, if someone on your staff *is* feeding them information, the only way to discover who they are is to draw their fire, smoke them out. Make them reveal themselves. I suggest, Shagger, that you put it about among all your staff here that I have discovered a means of curing your son and you know exactly who caused his injury, and why. And that I'm off back to London to do something about it. If there's an informer here, he'll pass on this information. Then they'll have to break cover. It means that they must show themselves. Instead of being on the defensive, we're doing something positive.'

'It seems a pretty risky operation,' said the Nawab dubiously.

'Life's risky,' said Love. 'If you knew how many million, germs were in a glass of water you'd never drink it, even with your religious principles.

'I suggest I go back to Gilgit tomorrow, Wednesday. I'll come back here early on Friday before whoever comes for the money. Then we can think again - together.'

'Why are you doing this?' asked the Nawab. 'This isn't strictly a medical problem. We're not even very close friends. After all, we haven't seen each other for more than twenty years.'

'There are several good reasons,' said Love. 'One is because I hate to see, time after time, the bully getting away with things. Everyone complains, but no-one *does* anything. Often they don't get the chance to do anything. Well, I've got the chance now. Also I've got two other reasons which seem pretty good to me.' He paused, thinking about the carpet-seller in 'Pindi, the unknown person who had searched his bedding roll. He wouldn't bother the Nawab with these details now. The man had enough on his mind.

'Now, Shagger,' he said brightly. 'What about that other Bacardi you didn't promise me?'

It was late when Love walked back along the dusty road to the rest house. The chowkidar had lit a hurricane lamp - for him and set it on the table in his bedroom, but he leaned over the rail of the veranda, looking down into the dark misty valley beneath. Here and there a few weak lights glimmered in windows, tiny tapers of flame from minute wicks floating in shallow glass bowls of oil. The roar of the river seemed louder in the darkness; ice must be melting higher up the valley. The night was very cold.

Love walked along the creaking grey boards of the veranda towards the guttering lamp that flickered in the dining-room. The chowkidar brought out a huge china plate, a set of cutlery in the dull, local silver of the kind that Love remembered from his last stay in India, a bowl of thick soup and a curry stew. Afterwards there was a pot of tea with goat's milk and brown sugar, a pile of Hunza grapes.

He returned to his room slowly, wondering who had spoken to the Nawab, whether his plan could work out; where he would be at the same time on the following night, whether he would be any nearer a solution then.

His thoughts were miles away as he lifted the open padlock off its staple and pushed open his bedroom door against the thick, red curtains. Then they rushed to the present like a boomerang.

Mercedes was sitting curled up in a chair, smiling at him.

CHAPTER FOUR: SHAHNAGAR, JANUARY 10 – 11

Love closed the door behind him, pulled the curtain carefully across it.

'I've just heard you are leaving,' Mercedes said. 'I wanted to see you before you go. Privately.'

'You mean, this is a professional call?'

'Well, yes. It is partly medical - about Iqbal.'

'I see.'

Love sat down, took out a packet of Gitanes, lit two, offered her one.

'Now, what about Iqbal?'

'I'm worried about him, about the treatment he's getting - or, rather, isn't getting. I don't want to speak out of turn, but, as you know, the Nawab took him to Switzerland especially to see Dr Grussman. We fixed an appointment, which wasn't easy, but the Nawab pulled strings. Then he suddenly changed his mind. Iqbal was to come back here with me. Then you arrived here to treat him. Now you're going.'

'True. But there's this difference - I know what's wrong with Iqbal. We'll have him cured soon.'

The girl glanced nervously, involuntarily, towards the door.

'Is there someone outside?' asked Love gently.

'No-one saw me come here,' she said.

'Does it matter if they did?'

'I - er - I suppose not. It's just that it's lonely up here. You get used to looking over your shoulder. I'm so glad - if you can really cure him. He's such a game little fellow, it's a shame to see him so gloomy. There's one other thing, Doctor. I've two letters here, and I wonder if you'd post them for me?

'If I put them in the mail box here it can take up to a week for them to reach Gilgit, let alone go on from there. If you could post them for me in 'Pindi, they'll be home within a couple of days.'

Mercedes stood up, took two air-mail letters from her handbag; their fingers touched as she handed them to him. She was only inches away; Love could smell the faint scent from her hair, see the slight down on her upper lip. Her teeth were very white and even; against her sweater her breasts were round and taut.

'Was this the only reason you came?' he asked, half smiling, hoping he knew the answer before he asked the question. Behind them a half-burned log collapsed in the grate, and a shower of sparks soared up the chimney. She turned at the unexpected noise, and then she was standing closer, her breasts against him, her heart beating on his. It seemed the most natural thing for him to put his arm around her. Close to, her eyes reflected the glow of the fire. They stood thus in silence while the river roared away, unseen and far away, an angry beast in the darkness.

'No,' she admitted in a whisper. 'There was something else. I'm frightened.'

'Why? What of?'

'I don't know.'

'You mean, you do know, but you won't say?'

She said nothing. Love moved his hand slowly down her back; she moved closer to him. He could feel the line of her spine, her breath on his face, on his neck, and he leaned closer, head bent. As they kissed, he thought, as though he were uninvolved, standing apart from the moment, simply looking on. You're an idiot if you become involved. Stay free, without anchors, without attachments.

But did he want this, anymore? The freedom of being alone, a loner, was also the freedom to be lonely; that was something you never thought about when you were in your twenties; but then with every year that passed you thought about it a little more, until suddenly you thought about it nearly all the time, and then it was too late, and you were on your own then forever.

There were moments when the telephone didn't ring, when the walls of a room became the walls of a solitary cell, and you admitted all this. And yet, and yet; he had seen too many marriages fade at the edges, too many instances of love growing cold.

A caution from Sir Thomas Browne touched his mind at a tangent: 'Break not open the gate of Destruction, and make no haste or hustle into Ruin. Post not heedlessly on unto the *non-ultra* of Folly ...'

But already the wheels were beginning to mesh and turn; signals stood at green, and he was posting on; it was too late for caution from another century. 'Tell me about yourself, Mercedes,' he asked gently.

She turned from him, drawing away slightly. His hand slipped from her shoulder on to her left breast; he could feel her heart beat, the answering awareness of a nipple hardening.

'What is there to tell? I was born in Hong Kong. My father worked there. He's dead now. My mother lives in Scotland. One of the letters is to her.'

He glanced down at the envelope: Mrs Irene Renfrew, MacBain Drive, Newton Meams, near Glasgow.

'Any other relations?' Did his questions sound like an interrogation, or simply friendly interest?

'A brother; Cameron. He's older than me. Ten years older.'

'What does he do?'

'He was missing in Korea., And then Mother got word he was safe. He was in a prison camp, but apparently he didn't want to come home. Anyway, he stayed in China after the armistice.'

Love remembered the handful of confused British prisoners who had elected to stay in China, bribed by the promise of degrees at Peking University, by the promise and illusion of equality, but in how unequal a world.

'Do you hear from him?'

'Sometimes.'

She threw her half-smoked cigarette over her shoulder into the fire.

'Well,' she began, and paused.

Love put out his hand; he felt her tremble under his touch. 'There's no hurry to leave, is there?' he asked.

She shook her head. Two solitary spirits had briefly reached out in the darkness of their individuality, and touched. And in that contact electricity had sparked, the alchemy of attraction flared; maybe it was only momentarily, and it would fade; but the important thing was that it was there, bright and warm and welcome. And in time to come it would be remembered; would return unexpectedly, unsought and unasked, the return of a loving spirit brought back by the chance burning of some other fire, the roar of some other river. Like a first love, it was something that would never quite die so long as either of them were left alive.

As Love kissed her, softly at first, then more fiercely, she put out her right hand, turned down the wick of the hurricane lamp. His hand moved beneath her sweater, over her warm, firm skin. His fingers found and released the metal catch of her brassiere; her breast grew in his palm, warm, firm yet yielding.

The log fell a little lower in the fireplace, but now they neither heard nor moved at the sigh of the rushing sparks. Love half carried, half led her to his narrow bed, she kicked off her skirt and they lay down together on the rough, male, blanket. And then, where it had been cold, there was warmth, and where they had been two isolated people there was one, and the soft and the hard and the inside and the outside did not belong to either of them, but to them both, equally.

But even as they lay in that timelessness after love, in the glow of giving and taking, in the warm, darkened room, Love knew that the tendrils of loneliness would entwine them again, yet in that rich, stolen moment there should be no time for thoughts of what would happen, would not happen, or when or where. He moved towards her again, thigh on thigh and felt his maleness grow against her, felt her breasts harden, her body open to him, her mouth meet his.

Afterwards, a long time afterwards, they slept, arms outside the coverlet, at peace, while the room grew chilly, the fire grew old and died.

A faint, insistent tapping broke Love's shell of sleep. He swung his feet on to the carpet, felt in his jacket pocket for his revolver, held it in his left hand, close to his body, padded across the carpet, opened the door.

The chowkidar, a blanket wrapped round his shoulders against the chill of the dark, stood framed in the doorway. The roar of the river filled the room like a living presence. A breeze rushed in like iced water and fluttered the curtain as the old man held out a letter.

'Dr Love sahib?' he asked, his breath like fog in the cold air.

'Yes?'

Who else could he be? Did he think he'd changed his identity in an evening? Perhaps he was right; perhaps he had changed, perhaps everything was changed.

'There is just now this telegram, sahib.'

Love ripped open the cheap, porous envelope, read the printed capitals of the unsigned message: 'REGARDING YOUR QUESTION OF FISHING TRIPS POSITIVELY NO REPEAT NO REGIONAL TOURIST OFFICER GILGIT.'

*

The sun was already high and bright over the whiteness of the distant hills when the old chowkidar tapped again on Love's, door, opened it, and drew the curtains with much heavy breathing. He deposited a china mug of steaming tea, thick with sweetened condensed milk, by his bedside, then left the room.

Love stretched luxuriously in the warm bed, sat up, lit a Gitane and looked out at the wide terraces sweeping down to the river, and then, up at the mountains beyond. Mercedes had left early, he was alone again. An image of Mercedes at Bishop's Combe; Mercedes married and ten years older, flickered through his mind. He shook the thoughts away. They scattered like dead leaves from the poplars in the valley. You had to live for the hour, not to hazard what future hours might hold.

Snow was late this year, but the early morning air felt so cold that it almost hurt to breathe. He drank the tea gratefully, climbed out of bed, washed in the ewer, in the tiny bathroom. He shaved with his battery razor, packed his belongings. Then he buckled on his magnetic belt, slipped the box of matches MacGillivray had given him into his jacket pocket, walked along the creaking veranda for the changeless Eastern breakfast of two minute eggs, a frizzled rasher of bacon, a small pile of mince. Akbar joined him as he poured the coffee.

'You wish to leave this morning, sahib?' he asked. He had heard rumours in the bazaar last night that the English doctor was able to cure the Nawab's son, but that he must return to Gilgit for some unexplained reason.

'As soon as you're ready,' Love told him, pouring him a cup of coffee.

Akbar nodded. He knew from his experience with wealthy tourists whom he had driven that the rich are subject to constant whims and indulgences; the poor man's lunacy is ever the rich man's eccentricity.

'It may be a little difficult,' he said awkwardly, looking down at his coffee.

'Why?'

'There's been a landslide, sahib. About thirty miles up from Gilgit.'

'Is there any way round?'

'It depends exactly where it is, sahib,' replied Akbar cautiously. 'There's a loop road for part of the way some distance from here.'

'Well, let's be off and see for ourselves. We'll start as soon as I've finished breakfast.'

'Very good, sahib.' He stood up, went out to start the Jeep. Love drank his coffee, walked into the chowkidar's room. A young boy stood rolling chaupatties, using a flat stone as his table; behind him, an oven built into a wall glowed with red ash. The chowkidar reached into a cupboard and brought out a cone-shaped basket of apples.

'For your journey, sahib,' he said.

Love paid the bill, told him to keep the change. Back in his room, he opened the clothes cupboard, took out a strip of mosquito netting that covered the shelf instead of newspaper, wound it round Bahadur's Smith & Wesson. If they were held up by this landslide, he could set up a stone as a target and see how it shot. A gun was of no serious use unless you knew its bias exactly. He came out, opened the dash locker on the Jeep, slipped the bundle inside.

While Akbar checked the level of the water in the radiator, Love unwound the net so that the revolver lay on the folded green muslin, which cushioned it against the bumpy road. In a Jeep again, with a bare revolver, it seemed almost like the war. But the years always gilded memories in the most outrageous and impossible way, and the more years, the more coats of gold old experiences wore. Probably, at the time, he'd found it all meaningless and distasteful.

Love bit into one of the chowkidar's apples, and they were off. Thick dust billowed up around them, stinging their faces as the wind changed. Love glanced at his watch; nine thirty. With luck, he should be in Gilgit after lunch, and then what? Maybe his bluff would be called. Maybe he'd be back on the following day.

He shut his eyes against the brightness of the sun, the prickling grains of dust, abrasive as iron filings, and let his mind freewheel.

A few miles outside Shahnagar, he opened them, saw a long wooden building to the right of the road. On one wall hung a red painted mail-box dating from the reign of Queen Victoria, and still stamped VRI. A radio aerial sprouted from the roof; telegraph wires ran in pairs like tramlines in the sky. This must be a wayside post office, possibly the last one they would pass.

'Stop here for a minute,' Love told Akbar on the impulse. 'I want to see a man.'

Akbar pulled into the side of the road, opened the bonnet, undid the two wires to switch off the engine. Two old men squatting on the veranda in the thin morning air looked up at Love with their oddly bright, beady eyes. Love nodded a greeting, walked past them, into the building.

A clerk in a khaki camp comforter, wearing two sweaters over his grey mazri shirt, was tapping out a message on an antique Morse key. Wires stretched up to the ceiling in coils, like an illustration of an early Marconi station. Love waited until the man had finished. The roof was high, ribbed with whitewashed rafters; several bats hung upside-down in one corner, paying no attention to the Morse. The clerk cleared the line and looked up questioningly at Love.

'Can I send a telegram from here?' Love asked him. To London?'

'But of course. To anywhere in the world. You write it just now and it will be going immediately.'

He pointed towards a sheaf of porous telegraph forms piled on a table under a piece of iron pyrites. Love pulled one out, put on his sunglasses, checked with his Diners' Club booklet for an address, decided to try Cape Town this time, printed a message to MacGillivray in block letters. Then he worked out the same message in the code that the booklet also contained, wrote that on a second form. He tore up the first one into tiny pieces, put them in a tin ash-tray, lit them with his cigarette lighter, powdered the flakes to black dust. The clerk watched him with interest.

'An old English custom,' said Love, feeling that his behaviour needed a rational explanation.

'Please?' asked the clerk.

'Nothing.'

'That will be 13 rupees 8 annas, then,' said the clerk, counting the groups. He asked no questions about it being in code, which was just as well, for Love could have given him no convincing reason except the truth.

Love walked back to the Jeep. Akbar went through the business of joining the two wires again, and they set off for the second time,

Ahead of them a line of men staggered along the road towards them, each with a branch of a tree tied to his back, torn from the forest to cut into firewood. They looked grotesque, as though a whole forest was somehow on the run; Birnam Wood was moving farther east than Dunsinane.

Women squatted on flat stories at the roadside, carding wool from sheepskins. Fifty yards farther on, other hacked circular slabs of rock from the hillside, fashioning wheels to grind the maize. Love watched them all incuriously, busy with his thoughts, his right foot braced against the cutaway side as the Jeep lurched and bumped, trailing its plume of yellow dust behind them.

He and Akbar were alone; the helper had not turned up for some reason that Love could not understand, and they had no luggage or provisions to carry to Gilgit, apart from his own bedding roll.

Love's thoughts moved at a tangent, remembering the helper's curious style in dress. Surely it was odd that a man who had apparently been indispensable on the way up could be so easily dispensed with on the way back? He asked Akbar about this but Akbar would give no explanation.

'Nay aya, sahib,' he said shortly. 'He hasn't arrived.'

Why not? And why hadn't they seen these people working at the roadside on their way to Shahnagar? They couldn't possibly have made so many stone wheels in less than a day. Yet the road still looked much the same, with the same red and white signs in English: SLOW, CAUTION; the occasional signposts with their abbreviated messages, 'GLT 59', to show the distance from Gilgit.

'We didn't pass these people on the way up,' said Love.

'True, sahib. We've left that road because of the landslide. It's nearer than I've been told. I asked when you stopped.'

'When do we cross the' river, then?' Love asked him.

'In a few minutes, sahib. In few minutes if Allah is good.'

*

Thirty miles to the south, in the shadow of a clump of trees, Ismail Beg sat at the wheel of his Jeep, his finger on the starter button. The battery was dead; the only result of his frantic jabs was to make the ammeter needle swing weakly to Discharge. Sweat ran down his back, soaking his shirt at his belt; his mouth felt dry as the dust on the road. Surely this couldn't be happening to him? It was impossible that his plan could be ruined by such an unexpected setback. He had stopped for a pot of tea at a dak bungalow, one of a chain built in the British time, about sixteen miles apart, the distance a horse and rider could travel in a day. Now his engine refused to start.

The battery was years old; it should have been replaced long since, but then his Jeep had been bought second-hand after being run without adequate servicing for years. There were always plenty of people in Gilgit willing to push-start it for him for a few annas backsheesh, and in any case he used his driver for short journeys, but on this road he could find no-one to help him. The chowkidar at the dak bungalow had disappeared and no one else was near. He had tried cranking the engine, but without any success, and he could not push it on his own.

What was he to do? The question beat recurringly in his brain like a drum, while the second hand on his watch swept uncaring round the dial, measuring away time lost, time he could never now make up.

This was maddening, for he had arranged with Akbar exactly where they would meet. Akbar would stop his Jeep on some pretext at the agreed place, and Ismail Beg, by then concealed fifty feet above the road, would simply pick off this English doctor with the rifle Mr Chin had supplied. At that range the wind would not affect his aim; he could not miss. Then they'd remove the doctor's watch, his passport, and any money he was carrying, and roll the body down the hill towards the river, where the hyenas would soon deal with it.

The risk of discovery was negligible; fatal accidents like this occurred frequently on the Gilgit road. There would be no witnesses, and in any case, who would inquire about the accidental death of an unknown Englishman? By the time any questions filtered through from the British High Commissioner, only a handful of bones would be left.

Akbar could easily memorize a story about the doctor wanting to make some inquiries on his own, or maybe that he felt ill or wanted to pass water. He was unused to the altitude, and the loose stones near the road gave no firm foothold. He must have plunged to his death, poor man.

But in this plan Ismail Beg had not reckoned with this ludicrous delay; now he would never reach the agreed rendezvous before Akbar. But surely Akbar would realize that something had gone wrong, and he would have to drive on, otherwise his passenger might become suspicious. He'd have to try again, but where, dear God, but where?

Ismail Beg did not dare to fail; the thought of Mr Chin's anger turned his bowels to jelly. Failure was unthinkable. He wiped the sweat of apprehension from his forehead, forced himself not to think of it, but with each minute that passed, its possibility grew greater. Panic began to rise within him like a tide, drowning positive thought and resolution.

There was only one place he could be sure that Akbar's Jeep would be stationary, and that was when it crossed the ravine. The landslide was a fiction, but the way in which they had to cross the river from this second road was fact. Years ago, arrangements had been made to build a suspension bridge, but either only the supporting pillars on either bank had been completed, or the bridge had been finished and had then collapsed. He was neither sure nor interested, but all that now remained of the bridge were two wire ropes to which vehicles were hooked and then winched across the ravine by a system of pulleys.

He would abandon his own Jeep where it was, walk on to this ravine, cross it and wait on the far bank, concealed in the trees.

He would not shoot immediately the Jeep arrived, because even with his telescopic sight he was not certain of hitting his target; the wind was strong and the distance deceptive. He would be more crafty, more cautious. He'd bribe the coolies who turned the winch, wait until the Jeep was more than halfway across, and order them out of the way. He could then shoot the doctor as he sat in mid-air - a stationary, captive, helpless target.

The thought cheered him; he was no fool, no fool at all, whatever Mr Chin might think.

There was a slight risk that he might hit Akbar, too; also, the doctor might be armed and use Akbar as a hostage for his own safety. He'd flash a mirror at Akbar, and hope the man had enough wit to realize that he should keep away. If he didn't, well, he'd have to take his chance. But Akbar was crafty; his firm handshake, his pleasant-seeming face were no clue as to the real deviousness of his nature. He'd realize that Ismail Beg would have to make an attempt later as he'd missed his first chance, and this ravine was the only other, place where he could be certain of success.

Ismail Beg climbed out of his Jeep, picked up his rifle, slipped a spare clip of cartridges into his trouser pocket. He took another look at the photo of the Englishman that Mr Chin had given to him, although he knew his face well enough, repeated once more the number of Akbar's Jeep, which he had written on a scrap of paper in case there should be any doubt; at a distance one Jeep looked very much like another.

Then he took a long drink of cold water from his canvas chagal that hung from the windscreen butterfly-nut, began to walk north along the baking road.

Love watched Akbar out of the corner of his eyes as he drove. Drops of sweat beaded his forehead, and he gripped the wheel so tightly that, his knuckles shone pale beneath his skin. What could have upset him? Something Love had done - or something he hadn't done? Or could it be something he had said?

He suddenly felt uneasy; he recognized the smell and sweat of fear easily enough, but why should Akbar be afraid? The road wound on, now with a fearful drop to the left of several hundred feet, now tunnelling through an archway where the exhaust echoed eerily. They turned into a long gentle bend where the rocks towered, bare at first and then bushy with shrubs and feathery trees. The mountains blocked the sun; the air grew suddenly cold and damp.

Akbar slowed and then stopped.

'What's wrong?' Love asked him.

'It's the engine, sahib. It has lost its strength.'

He climbed out, lifted the bonnet, peered inside, eyes narrowed against the blast of hot air from the fan.

'Sounds all right to me,' said Love; maybe this was where the other side would introduce themselves. He hoped so; he was an impatient man; he hated waiting. He glanced around him in case he could see someone half-hidden, watching him. He saw nothing sinister at all. They were parked in the centre of the curve. Above them, frowning in shadow, the mountain soared. On the other side, the road overlooked a sheer drop of several hundred feet to the pounding river beneath. All seemed well, yet still he shivered; this bend held all the shadowed dankness of a tomb.

'Come on,' he said irritably. 'That engine's as good as it'll ever be.' All, cylinders were firing; the exhaust sounded healthy enough; what the hell was Akbar worrying about?

Ah, well, might as well make use of the delay. Love opened the lid of the cubby hole, took out Bahadur's revolver, aimed it at a flat rock the size of a football thirty yards away, pressed the trigger.

The rock disintegrated. So the sights were true, without bias. That was reassuring.

At the sound of the shot, Akbar jumped round to the side of the Jeep.

'Sahib!' he shouted hoarsely. 'Are you all right?'

As he saw Love smiling at him, the gun in his hand, he glanced back towards the stone and then up at the side of the mountains.

'Oh, it was you firing,' he said flatly.

'Well, who else could it be?' replied Love. 'Come on, that engine's running well enough for this trip. We're not after the lap record.'

'Ji, sahib,' Akbar agreed. He slammed down the bonnet, climbed in behind the wheel. He drove on in silence, hunched up, looking neither to the left nor the right.

Love slipped his revolver into a side pocket of his jacket. A seventh sense, born in danger years before, lulled by security since, had not died but slept. Now, like him, it was fully alert. From Akbar's swift glance up the hillside, from his whole attitude, Love felt convinced that he had expected someone else to be firing. If he was right, whoever they were, they must make themselves known soon. He hoped he would be ready; if he wasn't, he would only have himself to blame.

Eight miles ahead by the mileometer, the road suddenly twisted to the right, then to the left, and fell away abruptly. The ravine loomed ahead of them, dark and deep, edged with rocks the colour of rust. Akbar stopped the Jeep. Two huge brick towers, eighty feet high and thick in proportion, marked the edge of the valley. Years ago they had probably supported a suspension bridge; now, only two steel hawsers remained, each as thick as a man's wrist, swinging nakedly in the morning wind from the tops of the pillars.

Across the ravine, 400 feet away, they were connected to two other similar towers. Halfway between these two sets of towers, and swaying slightly from side to side, hung a green-painted platform, like an upturned kitchen table, suspended from wires ropes by hooks around its legs. Beneath this the river cascaded in a white froth of fury.

'We hook the Jeep on to that, sahib,' Akbar explained. He lifted the bonnet and cut his engine.

The only sound now came from the roar of the angry river. Love saw that the far bank was shrouded in fir-trees. A gang of coolies in shabby white shirts and cast-off shorts had stopped work on the road to look at them. No birds were singing. The whole scene had the unreality of time suspended, the thin, remote quality of a nineteenth-century engraving. It reminded him obliquely of a print in his waiting-room showing Bristol suspension bridge on the day it had been declared open; except that here there was no bridge.

Love looked at Akbar; the skin on his face was tight around his mouth. So he was still strung up about something - but what? If he were one of his patients he'd recommend some phenobarb, a hot milk drink and an early night.

Akbar climbed out of the Jeep, holding a King Dick spanner in his hand. He banged it against a brass bell that hung from the left pillar. Close to, Love saw that these huge structures were in fact hollow, and stuffed with branches and straw. There was something symbolic in their emptiness; nothing was ever quite what it seemed to be. He would be thankful when he was on the other side.

Across on the far bank, the coolies waved to acknowledge the Dooming of the bell, and began to stream towards a winch. The distant, sunshine gleamed on its huge brass handle; worn smooth with years of use. As the coolies turned it, with many chants and groans to illustrate the extent of their effort, ropes tightened over pulleys; the platform began to slide creakily and jerkily towards Love and Akbar.

From a third, thinner wire to one side hung a square box, its floor-boards split and rotten, and held by supporting wires from each corner to a centre hook: Inside this box a rope was coiled loosely. By pulling on this rope, a passenger could propel himself across the ravine. Love shuddered at the prospect; he had no head for heights.

'For you, sahib,' said Akbar, indicating this swaying horror.

'Not on your nelly or your life,' said Love. 'I'm too old. Isn't there some other way round this landslide than over this Blondiri contraption?'

'No, sahib.'

'How do you cross, then?'   '.

'In the Jeep, sahib. It is only allowed for one man.'

120

'Then it's; allowed for me.'

'Nay, sahib. Not allowed for passengers.'-;

He held out both hands as though to push Love away.

'Balls,' said Love inelegantly. 'What's good enough for you is good enough for me. Otherwise; I'm staying right here.'

Akbar looked at him, and then across the ravine. Something bright flashed briefly from the distant trees; the sun must have caught a piece of glass or some such thing, thought Love. Or could someone be moving among the leaves?

Akbar cleared his throat.

'You go in the Jeep then, sahib,' he said, as though he was willing to oblige him. 'I'll follow in the trolley. One at a time. It is a rule.'

The platform bumped against the rocks at their feet. Akbar tied two loose ropes through rusty hinges in the brickwork to hold it steady, then climbed back into the Jeep.

He started the engine, banged down the bonnet, engaged four-wheel drive and began to edge forward slowly, inch by inch. The trolley trembled and dipped as it took the weight of the front wheels, and then the tie-ropes held it steady. Akbar accelerated suddenly, and the Jeep was aboard, the whole rickety contraption swaying alarmingly from side to side. Then he jumped out, slipped the two ropes from their rings, wound two loose chains from the supporting wire ropes to the front bumper to stop it shifting. Love climbed in behind the wheel.

Across the ravine, the coolies stood like figures in a tableau, a mezzotint of workers in the East, watching them. Akbar shouted something and two began to turn the brass handle, one on either side. From the driving-seat Love glanced back at Akbar; all the strain had left his face. What had been worrying him must have resolved itself. Well, whatever it was, it couldn't have been constipation.

For a moment the platform swayed from side to side on the wires, and then it began to go forward, jerking a foot at a time, as the coolies took up the slack at the winch.

Love looked down over the side. Three hundred feet beneath

him, the river boiled across the rocks, whiter than white, colder than cold. The sight held no comfort; he looked away quickly. High up above him, hiding in the sun like wartime pursuit planes, three vultures hovered, their dark wings spread widely as they slowly turned in the empty, burnished sky, watching him. In the swaying trolley that creaked with every jerk forward, suspended like a weight from a crane, he felt oddly vulnerable, naked to his enemies, but who could his enemies possibly be in such a remote and peaceful place?

To take his thoughts from the nearness and extent of the drop beneath the Jeep, accentuated by the shimmering sky, he took the Smith & Wesson from his pocket, polished the blue-steel barrel with his handkerchief. The solid weight of the gun gave instant psychological assurance; he was no longer alone.

He settled himself back more comfortably in his seat, gun across his lap, enjoying the warmth of the sun on his body, his thoughts turning to his practice; he wondered how that locum was making out.

Suddenly, the jerky movement of the Jeep changed. Instead of dipping fore and aft at each turn of the winch, it began to swing loosely from side to side like a ship becalmed. Love looked up and across to the far bank. The coolies had stopped turning the winch and were running away. Some had already disappeared; others were padding as fast as they could up the dusty, unsurfaced road, in a shabby cluster. But why?

The platform began to roll sickeningly from its supporting ropes. The pulling rope had fallen slack; the thundering river glittered like broken glass through spaces between the floorboards of the trolley. Above Love's head, one of the pulleys creaked with every movement, like the rigging of an old ship in a cross-wind.

Love's hand tightened round the revolver; the firm serrations on the handle poured comfort into his hand.

Crack!

The windscreen pane splintered in front of him; triangles of Triplex spattered his face and hair. He dropped down sideways, his face just missing the two black-knobbed gear levers. What the hell? The other side must be introducing themselves more violently than he had anticipated.

Love's eyes, on a level with the instruments, noted automatically that the oil pressure stood at 40 pounds a square inch. The dynamo was charging furiously at 10 amps., for as he ducked his right foot had gone down hard on the accelerator. The roar of the engine running light echoed back, booming from the rocky cliffs. Oil smoke blew out from beneath the rear edge of the bonnet, and seeped up by the gear lever. The noise was almost deafening, but he would have to endure it; he could not switch off the engine unless he opened the bonnet.

The attack had been so unexpected that Love still felt numb with the shock; he was out of practice for an ambush. There was always a time for heroics, but he didn't feel that this was it. He pulled his handkerchief from his pocket, knotted one corner, and tied it round the end of a rusty jacking lever that lay beneath his seat. Then he waved it furiously above the windscreen, a white flag of truce, still keeping down himself, trying to convince himself that the thin metal of the Jeep would give adequate protection from a bullet. *Crack!*

The glass, in the other panel of the windscreen splintered into an opaque frostiness. So this was a case of there being no surrender. Well, if he couldn't join them, he'd have to beat them; there was no other way. He lifted his foot off the accelerator long enough to give his words a chance to carry, and shouted: 'I've got something to tell you! Kill me and you'll never learn it! And you should, for your own life depends on it! And the life of the man who hired you!'

He repeated the words in Urdu, not pausing to be fussy over the points of grammar. He listened. Nothing but the creak of the pulleys and the roar of that blasted river. Then he heard an answering shout in English.

'Stand up, with your hands above your head, palms open to me.'

This was something, a breathing space. It might not be much

but at least it meant a change from crouching on the floor of the Jeep. He slipped the revolver into his right-hand jacket pocket, fished the starting handle from under the seat and jammed it down against the accelerator to keep the engine racing.

Then he remembered MacGillivray's box of matches, put an unlit Gitane in his mouth, palmed the box and stood up, his hands above his head, palms facing the far bank. He was ready to duck if he saw the slightest alien move of danger. As he straightened, he wondered, as he had often wondered twenty-odd years before, whether you ever heard the bullet that hit you. He heard nothing.

He stood upright, staring at the deserted winch. About thirty feet up in the hillside above it something moved. Branches parted; a dark-skinned man wearing khaki trousers and a white short-sleeved shirt stepped out. He held a rifle across his body in the way of a man who had been trained to use it. Love was close enough to see the venturi-shape of the telescopic sight. The man had tied a handkerchief round the lower part of his face as a crude mask. His hair was black and oily. He wore no hat. - 'Shut off your engine,' he called in English. He walked down towards the winch.

Love heard his voice above the iron thunder of his engine, but shook his head to show that he hadn't quite understood. He needed time to think of some way to escape, time arid luck; not much, but some; enough.

'Shut, off your engine!' the man shouted again.

'I can't!' Love shouted back. 'There's no key. I'll have to lift the bonnet to stop it.'

The seeds of a plan were germinating in his mind. For its success it was imperative that he, should open that bonnet.

'What have you got to tell me?' the man shouted again. 'Speak quickly!'

He raised his rifle briefly as though he were about to take aim. Love drew in his breath. Jesus, was he going to shoot him as he stood? What sort of madman was he now involved with And to think that if he hadn't faced a challenge nobody had made, he might have been enjoying a Bacardi and lime at Villars, watching all the girls go by; and maybe not just watching.

'I can't speak with this noise,' Love shouted hoarsely. 'If you let me raise the bonnet, I can stop the engine and we can talk. Nod your head if you agree.'

The man raised his rifle to his shoulder, drawing a bead on Love's forehead. Then he lowered it slightly. He'd got the range; he could take this doctor fellow any time he wanted. It pleasured him to, have an Englishman in this situation. Old debts were being repaid, a wheel was turning, full circle.

'All right,' he shouted. 'But don't try anything. I'm keeping you covered. And hurry.'

He began to raise his rifle again.

'Don't be a bloody fool,' called Love irritably. 'What *can* I try?' Why hadn't he been shot already? Was he wanted alive - or dead? Either way he didn't seem a very good insurance risk.

'I can't shut off the engine!' Love shouted. 'I've told you. There's no key. I've got to disconnect two wires under the bonnet.'

'Well, raise the bonnet with your left hand, keeping your right hand above your head. If you try anything funny, I'll shoot.'

Love lifted the T-shaped clips that held down the bonnet. He swung it up and back against the windscreen. Hot, oily smoke, a whiff of burning rubber from the spinning fan blew up into his face.

'Hurry up!' the man shouted irritably. 'Switch it off!'

He half turned and shouted something in Urdu to the coolies. Two came back reluctantly and stood by the winch. Love knew that it would be now or never; it had to be now.

'I can't see the wires,' Love shouted. 'I'm going to strike a match.'

He opened MacGillivray's matchbox, saw the row of black tips, like the busbies of tiny toy soldiers, and one green busby among them. He took this out, holding the box at eye level so that the rifleman could see it contained nothing but matches.

One of the coolies slipped the ratchet on the big cog wheel of the winch. Then they both threw their weight against the handle. The Jeep swung slightly from side to side as the wire rope grew taut. The man glanced impatiently at the two coolies, ran his finger along the edge of the trigger guard, facing Love, watching him, holding a bead on his navel.

He gave the handle a push with his left hand and the Jeep jerked forward.

'Hurry!' he shouted impatiently.

Love struck the green match, uttered a silent prayer that the gadget would work as effectively here as it had in MacGillivray's office, bent over the racing engine. 'All right,' he called, to give himself an excuse to stand upright and blow out the match. He pushed it back into the box, closed it, counted three and then tossed, the matchbox casually over the front of the Jeep towards the rocks.

The explosion beat his eardrums like a hammer.

A huge cumulus of white, choking smoke erupted in front of the radiator blocking all view of the bank. Love dropped down on his knees, and the bullet from the gunman's rifle whined softly over his head.

Love ripped off the high-tension lead from the front sparking plug, jabbed its bare brass end against the hot cylinder head.

Fifty thousand volts streamed through the Jeep's metal chassis, up through the chains, the hooks, along the wire rope to the metal winch. They poured through the hands of the coolies and the gunman, up their arms, down their bodies to earth.

The coolies screamed with him against the faltering roar, of the engine.

Love whipped the Smith & Wesson from his inside pocket, and fired once, twice, three times.

At the distance and despite the smoke, it was impossible to miss; Love didn't achieve the impossibility.

The smoke blew away to one side. The man rolled forward in slow motion, hands outstretched, head down. Love leaned over the engine and pulled apart the two ignition wires. The engine stopped. Wraiths of blue exhaust drifted across the ravine behind the cloud. Birds flew out screaming from the shelter of the trees, their bright wings turning like kites in the sky; even the vultures took refuge in height. Love could see the dark frightened faces of the coolies peering at him from the safety of the bend in the road. The noise of the shots had brought them back; they wanted to side with whoever was victorious.

'Idhar ao! Come here!' he bellowed. 'Five rupees each if you pull me in.'

He dug one hand in his back pocket, pulled out a wad of notes, waved them in the air.

'Jaldi! Hurry!'

For a moment, fear warred with greed; avarice tipped the scales. In ones and twos, and then in a crowd, they ran to the winch, and, ignoring the body of the rifleman, began to turn the handle. Within two minutes, the wooden platform was bumping against the cliffside.

Love jumped out, tied a loose rope round a ring set into the base of the tower, and ran to the dead man. He had fallen on his face, and lay head downwards. Blood, its first force spent now that the heart had stopped pumping, dripped steadily from rock to rock down the ravine. Strips of flesh, tufts of hair, were scattered on the bushes. Already flies buzzed noisily about the wounds; the smell and taste of death fouled the warm morning.

Love rolled the man over on his back, and the coolies gave shrill cries of horror at the sight of violent death. He ripped away the handkerchief from his mouth.

The dead face of Ismail Beg, the Regional Tourist Officer, looked up at him.

Love let go of his body; it collapsed like a dropped sack. God, what a mess. He went through Beg's pockets, but there was no identity card or passport, not even a rupee. In one pocket; reddened with blood, he found a piece of paper folded around something hard, the size of a visiting card.

Written in capital letters in pencil were the numbers SHA 1758. He looked across at Akbar's Jeep; this was its registration number. So he had been definitely waiting for this Jeep to make the crossing.

He unfolded the paper, turned over the small card it had contained. It was a head-and-shoulders photograph of a man in a bush-hat taken with a Polaroid Land camera, the sort that developed its own pictures. In the background was a small plane, a Fokker Friendship, the passenger door open. The hairs on Love's neck began to prickle with horror.

He was holding a picture of himself.

It must have been taken when he landed at Gilgit. Love remembered how Akbar had stopped the Jeep, farther up the road, his surprise when he found he was armed, the brief flash of light from the other side of the ravine. That must have been a signal; why Akbar had taken good care to stay on the far bank.

Love sat down shakily on a warm piece of rock, trying to sift his thoughts into some kind of sequence. But every permutation, every rearrangement produced the same answer: Ismail Beg, whom he had only met once, and then on friendly terms, had deliberately tried to murder him.

CHAPTER FIVE: LONDON — GILGIT, JANUARY 11

MacGillivray sat at his desk above the fruit importing business of Sensoby and Ransom in Covent Garden, his mind freewheeling.

Through the double windows with their aluminium-lined curtains, the morning hubbub of the market outside came up muted and remote, as though the ordinary sounds of an everyday world had no part in his life; and indeed they seemed to have little.'

On the black blotting-paper of the desk pad before him - black to minimize the risk of anyone reading in the mirror, what he might have, written with too full a pen - lay a single sheet of flimsy. A few paragraphs were typed on it, the digest of the previous twelve hours' Intelligence reports. They bore no heading, no date, no signature, and had been condensed from overnight messages sent in by various agents, from radio monitoring stations that the Foreign Office operated under such covers as a wireless research station and an experimental shortwave establishment and from other sources.

As MacGillivray read them no mark of his feelings showed on his face, but the feeling grew that with every day that passed, the more complicated his job became. Soon, it seemed to him, he could best be replaced by a computer, for each week the importance of electronics and other gadgetry in the gathering of information grew.

He remembered when the idea of hiding microphones in hotel rooms and elsewhere had seemed highly novel and hardly fair. As a result, it had become a standing order that British agents would never pass information within earshot of others, in cafes, or trains. If forced by emergency to exchange urgent messages, they would meet in a washroom, turn on the taps and talk against this noise. This was because tests had shown that even if the washroom were bugged, no known microphone could separate the sound of human speech from the rush of the water - a noise known electronically as 'white.

But now the first paragraph on the paper described how West German scientists had perfected a device that could wipe away this masking background and leave only the voices: Ah, well, they'd have to meet somewhere else. But where? Already long-range microphones could pick up a conversation from several hundred yards; the old plan of meeting in the middle of fields, on a moor, on waste land was not foolproof any longer. Something altogether more sophisticated would be necessary.

MacGillivray made a note on his pad to check with the electronics people. Could-agents carry midget transistors pre-set to transmit at will so that their high-frequency signals would block this new filter?

The next paragraph concerned one of Nasser's men who had been caught at night in the upper room of a West Berlin safe house with the lights out, the windows open; he had been transmitting classified material along an infra-red beam to an East German agent perched on the roof of a house over the Wall.

Only a few months ago this message would have had to be handed along a complicated network of go-betweens, with the risk of capture, of the double cross each time it changed hands, with death as the forfeit for failure. Now science had shortened the journey.

He read on without enthusiasm. In Lucerne, a tourist had been about to take a photograph of the Lake when his camera had exploded and killed him. The man had carried no identity papers, but a sealed envelope had been found in an inner pocket. Inside this envelope was a wad of paper sheets, each cut to the size of a Swiss fifty-franc note. In his right trouser turn-up was a claim ticket for the station left-luggage office.

The local police had presented this in exchange for a suitcase containing ski clothes, a .22 match pistol, several photographs of Ibrahim Khan taken from different angles and at different places.

A finger-print test, checked with Interpol, identified the dead man as one Kemal Sirokski, an Albanian subject, a professional assassin believed to have been implicated in the attempt to kill President Bourguiba, and in the abortive uprising against King Idris of Libya. In addition, he was thought to have worked for the nucleus, of agents that Red China maintained.

Well, thought MacGillivray dourly, he'd not work for anyone again. Like Cicero, the German spy who stole the details of the 1944 D-Day invasion while working as the British Ambassador's valet in Ankara, Sirokski had been paid in worthless notes. The means of killing him, too, reminded him of another wartime incident, the way in which two Bulgarians the Russians had chosen to kill von Papen had met with their death.

They had been provided with two camera cases of different colours. One contained a bomb to throw at von Papen, the other a smokescreen under which they could escape. But alas for them they missed von Papen - and the second case contained not a harmless smoke canister but a second bomb which killed them both immediately.

MacGillivray lit a cheroot, thought about the fearful complications of treachery, the ultimate wages of nearly every spy. He thought back to two more recent cases that had touched him closely. In 1957, a Ukrainian anti-Communist, one Lev Rebet, was found dead on his office stairs, of a heart attack, so a doctor said. Two years later, another anti-Communist, a Russian exile, Stefan Bandera, was found dying on his own doorstep. The verdict was suicide, while of unsound mind.

Then, in the early 1960s, a professional Russian assassin, Bogdan Stashynski, fled to the West, for he had served his purpose; he knew too much and his masters considered he had outlived his use to them.

He admitted he had killed both men with an electrically fired spray-gun which blew a whiff of prussic acid into their faces.

One breath would kill instantly; he knew this, for he had tried the weapon on his own dog. He reached Germany safely; was tried, sentenced to eight years' imprisonment, for the real murderers remained unknown. But so long were the tentacles of the Russian spy-net, so devious its web, that he is still being moved from prison to prison in secret, lest he is also murdered.

MacGillivray thought also of Nikolai Khoklov, another Soviet assassin, sent to murder Georgi Oklovich who led a Russian resistance group in West Berlin. Khoklov had two assistants, both East German Communists; they collected their weapons from the left-luggage office at Frankfurt station; electrically discharged guns built into cigarette-cases. They were to open the case, squeeze one end, and out through the cigarettes would go the bullet; no sound, no smoke, no smell. Their target would drop and they would lose themselves in the crowd.

Khoklov carried a second pistol, also electrically fired, in case their victim did not smoke. This had three sets of bullets one ordinary, one designed to stupefy, the third with cyanide in its head to make the slightest flesh wound mortal.

But Khoklov had second thoughts about his assignment; how did he know that he would not also die as soon as he had carried it out? He surrendered to the man he had come to kill, was given asylum - and a constant guard - by the Americans. Even so, he was poisoned by an unknown enemy, and only the fact that he was rushed to an American military hospital within minutes saved his life.

MacGillivray thought of the infinite cunning of political murderers. Although the fifty years between the two major assassinations of the century - in Sarajevo in 1914, in Dallas, Texas, in 1963 - had seen phenomenal advances in scientific and electronic technology, the means of murder remained the same: the bullet.

Now this was at last becoming obsolete. French OAS terrorists, out to murder President de Gaulle during a visit to St Hermine in Vendee province in France, had concealed a radio-operated bomb in an ornamental vase near the dais' where he was due to speak. It was controlled by a man a hundred yards away - through a midget transmitter in his coat pocket. Fortunately someone talked, the plan was discovered. Despite all electronic progress, the human element remained the weakest in any chain of events.

He read on.

The CIA Liaison Division were reporting on their latest experiments with lasers; one had carried more radio messages than all the cables under the Atlantic. At this rate, he thought, soon even the infra-red ray would be obsolete, and then, in time, something else would supersede the laser. And what would be new then? He looked out through the dusty windows, seeing nothing, thinking back to his own first case in 1935. No lasers, no infra-red beams, no lethal cigarette-cases or exploding cameras; simply suspicion - and a bit of luck.

A Margate landlady complained to the local police that a German photographer had rented her bungalow and left without paying his bill. Going through some belongings he had left behind, she found a roll of film in a suit of dungarees. When developed, it showed various views of local airfields. Then the German returned unexpectedly - and turned out to be Dr Hermann Goertz, one of Nazi Germany's senior espionage photographers. He was tried, convicted, imprisoned, but released just before the war - in time to parachute into Southern Ireland, where he operated a sabotage group until he was captured for the second time. After the war Goertz committed suicide by swallowing an 'L' pill which had been smuggled in to him, rather than return to Germany. Sometimes it was better to die than to live and report failure.

MacGillivray lit a corner of the paper with his lighter; it was chemically treated and burned fiercely, curling into a crumpled brown skin. He crushed this to powder, blew the dust into his metal wastepaper basket, picked up a copy of *Country Life*. How refreshingly, friendly and honest the advertisements seemed after the cold facts of electronic espionage. Two hundred acres in North Wales, with 'mature standing timber' - why the devil couldn't they simply say big trees? Another estate with what the agent described as 'much valuable land', apparently so valuable that he gave no price.

Very pleasant thought MacGillivray; very pleasant indeed. If he had, say, a million pounds deposited with a Swiss bank, he could easily spend £50,000 on such a house, and still have as much to spend on renovations and improvements, without feeling the draught. The phrase, a million pounds, had a nice round ring; a cool million was the cliché. But why not a hot million? Hot. Tainted. Stolen. The great train robbery. The wages of sin were often immediate and tax free. Such thoughts led him back to the Nawab of Shahnagar and his problem.

MacGillivray's acquaintance in the Treasury had raised no objection to delaying by ten days the Nawab's request to transfer his second gift of two million pounds, so long as the Treasury were not implicated in any way. Although the man had first pointed out the anachronism of a big-game hunter wishing to subscribe to an organization dedicated, to preserving big game, he now wished fervently that he had never done so. He was due for retirement in less than a year, he didn't want to become involved in anything that could conceivably affect the CBE he was bound to receive if he stayed the course uncontroversially.

But already five days had passed, and the only word MacGillivray had received from Love had been a request to find out whether the Pakistan Government maintained a Regional Tourist Officer in Gilgit. MacGillivray thanked God he'd been able to intercept this message before Sir Robert could read it, and pass his comments. Sir Robert knew, of course, that Love was in Shahnagar and why, and his presence there had drawn forth, some hard remarks, even though MacGillivray had assured C that Love was travelling purely as a doctor to see a patient.

He had added, against C's derisive remarks, that if Love were unsuccessful in helping the Nawab, then Six would take no blame as he had nothing to do with him. But if he succeeded, they would naturally claim full credit at the bank of governmental goodwill. Sir Robert had retorted that at the rate of progress so far, all they'd have was a debit balance.

MacGillivray turned the page and marked another advertisement. A Victorian house, four miles from Pitlochry. Formal gardens, grass tennis court, three acres rough pasture, outbuildings, coach-house; Could be converted. Lodge at present untenanted. Whole for sale unexpectedly owing to bereavement.

That sounded more like him. He remembered spending his school summer holidays in the Trossachs, standing up to his thighs in the river, fishing. He hadn't been back for thirty years. He began to wonder how much it had all changed, whether the roads were still surfaced with gravel, whether any air could feel as fresh, whether any other water could be as clear. He felt a sudden longing to return, to walk the springy peaty turf again, to escape from the convolutions of spying, the double agent, the treble cross. He had four days leave due; but, no, he'd never get away. He'd too much in the pipeline; the almost impossible business of infiltrating the Chinese Arms Mission in Tanzania; how to devise a safe cover for two men in Indonesia; the worry of a trusted agent who was two days overdue with his routine signal from the Yemen.

His adjutant knocked on the door, paused and came in holding a folder with the familiar red star on the cover. To underline the secrecy of what it contained, the folder was tied with pink tape, and the bow sealed in glossy red wax.

MacGillivray nodded a dismissal and snipped the tape irritably. These futile precautions always annoyed him. *Quis custodiat custodies?* What use were all these seals and stars if the man who had typed the message simply took; another copy for the other side? That had happened embarrassingly often before now; doubtless it would happen again...

He opened the file. Inside lay a sheet of flimsy on which was typed a decoded message from Dr Love. It had been sent to Cape Town, then on to a wood-carving shop in Colombo, across to Nassau as a request for holiday bookings, finally to Sensoby and Ransom as an order for Israeli melons to be delivered to an hotel off Oxford Street. Such a roundabout route took a few hours longer, but it made every message immeasurably more difficult to intercept.

At least the doctor was still alive; that was something. He read on. The governess to the Nawab's son had given him two letters to post, one apparently to her brother and the other to a man friend, a mechanic in a garage outside Perth. So?

MacGillivray read the rest of the message twice, and then put down the sheet of flimsy on his blotter, lit another cheroot. He had dwelt for so long on the shadowy, undefined frontiers of espionage and evil that he knew instinctively how agents reacted, what motives worked within them; thus answers sometimes came before questions. This could, be one of those times.

He pressed an intercom button on his desk and his secretary entered. The door closed soundlessly behind her on its vacuum stop. She stood, sexless, all other thoughts sublimated in her concentration, awaiting his command like some Pitman-trained genie, pencil poised above her short-hand book.

'Ah, Miss Jenkins,' he said, focusing his thoughts. 'A high priority to Hong Kong. Coded top secret message begins: Find and report whereabouts, condition, health and political inclination former British soldier with Glosters, Private Cameron Ryan captured Korea, believed remains with Chinese. Undertake assignment without subject's knowledge. Advise urgentest. Message ends.

'Before you send it, get his army number from Records at the War Office. And ask them to dig out a photo. Put it in the next bag for Hong Kong just in case he hasn't changed too much since it was taken.'

She snapped the rubber band on her notebook, left quietly on her sensible, low-heeled shoes.

MacGillivray pressed another intercom key; Superintendent Mason of the Special Branch answered.

'Mac here;' said MacGillivray. 'Going over now.' He pushed the scrambler button.

'I wonder if you could do a small job for us?'

'How small?'

Mason's voice was wary. When Six started with a request like that, you never knew how or where or when it would end. Or if.

'Almost minuscule,' MacGillivray assured him soothingly. 'To look into the background of a couple of people in Scotland. One's the mother of a young girl out in the Himalayas. I'd say she's harmless. In fact, we could leave her out of it altogether. The other is the girl's boyfriend. I've got his name and address.'

'We'll do our best,' said Mason without enthusiasm. 'But we're a bit pushed at present One of those bloody demonstrations at Holy Loch that we've got to cover. And we just haven't enough people for everything. You know how it is? Even policemen like to sleep at home occasionally.'

'It must make a change,' MacGillivray agreed. He paused to let what he had decided to say sound spontaneous. He might not be able to return to Scotland himself, but at least he could travel by proxy; he'd send his adjutant. Give the fellow a change from polishing his arse in an office.

'Look,' he went on. 'My adjutant's got a few days free, and he's going to Scotland in any case.'

This was not strictly true; but he was going all the same.

'If it would help you, he could dig about. Give him a bit of practice. But I don't want to poach on your territory.'

'No question of that. Poach where you like, so long as we're not involved if there's a balls-up. You know how lines get crossed and people think they're being slighted. But in case he runs into trouble, I can give you a couple of names. OK?'

'OK. And one other thing. This boyfriend works in a garage. Can you rustle up some old car from your brother-in-law so that my adjutant could use it as a card of entry - something to get this character talking?'

MacGillivray knew that the Superintendent's brother-in-law ran a garage specializing in vintage sports cars; he would not be unwilling to hire one out if business were slack.

'I'll have a word and ring you,' Mason promised him. 'Anything else?'

'Not this time. Be seeing you.'

MacGillivray flicked up the switch, and went back to *Country Life.*

Could be a lot worse: he would mark two definite houses for the adjutant to look at and report on, plus one or two, possibles. Yes, from where he sat, it could be a hell of a lot worse. He pressed the buzzer to break the news.

*

From where Love sat, on a round rock at the side of the Gilgit road, it seemed enough that he was still alive; that he could feel the sun warm on his back, hear the roar of the river and the scream of the screeching birds. For a moment it had been touch and go whether he'd end up like Ismail Beg. He had touched and gone; but the nearness of his escape made his hands tremble slightly as he lit a Gitane, drew in the smoke gratefully. He still felt a little sick from reaction, the aftermath of danger. In the war he had had friends, companions in danger; now he was alone and a long way from home. What a bloody, quixotic idiot he had been ever to become involved in events so far out of his experience; what an unbelievable cretin to draw the fire of another man's enemies deliberately. Well, he had only himself to thank for what might happen. This thought gave him no comfort at all. He stubbed out his cigarette; even that tasted sour today;

One of the coolies approached him. He was taller than the rest, with a lined, sad face, as though he had discovered all that was wrong with the world long ago but could put his knowledge to no use. His teeth were reddened with betel-nut so that his mouth seemed perpetually full of blood.

'You. promised us five rupees each, sahib,' he began reproachfully.

'So I did,' Love agreed. Memory floated up through his other thoughts. 'How many of you are there?'

'Ten, sahib. I'm the leader.'

'Ten at five; fifty chips. Love undid the button of his back trouser pocket and nicked his thumb along the edge of ten notes, without taking the whole bundle from his pocket. He did not want them to see how much money he was carrying; violence could be an infectious virus, and at ten to one the odds were unwieldy.

'Cover the body and put it in the back of the Jeep,' he told them. 'Then you'll get the money.'

The coolie unwound his turban; bandaged the dead man's hands across his chest. Love looked away across the ravine. He wondered where Akbar was, but the road was empty and the sun was in his eyes: he could see no movement.

Four coolies carried Ismail Beg's body to the Jeep, heaved it in the back, next to Love's bedding roll, covered it with a tarpaulin. Then they all lined up, as though on pay parade, left hands outstretched, right hands ready to salaam as soon as they received their money. Each in turn touched his forehead with the five-rupee note as Love paid them.

'Who was this man?' Love asked the leader casually, pointing to the hump beneath the tarpaulin.

'Nay malum, sahib. I don't know.'

He spoke so quickly that Love guessed he had been told not to talk, or else was afraid to.

'Did any of you see him before?' Love went on, looking at each man in turn. They shook their heads, their faces blank masks, registering nothing, admitting nothing.

'I have ten rupees more for each man if *anyone* tells me.'

Still they stared back at him blankly, not wishing to admit that they understood the question, knowing he could not force an answer. In their minds greed fought with fear, but fear was victorious; the price was too low, the risk immeasurable. They had to go on working here; there was nothing in this for them but trouble if they became involved. You could not buy safety with ten rupees; you could not buy it at all; the sahib must be mad.

'What is your name?' Love asked the head coolie.

'Nay malum, sahib,' he said. 'I don't know.'

It was useless to go on. He would only come up against an endless wall of silence. Yet someone must have built that wall with fear and threats; someone was sheltering on the other side. But who?

He bent over the Jeep's engine, reconnected the plug lead, joined the two ignition wires together, started the engine.

Then he drove off the trolley on to the road. No-one moved to help him, but, equally important, no-one tried to stop him leaving. His last view of the coolies in his driving mirror was of ten men in a line, watching him. Possibly they were as puzzled as he was himself.

Love trod down the accelerator, and took the first bend. The steering wheel had five inches play each way, and the brake shoes were worn to the rivets, but the engine seemed healthy enough. Even so, he did not risk stopping until he reached the Political Agent's bungalow.

The same sentry saluted as he turned into the drive; or at least, he looked the same. Love wondered whether he did, too; he climbed out in front of the bungalow, smacked dust from his trousers. It was only when he stood upright that he realized how cramped he had been on the journey, what an effort it had been to control the creaking vehicle.

A Pakistani in sports coat and flannels came out to meet him as he walked up the steps to the bungalow.

'You wish to see the Agent?' he asked in English.

'Yes,' said Love, wondering whether the Agent would wish to see him when he knew what the tarpaulin concealed.

'Please come inside.'

The Political Agent sat on a sofa under the broad blades of a slowly turning fan, reading *Last Essays* by the Earl of Birkenhead. What a man, he thought in admiration; what an advocate; what a decade in which to live. He put down his spectacles on a side table and stood up, hand outstretched. Love sat down wearily.

'You look tired,' the Agent said politely. Would you like a drink?' He pressed a bell. An orderly came in with a jug of *nimbu pani* covered by a square of beaded muslin. The Political Agent poured out two glasses; Love drank gratefully.

'I've come to report something rather serious,' Love began, choosing his words carefully. Then he paused. Really, the whole episode sounded ludicrous; only the body humped in the Jeep outside proved that he hadn't imagined the whole thing.

The Agent looked at him, spatulate fingers pressed together, eyebrows raised expectantly. He was paid to hear everything, serious or not. The breeze from the fan fluttered the pages of his open book; he placed a polished piece of pyrites on it to keep his place.

'Yes?' he prompted patiently.

'I was driving back this morning from Shahnagar in Akbar's Jeep,' began Love. 'One road was blocked, and so we crossed the river by some sort of winch and rope and tackle. Halfway over, a man fired at me with a rifle from the far bank. He smashed half the windscreen. He fired again, and broke the other half. I had a pistol with me, so I shot back. Then the coolies pulled me in. I regret to say I killed him.'

Well, there it was, a confession of murder.

'You *killed* him?' asked the Political Agent in a horrified voice.

'Yes.'

'Who was he?'

'A man I mentioned to you when we last met. The Regional Tourist Officer.'

'But we have no such officer. I think I told you?'

'You haven't now, anyway.'

'Where is the body?'

'In the back of my Jeep outside. Under a tarpaulin.'

'Were you wounded at all, Doctor?'

'No.'

'You are sure you recognized the man?'

'Positive.'

'Why do you think he shot at you?'

Love shrugged. He said nothing about the photograph and the folded paper; nor about Akbar stopping the Jeep in the lee of the mountain. The fewer people who knew these things, the better.

'And how did you have a pistol with you. Doctor? It is forbidden to carry arms without a licence.'

The Agent's eyes were hard as pebbles; he was no-one's fool.

'A friend gave me one,' said Love lamely.

'I see.'

Disbelief edged the Agent's voice.

The Commissioner of Police is away in 'Pindi. An officer in the Scouts is standing in for him. I'll give him a ring. Were there any witnesses?'

'Only the coolies on the winch. And they ran away.'

'What about your driver, Akbar? Did he see this?'

Love shrugged.

'God knows. He stayed on the near bank when, I went over. I haven't seen him since. Maybe he ran away, too.'

'No doubt he'll turn up here in Gilgit in due course. Meanwhile, please leave his Jeep here with the - ah - body. My driver will take you back to the Rest House.'

The Agent opened the door, and led Love out into a courtyard behind the, house. The Agent's Jeep stood waiting, agleam with polish; the Pakistan flag drooped at its bonnet. The driver saluted; Love climbed in; they moved forward with a discreet putter of exhaust.

News of Love's ambush and his escape had somehow preceded him. The Rest House bearer, the gardener, the chowkidar, stood in line on the veranda to salaam him, their left hands already outstretched for the expected backsheesh. He nodded to them all and went into his room. The bearer padded after him carrying two old oil drums full of hot water suspended from a wooden yoke like milk churns across his shoulders. He emptied them into the bath. Love undressed and sank gratefully into the steaming water.

It was dusk by the time he had towelled himself down and dressed in the clean clothes the bearer had laid out for him. After he saw the Scouts' officer, he might, or might not, be free to return to Shahnagar. And then what? Would there be yet another attempt on his life - and where and by whom, and why? If all the bearers already knew he had escaped an ambush, so would those who had arranged it. They would also guess he'd want to leave as soon as possible. And since it would obviously be easier for them to make another attempt on his life when he was here, rather than wait until he had returned to a city, the Boy Scouts' motto had best prevail; he'd be prepared.

With some luck, events might carry him on the swell of their tide. With a little more luck, he might yet reach harbour safely.

The bearer brought in a plate of lamb curry and a bottle of Murree beer. He ate his supper in his room and then pulled the curtains together closely and stood the bed-light on a small table so that any watcher outside would think he was sitting at the desk. He put his pencil torch in his pocket, wedged open the bathroom door with a piece of wood from the fireplace, removed the electric bulb from its holder in the ceiling.

The uncurtained bathroom window was set high up in the wall, a square of deep blue cut into the darkness. Through it he could see the rising moon. Love let himself out of the bathroom door, locked it behind him, pocketed the key. He paused for a moment, back pressed against the outside wall, to accustom his eyes to the darkness. The night air smelt of wood smoke; the brickwork was still warm under his fingertips. Somewhere in the gloom a cricket whirred like a rusty ratchet; another hidden unknown creature croaked in reply. Love remembered the unseen lizards that would cough, Tuc-too, tuc-too, in the jungle during the war, and the rhyming replies from his platoon. Odd, the long forgotten memories a chance sound, a scent, a taste could evoke.

He tiptoed along the wall of the building until he reached the back door of the bathroom of the next room, and tested the handle. It was unlocked. He opened the door, closed it silently behind him.

In the thin, unexpected beam of his torch, a stone-coloured lizard scuttled across the damp concrete floor; in one corner the lavatory cistern dripped like a metronome.

He went on into the bedroom. The red-and-white striped mattress was rolled up on the bed with three folded blankets and a striped pillow pulled on top of it. The air smelt musty, as though the doors and windows had been shut for too long; clearly the Rest House wasn't so busy that it was turning away trade.

Love flicked off his torch, sat down in an easy chair, put his feet up on the bedside table and tried to doze. He was tired, but his nerves were taut and sleep was impossible until he gave up trying.

He awoke suddenly, instantly alert. The faint scratching noise from the veranda that had woken him was repeated. It could be a pi-dog rooting for scraps, or someone outside his room carefully trying the door. He decided it must be a dog who walked on two legs.

He looked at the luminous hands of his Juvenia watch; half-past one in the morning, an odd time for anyone to come calling. He swung his feet off the table, flexed his arms to rid himself of stiffness, and tiptoed out through the bathroom, round the back of the building and into his own bathroom.

A tap was dripping, glob, glob, glob. In a damp corner, mosquitoes whined complainingly. Love moved silently into the bedroom doorway. The moon had risen and it shone through a fanlight above the curtains. The bearer had turned down his bedding and laid out his pyjamas invitingly on the white sheet. A carafe of water with an inverted glass on top stood near the lamp he had left alight.

To the right of the room, the cupboard doors were still closed; the silvered oil drum gleamed dully in the fireplace; the curtains were drawn behind the door. Perhaps he'd made a mistake? Perhaps he was imagining things? Perhaps he wasn't.

He put his hand into his pocket and flicked a two-anna piece across the room. It hit the mirror at the back of the dressing-table and slid along the floor. He heard a sharp intake of breath on the other side of the cupboard. So he had been right; he was not alone.

Love took one pace forward and then jumped to the right. A quick whip with the edge of his left arm against a bony wrist, then a pull on the right shoulder with his right hand. (How often he had taught this basic defence to his British Legion judo class in the village hall at' Bishop's Combe; Lesson four: defence against an upward stab with a knife.) The preaching worked in practice, too; a knife clattered uselessly to the floor, just as the training manual said it would.

He stopped himself making the follow through, the ferocious upward blow with his right knee into the hidden face. He had to discover who his caller was; if he used that blow, he would discover nothing except that he had another body on his hands. He spun the man round so that the light shone on his face. And then he let him go. He was holding Akbar, his Jeep driver.

Love released him and stepped back a pace, watching him warily, prepared to parry any judo movement. But the man made no attempt to attack him. He simply pushed himself farther against the right angle of the wall and the cupboard, his mouth agape with fear, his eyes clouded with alarm.

'You,' said Love, releasing his arm in surprise. 'What the hell are you doing in my room? What happened to you when I was shot at?'

'Sahib, I ran,' explained Akbar simply. 'As I told you, I have one mother, three children, two wives and my mother's mother, all dependent on me. What is to happen to them then if I am killed, sahib?'

'But why the knife?' Love kicked it under the bed; he didn't want Akbar to get any ideas beyond his capabilities.

'I was afraid, sahib. There are evil men in this town now. I could get no answer from my knock, sahib. I saw a light in your room and came in. All times was I tapping on the window and not any reply did I hear.'

The explanation sounded plausible, and yet it did not convince Love entirely; he had heard too many edited confessions in his surgery not to recognize the wheedling tone of someone willing his hearer to believe that half a story was the whole.

'That's not the real reason,' said Love softly. 'Now, why did you come here?'

'I'll tell you,' a voice said in English behind him. 'He came to collect you.'

Love turned, but too late. Hands pinned his arms to his sides. Akbar's face split into a grin. Then he spat into Love's face.

'There's your answer - *sahib,*' he sneered.

'Who are you?' asked Love angrily, twisting his head round to see the heavily built Pathan who held him. The man deftly slipped his wrists under Love's elbows; if Love moved suddenly, he would only break his arms. The Pathan did not bother to reply. He frisked Love's jacket, took out the Smith & Wesson, put it in his own pocket.

'You're coming with us,' he said simply. 'And do not try to escape. You will only break a bone if you struggle, and you will not escape. There is nowhere to escape to, in any case.'

He nodded towards Akbar, who switched out the light. Then he pulled the curtain, opened the door. A chill wind blew in from the darkness. Love shivered; the taste of sleep was still in his mouth. What a bloody fool he was, to imagine that he could beat professionals; he was playing out of his league, the Bishop's Combe Second XI against Real Madrid.

The two men marched him into a Jeep parked round the side of the Rest House, beneath the trees. Akbar drove and the Pathan sat behind, holding Love's right arm up behind his back. Love wondered briefly whether this was Akbar's Jeep, but in the darkness he could not be sure, and, in any case, what did it matter now, what the hell did anything matter now?

But the rush of night air refreshed him, so that by the time they reached the empty main street where the dust lay inches thick, white as flour under the high moon, he felt more relaxed, even slightly more cheerful, although he had little enough to be cheerful about. Sleepers lay on the shop verandas, brass bowls at their heads, their bodies wrapped in white sheets, like shrouds. He remembered, without, enthusiasm, Sir Thomas Browne's words, 'Sleep is, in fine, so like death, I dare not trust it without my prayers.' He wished he had said his own.

Akbar turned off between two shops, and bumped up a dirty, unmade alley. The boom of their exhaust beat back from mud walls, scrawled with Urdu slogans and cheap advertisements sprayed on to the crumbling houses. A few chickens, disturbed under a box by the lights and the engine, squawked away in a flurry of fear. Love knew how they must feel; he felt much the same himself. The Jeep stopped.

'Get out,' said the Pathan.

He jumped down and pulled Love roughly after him. A door opened in the wall and shut behind them on a vacuum stop. A light clicked on; Love was standing in an office with pale paint and panelled walls. In one corner was a heavy desk. He noted the telephone, the shaded lamp, the bowl of pins and rubber bands, the sickly scent of flowers. Mr Chin sat in a black leather swivel-chair behind the desk, watching him, his face round as a bladder of lard, and wearing about as much expression.

'What the hell is all this rubbish?' asked Love angrily. 'What is this - an inquisition?'

'I'll ask the questions,' said Mr Chin smoothly. 'Why are you in Gilgit, Dr Love?'

'Because I can't get out to Rawalpindi without passing through. Anything else?'

'We believe you are some kind of agent. Doctor, here for a purpose that we feel is hostile.'

'If you believe that you'd believe anything,' said Love, misquoting Samuel Johnson (or was it the Duke of Wellington?). 'I'm a doctor who came here to examine the Nawab's son.'

'We know all about that. But what we don't know all about is *you,* Doctor. And that interests us.'

'What do you want to know?' asked Love. 'I've survived two, possibly three, attempts to kill me. I've had my baggage searched. Now I've apparently been kidnapped. Who the hell are *you,* in any case?'

'Please don't treat this as a joke. Doctor,' warned Mr Chin. 'We do not like violence in my country, but we have a proverb my old father likes to quote. *Yi yi chih yi,* which means, roughly, "Use one barbarian to checkmate another." My friends here can be barbarians at times:'

'So I've discovered.'

'Then spare them the excuse to be barbarians again. Who sent you here?'

Love said nothing. What could he say that this man would believe, that would even sound believable? Who was this man, in any case? One of the Committee anxious to preserve big game?'

Mr Chin gave a slight nod. The Pathan hit Love across the back of the neck with the edge of his hand. Love staggered forward on his elbows, half falling over the table. Without leaving his seat, Mr Chin drew back his left hand and flicked his fist into Love's face.

Love tried to ride the blow, but lost his balance, and fell back on the stone floor. Akbar prodded him in the kidneys with his boot.

'Get up,' said Mr Chin. 'You're making things hard for yourself. Doctor. We cannot spend all night here with you, so I'll give you three to talk. *One.*'

'There's nothing more to say,' said Love. 'I've told you, I'm an English doctor, here to see a patient.'

'*Two.*'

Love shrugged; they were determined to rough him up; nothing he could say now would alter this intention. '*Three.*'.

Again Mr Chin nodded, but this time Love was better prepared. He heard the slight intake of breath behind him that presaged another blow, and kicked back with his right heel. Akbar screamed in pain as the unexpected metal tip bit into his shin bone.

Love spun around in the judo move, and cut across the Pathan's throat with the edge of his left hand. He staggered back, bumped into Akbar. Love thrust his left knee under the desk and heaved it up and over on to the Chinaman. Then he jumped for the door and tore at the handle.

The door stayed locked.

Mr Chin stood up slowly. His flabby, pale face was flushed; he had lost his most precious possession; he had lost status. He would make this sweating, long-nosed barbarian repay the loss. From, his side pocket he took what Love recognized from a book of firearms MacGillivray had once shown him as a .35 Luger.

'Do not move Doctor,' he said quickly, neither surprise nor anger in his voice. 'You have left me no alternative but to kill you. I may say that you seem to have been extremely clever - or extremely lucky - to avoid the earlier attempts you mention. I'll never know which now, but this I do know. Fourth time will be unlucky for you.

'I have asked you some civil questions, but instead of answering them, you persist in these foolish heroics. We have no more time to waste. Doctor. No more time at all.'

He paused. Love tried to speak, but his mouth was dry, he could not find any words. The moment was etched in his mind with the acid of experience; the strange room with the smell of flowers in his nose; Akbar breathing heavily; the Pathan watching him through narrowed eyes; the fat man with the blue-steel gun in his hand. This was the end, then. To be killed by a man he had never met before, for a reason he would never know. The irony was almost unbearable. He found a voice, not the voice he remembered as his, but someone else's, a voice that could only speak one word.

'Wait,' he said hoarsely, with this other man's voice.

At that moment the telephone rang on Mr Chin's desk.

He looked first at the Pathan, then at Love. 'Don't move,' he said. 'Stay exactly where you are.' He jammed the muzzle of his Lüger against Love's stomach. Love stayed, he thought what an enlargement a .35 bullet would make of his navel if he moved; it was not a comforting thought: He hoped that Mr Chin had a steady finger.

Still watching him, Mr Chin picked up the telephone.

'The Himalaya Travel Agency here,' he said.

'Oh, great.' A woman's Texas drawl filled the room. 'Say, I've been trying to get you for ages, but there's been no reply.'

Love could imagine her; a complexion ruined by too much steam heat, her hair rinsed blue, fingernails painted metallic mauve, her husband somewhere in the background, somewhere far in the background, ineffectual but rich.

'It is after hours. We are officially closed,' Mr Chin said, still watching Love, the barrel of his Lüger pressed like a steel finger into his body.

'That's just what I told my husband, but he's still coming right on down to meet with you. As you know, we've booked through you to Rawalpindi and then on to New Delhi this afternoon - name of Wilbraham - and we're out on the first plane tomorrow at six.

'I can't find my health papers, and I'm sure I gave them to your clerk in your front office. So Maxie - he's my husband - he's on his way now to try and find them.'

'But I have said we are closed, madam.'

'I know. You told me. I told him. But even so it won't take a minute to find them, and I won't have time in the morning, we're off so soon. 'Bye!'

The phone whirred as she put down the receiver. Mr Chin said, 'Some American's on his way here, as you heard. You, Akbar, see if you can find that form. It's a yellow booklet, an international form. Hurry. He'll be here any minute.'

The back door bell rang.

'He's here now,' said Love.

'You keep quiet,' whispered Mr Chin. He turned to the Pathan.

'Put him in the cupboard until we're clear. He can't escape.'

The Pathan seized Love's right arm while Mr Chin pulled on a filing cabinet door. The whole cabinet swung away from the wall, revealing a small inner room. They pushed Love inside, the door shut behind him; he heard the click of the double Chubb locks.

This room was virtually like a cell. It had no light, no seat, was barely twelve feet square. A small window, about eighteen inches across and six feet up, allowed a square of moonlight to shine on the floor, bisected by an iron bar. Mosquitoes sang and whined, but at least they were free; they could go out through the window whenever they wanted. Love was determined to follow their example. He gripped the iron bar across the window and pulled. It stayed firm. The way things were going, he wasn't only out of his league, he seemed set to lose the match.

Then he remembered the shoe-laces MacGillivray had given him, and took back some of the things he had thought about the Colonel. He knelt on one knee, ripped out the lace from his left shoe, put it in his mouth, gnawed through the brown cloth covering. A thin, flexible trepanning saw with a loop on each end glittered like a steel worm in the moonlight.

He pushed his fountain-pen through one loop, his thumb through the other and then, standing up against the window, he began to saw the vertical bar.

The blade was new, and its tiny teeth, although seemingly no rougher to the touch than a cat's tongue, bit steadily into the metal. It was exhausting work with his hands above his head, but Love was under no illusions as to what would happen if he were still there when the Chinaman returned. Sweat streamed down between his shoulder blades, his arms ached, his whole body throbbed like one gigantic bruise that had been hammered and hammered again. Once, twice, he stopped and leaned back against the wall, his arms down by his sides, to let the blood return to his wrists. Then he forced himself to continue. If he couldn't escape now he would never have another chance. He heard voices on the other side of the wall; someone with an American accent said: 'Is that right?'

Finally, the blade slipped through the bar. Bracing himself against the wall, he pulled at the two pieces with all his strength. Slowly and steadily, they began to bend.

Holding the bottom half of the cut bar with both hands, he gave an upward leap, and, digging the toes of his shoes into the rough bricks, he clawed his way up to the window. He hung there, balancing on his elbows on the sill.

He was looking out into the back alley. Dust lay thick on the ground; a dog was rooting beneath a bush. It looked up, at Love, gave a frightened yelp and scampered away, its long yellow tail curled up under its scabby body.

The cool night air chilled Love's face. Slowly he heaved himself through the window, until he was balanced half in and half out. He could see no gutter, no drain pipe, nothing to break his fall. He pulled his handkerchief from his breast pocket and wrapped it round his hands. Then he held them out in front and wriggled with his hips until he, overbalanced.

He hit the ground on his fists, then rolled forward in a somersault. He was out, free, with only a few grazes on his knuckles where sharp flints cut the protecting handkerchief. He stood up, smoothed back his hair, started to run.

Immediately, he fell flat on his face.

He'd forgotten he had no lace in his left shoe. He took off the shoe, stuffed it in his jacket pocket, and ran on lumpily, one shoe off, one shoe on, through the dust into the main street of Gilgit. The shops were all shuttered and dark. Where the devil could he go? It would be suicide to return to the Rest House, and the Political Agent's bungalow was too far away. They'd be after him within minutes at the most, and he'd never make the distance, especially as he was not too sure of the way.

He thought briefly of running to the airfield, but he could find no shelter there, and maybe the radio operator would be off duty at this hour. Then he remembered Mogul Ahnsullah of the Gilgit Scouts. Their officers' mess lay somewhere between the Rest House and the Agent's bungalow, possibly only 500 yards away. This was his best chance; possibly his only one.

He began to run towards it, through the huge stone gates with their kite-shaped Victorian oil lamps, past the Jeep park, following the painted arrows: 'Officers' Mess.' Thankfully, he climbed the stone steps, pushed open the heavy door, bolted it behind him, and then leaned wearily against it while he regained his breath; his heart was leaping within him like an imprisoned bird.

The hall was lit by two electric bulbs in china shades. An unseen clock ticked somewhere and began, to clear its throat before it struck the hour. From the walls on either side yellowing photographs of groups of officers looked down disapprovingly at him. This sort of thing never went on in the old days, he thought; but then the old days were never like these.

He brushed down his jacket, put on his left shoe again, and walked slowly through the hall to a door at the far end marked Captain Ahnsullah. He knocked on the wood and waited.

'Come in,' said a voice.

Love turned the handle and went in. The room was lit by a red-shaded reading lamp; a log fire glowed in the grate. In the corner the mosquito net was lowered around a single bed. Along one wall ran a shelf of books; a table covered with a blanket; a framed photo of a girl in a sari looked down from the writing desk.

Reading in an easy chair, pipe in mouth, Mogul Ahnsullah stared at him in amazement.

'You,' he said slowly, lowering the book.

'Yes, me,' said Love urgently. 'I. may not have much time to explain, but it's a matter of life and death. You've got to listen to me.'

Ahnsullah stood up. Even in the dim light his face seemed cold and hostile.

'Why the hurry, Doctor?' he asked. 'You'll have plenty of time to say whatever you have to say to the appropriate authorities.'

'What do you mean?'

Events had moved too fast altogether for Love. Wheels spun in his mind like a tape machine gone mad, but the message itself was missing, nothing made sense any more.

'What do you mean?' he repeated.

'What I say, ' said Ahnsullah. 'But at least you've saved me a journey. I was coming to see you tomorrow, or, rather, later today.'

'Me.? Why?'

Love put up one hand to steady himself. Reaction was setting in, a cold hand that clawed at his heart. His shirt was clammy with sweat, his body drained of all effort. He caught sight of himself in a mirror, saw the dark bruises on his face; blood from his nose had run down his chin, soaking into his shirt, staining his light suit. He looked as though he'd been in a rough-house, but then he had, he had. Then he remembered why Ahhsullah must want to see him.

'Oh, yes,' he said, relieved. 'The man I shot on the ropeway yesterday.'

Was it only yesterday? It seemed ages ago, in another life, another world. And how far along the road to violence had he travelled when he could speak of a dead man thus; worst of all, a man he'd killed himself. What price the Hippocratic Oath now, Dr Love?

Ahnsullah shook his head gravely.

'Not only that,' he said. 'I've also been asked by the Rawalpindi police to investigate another possible charge of murder.

'A man named Bahadur, who was found dead of cyanide in your room there in the McDavid Hotel.'

CHAPTER SIX: COUPAR ANGUS, SCOTLAND - GILGIT - SHAHNAGAR JANUARY 12-13

The little red BSA motor-cycle puttered into the garage off the Coupar Angus road and stopped in front of the petrol pumps. Rain beat down on the corrugated-iron awning above them with impatient, angry fingers. The GPO messenger swung his leg off the saddle, shook the rain-water from his streaming yellow oilskins, looked about hopefully.

The door of the tiny office to one side of the repair shop stood open. An old-fashioned one-bar electric fire glowed on a nail from the distempered wall. A pneumatic blonde smiled from a trade calendar at the crude kitchen table, scored with telephone numbers and doodles, at the old pistons used as paperweights for unpaid bills; at the dashboard clock from an Austin Heavy Fourteen that ticked away the minutes.

Lubrication charts of obsolete makes of cars - Arrol-Johnston, Argyle, Bean, Clyno - were pinned around the walls: A circular Bakelite wireless, a refugee from the 1930s, with its aerial strung along the picture rail, played 'Music While You Work'. But no one seemed to be working.

A man with reddish, tousled hair and smuts of oil on his cheeks came in from the brick building at the back, wiping his hands on a piece of rag; he was in his late thirties, thick-set, with a large, heavy body, and a sullen face. His nails were ingrained with black oil; one of his knuckles red raw where a spanner had slipped.

'You want me?' he asked, more a statement of fact than a question.

'Are you Mr Rafferty?'

'Aye.'

'A telegram,' said the boy.

He handed over a damp yellow envelope. Rafferty ripped off one corner, stuck a blunt forefinger through the hole, tore it wider, took out the cable form. He read slowly, his lips mouthing the words as though he had difficulty in understanding them: 'arrived safely letter follows love mercedes'

He folded the form carefully, pushed it into his back trousers pocket.

'No reply,' he said briefly. As he sucked his split knuckle, the boy saw that his teeth were yellow and uneven. He stood for a moment, as though unwilling to return to the streaming rain and the discomfort of his motor-cycle. He peered over, the man's shoulder into the little workshop. The district nurse's black Austin A35 stood in one corner minus its engine. Next to this, the local baker's van, that had snapped a half-shaft in Scone earlier that week, was up on a trolley jack.

'Saw an old car outside here this morning,' the boy said conversationally. 'Long bonnet with lots of louvres in it, great big lamps like soup-plates with wire screens in front of them. Green. Looked a real treat.'

'Oh, that. Aye, it's a rare one. An SS100. Bit before your time. Forerunner of the Jaguar. Belongs to a gentleman up from London.'

The boy walked into the workshop under the fluorescent lights. The music followed him, through the smell of oil and petrol: 'I want to be Bobby's girl.' 'Anything wrong with it?' he asked.

'Electrics,' replied Rafferty briefly. 'It's about ten years older than you are, so it owes its owner nothing. Runs for half an hour and then packs in. Query condenser.'

'The owner's staying here?'

'Aye. Young fellow. Think he's in the army. Calls himself Captain, anyway.' Rafferty hawked in his throat and spat green phlegm on to the oily concrete floor to show what he thought of people who called themselves Captain.

'Oh, aye,' said the messenger. 'I ken the man. He's up at the Station Hotel. I've had to take five telegrams to him since he's been here.'

'Five?' repeated Rafferty, scratching his hair with his thumb nail so as not to dirty his scalp.

'Aye. And they didn't seem to make any sense to me at all.'

'What do you mean, they didn't make sense? How did you come to read them, then?'

'Saw them back in the office. They're in groups of letters. Sets of five in each. I counted them. Some sort of code, I should think.'

'Code?'

For the first time a bead of interest gleamed in Rafferty's eyes. He took out a packet of Weights, offered it to the boy.

'Let me know when he gets six, will you?' he said conversationally. 'Then I'll fix you up for a run in that SS. It's coming in again later today. I can take it up the road for testing, so there's no reason why you shouldn't come with me.'

'Wonderful,' breathed the boy rapturously. 'I will, indeed, Mr Rafferty.'

He walked out to his BSA, kicked down the starter, and was away. For some time after the little motor-cycle had disappeared along the streaming road, Rafferty stood under the corrugated-iron roofing, his hands in his pockets, a vague feeling of disquiet spreading through him like indigestion after a bad meal. Then he ground his cigarette into the wet tarmac with his heel, walked into his office.

He pulled the door shut behind him, sifted through the untidy mass of bills and receipts darkened with greasy thumbprints until he found the telephone book. The number he wanted wasn't listed, but he'd written it inside the back cover.

He dialled it and then stood, waiting nervously. The tick of the little clock was the only sound, apart from the distant burr-burring of the telephone bell in the house of the man he was calling. Perhaps he was out? He half hoped so, for there was something about the man that frightened him; something dead, evil. He was consumed by an animus that had fed for too long on bitterness and hate, that threatened to engulf not only the man who succoured it but others also.

Rafferty breathed at the mirror and with his fingers drew the sign of the cross on his breath. Then he gave ends to the arms, and found that a swastika looked back at him. As he blurred it out with his hand, the burring stopped and the harsh, cold voice he knew so well spoke in his ear.

Rafferty bent down before he replied and looked out through the glass window of the office, to make sure that no one could possibly be outside, waiting for petrol. But the forecourt was empty.

Three globes glowed on the petrol pumps, lit from within like turnip lanterns; the homely green Castrol dispenser, and beyond that the shining road stretching away emptily in the rain. An intermittent red neon sign, flickering on and off from the roof, turned the shining concrete to blood. Rafferty straightened up, took a deep breath. His orders were never to ring unless in a definite emergency, and he felt hesitant now. Then he let out his breath slowly and began to talk.

*

Four miles up the road, the estate agent was showing MacGillivray's adjutant out of a gate. He was a round, dumpy man, who wore tweed plus-fours with little green forked ribbons peeking from the turnover of his socks. Every time he showed a prospective customer over a landed property that was for sale, he hoped that he'd be taken for the owner of the estate, not just the, man who was trying to sell it.

His domed, bald head gleamed as though it had been French polished; now and then he stroked the brown skin with his right hand as though to reassure himself that he had grown no hair since he touched it last.

'Marvellous place,' he said, his voice thick with whisky and professional enthusiasm; he threw out an arm towards the derelict house that stood behind them in a wilderness of thistles and dock.

'Only wants a bit of loving care. Magnificent views. Running water in all rooms. Three lavatories. Offices. Garage for four cars. Stable. Even a peach tree in the kitchen garden - something I've never seen in Scotland before.'

'Nor me,' agreed the adjutant. 'And while we're on that, subject, I've never seen a place like this, either. You can smell the damp from here. Don't know what my colonel would say about it, but I can imagine.'

The agent looked pained. This fellow was really a bit much, with his ridiculous narrow trousers and suede boots. Damned southerner. Couldn't wonder there were so many Scottish Nationalists.

'Bound to get a bit in a house that's been shut up so long,' he pointed out defensively. 'Only natural. Can't expect otherwise. Have a fire for a couple of days, and it'll be dry as a bone.'

The adjutant grunted with disbelief. He was enjoying himself. It was a long time since he'd been able to swan off like this, and be paid for it. And there was a girl in his hotel, just up for the week, who looked an absolutely certain lay. He'd book her down to expenses as a secret contact. Which reminded him; he hadn't all the time in the world; this estate agent buffoon had rather dragged things out. He led the way through the tangled drive to his borrowed SS100 and climbed in. The estate agent groaned for breath at the unaccustomed exertion of folding himself into the narrow cockpit.

'What do you think, then? Will you make an offer?' he asked, as the adjutant let in the clutch.

'No, I fear not. Your description did that place a bit too much honour.'

'*Any* offer?' said the agent, as though he hadn't heard. 'My client is not an unreasonable man.'

'With that place on his hands, he can't afford to be. But, no, it's not what my colonel's after at all.'

They drove in silence to the agent's office.

'You have my address,' said the adjutant, as he stopped the car. 'I'm at the Station Hotel in Perth. If you find anything else within the next day or two, anything that at least keeps out the rain, please give me a ring.'

'I'll do just that,' said the agent. 'Damn' small doors you have on this car.'

'It was built for a small world,' the adjutant replied. The agent heaved himself out, gave a wave with his stick, and was away.

The adjutant looked at his watch. Four-thirty. He had killed a couple of hours very pleasantly. They'd seen three houses, all mostly ruins, full of dry rot, probably even foot rot. None was even worth reporting on to Colonel MacGillivray, and yet all had sounded idyllic in the advertisements. The adjutant couldn't understand it; despite his pretence at sophistication, he was a young man, and still believed what he read in print, even in advertisements.

He turned his thoughts back to the task in hand, wondering what luck they were having on the telephone wire. It had been a bit dodgy, actually, faking that telegram; the whole scheme could easily have fallen down if this woman Mercedes had some sort of nickname with which she always signed herself, but that was a risk there was no way round. After all, old MacGillivray had sent him off to do what he could on his own initiative. And he was proud of the idea of having five meaningless telegrams sent to him, just jumbles of letters, in groups of five. Touch of the old mystery there; he rather cared for that.

His thoughts wandered. Mercedes SSK, SL300, 32/220S; all legendary cars, men's cars, with no concessions, nothing feminine about them. He wondered what the girl was like, whether she was legendary, too, whether this Dr Love fellow had done her a bit of good yet; or perhaps he wasn't that type. Maybe he was a bit old for it, too, he thought sympathetically. Must be around forty, although from what the colonel had said he didn't act like an old man. He wondered what he'd feel like at forty; whether he'd feel any different from twenty-four.

He knew how he felt now well enough; that girl back in the hotel, the one in the tight, gold lame slacks, had a very interesting effect on him. He'd caught her bending down to pick up a letter, and there was not even the suspicion of the line of her pants. That intrigued him; it always did. You never knew what sort they'd be wearing -.if any. The permutations, the possibilities of the unknown were fascinating. She'd sensed him looking, and had stood up and their eyes had met and they'd smiled; they couldn't help smiling, because each knew what the other was thinking. What she wanted was a bit of bedroom bayonet drill, he thought, reverting to the crude phrase current when he'd been a cadet at Sandhurst; in, out, on-guard, follow through. And unless the good Lord willed otherwise, that's just what she'd get. Tonight and every night, until MacGillivray called him home.

He remembered a time in Barcelona when his cover had been the post of an assistant, on a stand at a trade fair, for a Birmingham firm, exporting jigs and portable lathes. There had been a girl, Juanita or Dolores, or some other Spanish name, with one of those skirts that flared out when she turned, and you thought you'd see something, but somehow you never did. He had, been young then, of course (though he wasn't so old now) and eager for experience.

She'd had a wonderful pair in a tight black sweater, firm and with the tips of the nipples sticking out like buttons, and he'd been chatting her up about how lovely she was, and how well she spoke English, so that when the fair closed about midnight she was delighted to join him for supper, paella and red wine. She could drink from the small glass spout on the decanter, holding it away from her mouth, so he complimented her on that, too. He tried it himself and only succeeded in spilling the wine down the front of his shirt, which gave her that edge of superiority all women like.

In the car going back she had nestled against him and made no effort to check his caressing hands. Only when he had tried to undo the clip of the brassiere between her shoulder blades had she protested, 'No, no. Not yet. *Please.*'

But the night had been warm, the wine red; and he had persisted, and suddenly, almost by accident it seemed, the clip sprang open. His hands had moved against her warm, young body, round her ribs, and then - nothing.

She had been the victim of some fearful surgery; her chest was as bony as a scrubbing board. The breasts were foam rubber, built into the bra. The memory still made him feel ashamed: Christ, what a heel he'd felt.

There would be nothing like that with this girl tonight, though. Hers were real. He knew that. He was older now; he could tell. He thought of a story the duty officer had told him on the night before he left for Scotland.

Apparently a fellow had had too much to drink, and by mistake, went into a ladies' lavatory. A girl surprised him there, .and pointed but coldly: But this is for ladies only.'

'So's this,' replied the man, 'when I've got the water out of it.'

The adjutant laughed at the memory; hell of a good joke, that. The duty officer was full of them; could go on for hours without repeating himself once. You'd wonder how he remembered them all. Life was really very good.

The old car growled along through narrow, almost empty lanes; there was something wolf-like in the vehicle, in its long searching bonnet, its huge round headlamps, the impatient male snarl of the exhaust.

He turned happily into the Perth road out towards Coupar Angus, the boom of the copper, straight-through exhaust echoing pleasantly in his ears. Half a mile past Balbeggie he saw the big khaki GPO repair van pulled up to the left-hand grass verge. It was shielded by a portable trellis, two red flags and a road sign that exclaimed dramatically: DANGER, GPO WORKS, as though it was news that the GPO did actually work. Bit of a gag, really. He'd try it on the duty officer when he got back, although it wasn't really up to his standard.

Two men in overalls were brewing up tea in a soot-stained dixie at the side of the ditch; a third was halfway up the nearest telegraph pole, a pair of rubber insulated pliers in his hand. The adjutant slowed, checked the van registration number against the number he had written on the top of an envelope - never do to get mixed up with the wrong van on his first job in the field - and then pulled up beyond it, off the road:

He climbed out, still thinking about the girl, nodded to the men with the dixie, knocked with a peculiar tattoo on the side of the van as he walked past. The door at the back opened and a man of his own age looked out inquiringly. He had a fresh, scrubbed face, very blue eyes; he wore a light cavalry mackintosh over sports coat and flannels. He couldn't be anything but a plain clothes detective.

'Anything?' the adjutant asked.

'Half a tape here, sir,' the young man told him briskly.

'Then I'll come in and hear it.'

The adjutant climbed up the steps into the van and closed the door behind him. He glanced through the small window, reinforced with wire mesh, at the shoes of the man on the rungs of the telegraph pole. Two wires ran down the side of his legs to the van window. Inside they were connected to a transistorized tape recorder mounted on Sorbo rubber feet. The adjutant was enjoying himself; this sort of job gave a chap a chance to show whether he had any push and ideas or not.

Too much of the work he'd done so far had been waiting for others to make a move; to break cover, maybe in so doing to give themselves away. And often when they did, you couldn't believe they had. There wasn't much excitement; wasn't much of anything, really, but boredom and frustration. It was a treat to have something definite like this to do.

'When did he come on the phone?' he asked crisply.

The other man checked a report pad.

'Ten-thirty-five this morning, sir.'

'Who did he ring?'

'A Mr MacLeod. He's got a hairdressing shop in Midlothian Street, Dundee. Number 27.'

'Anything known about him?'

'We've put a call through, sir. A great CND man. Took part in two Aldermaston marches. Then was arrested after a lie-down strike at Holy Loch last year. Fined forty shillings.'

'Mm-hm. What else?'

'Single. Fiftyish. Almost certainly an undercover commie. Could be a queer. Came over from Ireland about two years ago. Seems to have no relations, no background we can trace, but gets a lot of mail from London. Sends letters regularly to - he glanced at his pad again - to a Mrs Rooney, 145a Caledonian Road, near King's Cross Station.'

'I see. Well, I'd be most grateful if you'd ask your people to keep an eye on this MacLeod character. Put a tap on his phone, if you can. It's the easiest way to find who he knows. And do a Telex to London about Mrs Rooney. Ask them to take a look at her post for the next day or so. Now what's our character got to say?'

The young man rewound the tape and threw the switches. The machine's green electronic eye flickered knowingly at the adjutant as Rafferty's voice began to speak. The adjutant nodded, halfway through the reel, and the young man switched it off.

'Looks like your idea of putting your car in there paid off, sir,' he said, anxious to make conversation with his visitor. He might not have another chance for a long time.

'Could be,' the adjutant agreed noncommittally. 'And while we're exchanging compliments, it was a pretty good idea of yours to get your young nephew to do that little job.'

'I know he's on the small side for the police, but I'll ask the colonel to have a word with the Commissioner. After all, they can't all be six-footers. I'm sure they can use a lad as bright as that.'

'Thank you very much, sir. He'll be very pleased.'

'I'm glad someone is.'

Rain began to fall, blotting out the Sidlaw Hills; rolls of mist billowed down, shrouding the tops of the fir-trees. That was the worst of Scotland; the weather. It could be even more depressing than in England. He began to think of an evening with that girl on. a huge settee, near a log-fire, with the lights dim and a record-player giving out that old, soft, sexy smooch.

'Do you want us to keep tapping the line, sir?' The young man's question brought him back to the present, the cold, functional van, the smell of rubber adhesives and new paint.

'Has he made any more calls?'

'Nothing but routine, sir. To the Dunlop factors about a pair of tractor tyres and then the Austin main agents for a set of cylinder head gaskets.'

'No,' said the adjutant, savouring the power of making a decision for himself. 'I'd pack up and get the van back to the Post Office people as soon as you can. We don't want to abuse their kindness. Do the men out there know whose line we're tapping?'

'Oh, yes. But they think he's a Fascist, so they've no sympathy with him. If I'd said he was a Red then they might have turned funny. I reckoned that it would be back to him by tonight, one way or another, that we'd put a hook on his line, and there could be hell to pay. Liberty of the individual, and all that chat. Odd, isn't it?'

'Very.'

'Right, sir. Will you have a cup of tea before you go? You probably saw, they're just brewing up outside.'

'I'd love to,' said the adjutant, and began to think about the girl in Perth. 'One thing I learned early on in this business, and I'll pass it on for free. Never ever refuse a good offer.'

*

'Mind if I sit down?' asked Love.

'By all means,' said Ahnsullah. He pulled up a chair.

'I don't know whether the Political Agent told you, but as the Police Commissioner is away, I'm doing his work.'

'Yes, ' agreed Love. 'He mentioned something about it.' He'd had so many other problems that he'd forgotten all about Bahadur in 'Pindi. This was going to be difficult. Even if the dice didn't go against him, and he escaped a charge of murder, he'd probably be up before the General Medical Council; withholding evidence, even falsifying evidence. It was not a happy thought. He tried not to think about it.

'This is a long and complicated story,' he went on, 'and before I begin I want to know who I'm speaking to - Mogul Ahnsullah the policeman, or Mogul Ahnsullah the Nawab's nephew?'

Ahnsullah smiled.

'Let's say both are on duty.'

This was not quite the reply for which Love had hoped, but it was better than nothing; not much, but a little.

'All right,' he said. 'Well, to begin at the beginning. I first met the Nawab in Switzerland. It turned out that we'd both been in Burma together during the war. He asked me out here to examine his son's sight, In 'Pindi, in the hotel, on the way here, this Bahadur character came to sell me a carpet. I didn't want one. He followed me into my room and pulled a gun. I managed to get it away from him and threatened to call the police. Bahadur took a cigarette out of the packet, chewed the end - and fell on the floor. Dead. I smelted cyanide. No doubt the police found traces in his body?'

'They could hardly fail to,' Ahnsullah pointed out. 'He'd eaten about six grains.'

'As much as that? Quite a dose to take between meals. But to continue. I came out to Shahnagar, and on my way back here I was ambushed, I'd still got Bahadur's gun, and I shot the fellow who ambushed me. Unfortunately for him, and maybe eventually for me, if you don't believe my story, I killed him.

'Then tonight Akbar, the Jeep driver - who'd run away when the shooting started - came into my room with another man and they carted me off to the Himalaya Travel Agency - again at gun-point.

'There have been more guns around here in the last few days than you'll see at Bisley rifle-range in a year, I tell you. A fat Chinaman with the travel agency says he wants to know what I'm up to. I don't know what I'm up to myself, so how can I tell *him*? He starts being a bit rough, but I managed to get away. As I didn't fancy going back to the Rest House, I came on here. That's the action so far.'

'All the action?'

'Not quite. But give me time. This has taken some of the best days of my life to live through. It still takes a few minutes to tell.

'Now here's the difficult bit. Your uncle told me in Switzerland that he was being blackmailed for £2,000,000. This money is to be paid to some international committee interested in preserving big game.'

'Impossible!' exploded Ahnsullah. 'My uncle would never support such a cause. He's one of the best shots in Pakistan.'

'So I believe. Anyway, to cut a story short, the Treasury delayed paying out the money over some technicality, and I've been trying to find out who is putting on the squeeze. Entirely unofficially, of course. And so far, entirely unsuccessfully.

'I don't represent anyone but myself, and at this rate of progress I'll never be asked to. Not to put too fine a point on it, I don't know one single damn thing more than when I was in Villars - except that a number of people seem to think I do, and want me out of the way. Which is flattering, but a strain on the nervous system.'

Ahnsullah lit two cigarettes, handed one to Love.

'Are you certain about this blackmail business?' he asked, his manner thawing.

'I know,' Love told him firmly.

Ahnsullah blew a smoke ring towards the ceiling, still not completely convinced.

'I'll be quite frank with you, Doctor. I had orders from 'Pindi to question you, and detain you if need be, on a charge that could be anything from concealing or falsifying evidence, to murder.

'But what you say - if it's true - makes what seemed a relatively simple matter bloody complicated. Not an open-and-shut case, a beginning and an end, but very much a beginning, a part of something else that seems much bigger.

'There's only one quick way out of Gilgit, as you probably know, and that's by plane. So I'm going to take you away from the plane and from any temptation you may have to use it.

'I'm going to take you north again to Shahnagar. Then I'll ask my uncle what the hell is happening. I've got to call at an army unit about fifty miles up the road in any case, so there'll be no strain at all in going on to Shahnagar. Maybe we can then clear all this up - one way or the other. Meanwhile, you can have a bed here for tonight in the mess.

'But don't think about running away, Doctor. There's nowhere you can run to.'

'I feel too tired to run anywhere,' said Love. 'I prescribe sleep for myself. What about my luggage?'

'I'll send a bearer over to the Rest House.'

'For these small mercies, many thanks. What time do we start tomorrow?'

'About seven-thirty. In the meantime, you'd like a bath?'

'Only one thing I'd like better,' said Love.

'Well, you won't get that here,' retorted Ahnsullah, grinning. 'That's against my religious principles.'

'Then your principles must be different from your uncle's. His only extend to drinking alcohol.'

They both laughed together and shook hands. For the first time in Gilgit, Love felt relaxed, almost at ease.

'One last question,' he said, remembering something. 'Who suggested in 'Pindi that Bahadur was poisoned?'

Ahnsullah picked a telegram from out of his book, where he had put it as a marker.

'A man at the McDavid Hotel named Fernandez. Know him?'

At seven o'clock on the following morning a bearer came into Love's room, rolled up the mosquito net and set down the *chota hazri* by his bed, a tray with tea, a dry biscuit, an apple. Love had a bath, was waiting in the sunshine on the veranda when Ahnsullah came out.

'This unit I've got to see,' he explained. 'I'm taking up some detonators for the Sappers and Miners who're doing practical training in road repair. They've enough explosives, but the CO's been on to our adjutant over the field telephone for more detonators.

'The last lot were in a mule pannier that broke a strap and dropped down the kud-side. But we don't need to go out of our way for more than a few hundred yards, so don't be alarmed.'

'If that's all I had to be alarmed about, I'd be putting on weight,' Love said. 'Let's go.'

Ahnsullah drove fast and ruthlessly; also, his Jeep was in good trim and well maintained. When they stopped to leave the detonators, Love felt he was stepping back twenty-odd years; the soldiers in jungle green battle-dress, their neat tents with scrubbed guy-ropes, the hand-painted regimental signs, were all part of a shared experience of long ago. He would have liked to stay longer in this peculiarly ageless atmosphere, but Ahnsullah was restless and impatient. There would be time for another visit on the return journey, he said. He wanted, to reach Shahnagar as quickly as possible. But Love was older; he knew that when you missed a chance at the first turn of the wheel, it rarely came again.

By half-past two they were in Shahnagar. Ahnsullah drove straight to the Rest House and kept his thumb hard down on the horn button until the chowkidar came running out to unload the Jeep. This was all rather different from Love's earlier arrival; he didn't mind the difference.

They had a wash in a bowl of gritty, cloudy water, and went straight up to the palace. The Nawab was waiting at the top of the wooden stairs. He had seen the Jeep arrive.

'Can we talk privately?' Ahnsullah asked him.

'Certainly,' said the Nawab immediately. 'Come to my study.'

The Nawab closed the door behind him and threw the catches.

'Now,' he said seriously. 'What is it you want to see me about?' Then he smiled. 'As if I don't know already!'

'Then you know that the doctor here was ambushed, and nearly killed when he left you. Uncle?' Ahnsullah began.

'I do know,' said the Nawab. 'The PA was on to me from Gilgit' He turned to Love.

'I'm sorry, Jason, you've had this experience; But you must

have half expected something Like it when you suggested being a stalking horse. The only good thing seems to be that you're still alive - and, I hope, unhurt?'

'Those are negative benefits,' said Love. 'What we need is something positive - a bit of action. Instead of all these things happening to us, we should be making them happen to *them*, whoever they are. I was always taught, Shagger, that attack is the best method of defence.'

'Agreed,' said Ahnsullah. 'But it helps when you know who you're defending yourself against, and who you're supposed to be attacking before they attack you.'

The Nawab looked at his nephew.

'Dr Love's told you something of my problem?' he asked.

'Something. But not all, not even much. Who exactly are these bloody big game people, then?'

'God knows. I've no idea. I've had a private inquiry agency on to them, working through a friend in New York, in the hope that the questions wouldn't be traced back to me. And nothing detrimental is known at all. They seem to be a perfectly straightforward charity interested in animals.'

'To hell with private inquiry agencies. What about the police?'

'As Dr Love knows, I daren't bring the police into this because these people - whoever they are - seem to know my movements.'

'And I'd say they know the doctor's, too,' said Ahnsullah dryly.

'In that case, there's nothing I can do but pay,' replied the Nawab quietly. 'I can't risk my son's sight - or the doctor's life.'

'Don't let's be so bloody defeatist,' retorted Love. Whoever this Committee is - and while we don't know they *are* behind this attempt, it seems fairly clear there must be some connection - they're not supermen. I know I'd recognize the Chinaman in the Himalaya Travel Agency again. And Akbar, my driver.'

'They're both likely to be over the border now,' pointed

out Ahnsullah.

'Maybe they are, but they must have someone left around here, if they're using a laser gun. They can't aim that by remote control.'

'What do you suggest then, Doctor?'

'Simply this. At the worst, the Nawab's got to shell out £2,000,000. But we're a long way from the worst yet.'

'I suggest we put his son under guard - and if necessary you stay here with him yourself, Shagger - while Ahnsullah and I, with a couple of men you can vouch for, get up into the hills and see what we can discover.

'Any sort of action is better than just sitting here and waiting for others to take the initiative. If we find out who's got the laser gun, then we're halfway home. And if we find out damn-all, at least we won't be worse off than we are now. Don't you agree, Ahnsullah?'

'Entirely,' said Ahnsullah. 'What do you say, Uncle?'

The Nawab nodded.

'I'm with you,' he said. 'The way you put it, Doctor, it's the most - and the least - we can do. Let me tell you about one of my early ancestors, a Ra, or ruler of Gilgit.

'As with all Gilgit men - and as you'll have noticed, even with the children - he was a great polo, player. One day, he challenged a team to play for a prize of some goats. They won.

'He challenged them again, with their horses as the prize. The other side won and so they issued the challenge. They played for their slaves, for their jewels, for their land. Finally, they had played for every possible prize except the last - their own lives. His team challenged his rivals to a game to the death - losers to forfeit their heads to the winner.'

'And?' asked Love.

'He won,' replied the Nawab. 'And they beheaded their opponents.'

'Amen,' said Love, 'After that, our little encounter should seem like a friendly match. Now let's see what we know already about the rival team.

'Someone must be up in the hills, or your son couldn't have seen this light. Is there any other way up there from this side except through Gilgit, Hunza and Shahnagar?'

'No. None at all.'

'Could anyone come in by helicopter?'

'It's possible, but very unlikely. Of course, they'd be screened by the peaks from our side here if they did. But I wouldn't give much for their chances. The air currents are tricky, and the altitude's very high for a helicopter.'

'How long would it take us to reach where Iqbal says he saw this light?' asked Love.

'Probably four or five hours' walking.'

'Are you certain of the place he says it came from?'

'Absolutely. Here, I'll show you.'

He handed Love a pair of Zeiss prismatic field-glasses, took him across to a window that overlooked the valley. Love raised the glasses; the side of the white mountains instantly rushed into the room. He could see crevasses, pinnacles of rock encrusted with snow-like pillars of salt, and then a slightly darker patch as though the sunshine never reached it, as though it always stood in the shadow.

It took several seconds before he realized that it must be the mouth of a tunnel or a cave.

'That's the place,' said the Nawab.

'Have you a compass so that we can get a bearing on it?' Love asked him. The opening might seem easy enough to find from the comfort of the Nawab's palace, viewed through a set of two-hundred-guinea glasses. It would be a totally different matter up there at night in the freezing snow, with a gale blowing around the peaks, and no moon.

'Surely. I've got my army one,' said Ahnsullah. 'I'll lay on that part.'

'What about arms, then?'

'I've two rifles that should be useful,' said the Nawab. 'And a couple of .38s. They should give us enough protection, and yet not arouse suspicion here. No-one need know we're going armed but I'll have to say we're going out, otherwise it would look suspicious. Everyone knows I'm laying on a shooting party for the President next week. This jaunt can be a rehearsal.'

He turned to Love.

'Now, Jason, I suggest you try on a pair of spare mountain boots I've got. It's too rough up there for ordinary shoes. The rocks would just rip them to pieces. You'll also want to borrow a couple of sweaters.'

They started towards the door. As they reached it, someone began to beat urgently on the other side.

'Your Highness! Quickly!' a man shouted in Urdu. The Nawab unlocked the door, one of his servants stood in the corridor, his face lined with fear.

'Your son, sahib!'

'What's the matter with him?'

Instantly, tension flared in the room. The Nawab seized the sash of the man's uniform and shook him.

'Answer, you fool!'

'He's hurt, sahib, Mercedes memsahib sent me to find you.'

'Hurt?' the Nawab repeated as though he could not understand what the man meant. Then he turned to Love.

'Quick, Jason. Come with me.'

Together they raced up the wooden stairs and along the corridor to Iqbal's room. The door was open; Mercedes sat on the bed, cradling the boy's head in her lap. He was crying silently as though the pain was too great for tears.

'It's his eye,' said Mercedes tensely. 'The other one. He was near the window and suddenly he screamed. He says it's the same light he saw last time.'

'And from the same place?' asked Love.

'Yes, so far as I can tell.'

He crossed the room, knelt down by the bed, raised Iqbal's head. The boy held one fist screwed up into his eye. Love moved his wrist and gently rolled up Iqbal's eyelid. The boy squirmed with pain; Love lowered the eyelid, patted him on the back. The symptoms were the same as before; he had obviously been dazzled by a light of ferocious intensity. The beam must have been so narrow and so controlled that it could be directed at some precise target from a distance of miles. Both these characteristics suggested a laser. Love turned to Mercedes.

'Was he actually looking out of the window when this happened?' he asked her.

'Well, not quite, Doctor. I think he was crossing the room towards it. He was very near it, though.'

'Is that important?' asked the Nawab impatiently.

'Yes; it means that I'm virtually certain what's causing this. It must be a laser. There's no other ray of light that could be aimed with such precision from so far away.'

'Then?' the Nawab began, when someone knocked on the door. A servant entered, bowed.

'Salaam, sahib,' he began, looking nervously from the Nawab to the whimpering boy. 'There's a wireless message for you.'

'You stay here,' the Nawab told Ahnsullah. 'Close the shutters and see that Iqbal doesn't go near any window at all. Come with me, Jason. I want to hear your theory.'

Love paused, turned back to Mercedes.

'Carry on with the treatment as before,' he said. 'Keep a compress on each of his eyes, see the room is left in darkness, and use the drops the Gilgit doctor has already prescribed. Then come down to my room at the rest house where I've got a new American drug that should help him.'

The Nawab led the way down to his study. On the far wall, above a small door that looked as though it led into a wall cupboard, a small red bulb, that Love, had not noticed before, flashed intermittently. The Nawab produced a key from his pocket, turned it in the Yale lock, opened the door into a room about eight feet square.

Along the far wall stood a huge Decca ultra-short-wave transmitter and receiver, business-like in its grey hammer-finish; in front were two swivel chairs. Two pairs of earphones were plugged in, and static hummed restlessly from the circular speaker behind its protective wire mesh. A small red warning light flickered in unison with the bulb above the door.

'What's all this?' asked Love.

The Nawab closed the door behind him, flicked on a shaded lamp, motioned Love to one of the seats.

'Several of us have these sets up here,' he explained. 'We're all damned isolated, and telephone lines can be cut so easily. If we had any trouble - revolution or invasion, that sort of thing - we'd never get the news out - or help in. I keep this set locked away, and always tuned, so that if anyone does call me, the signal light flashes outside. The other rulers round about do much the same. We each have our own frequencies, so we can call each other up whenever we want. It's the next best thing to having neighbours. Now, grab those earphones.'

Love clipped one set over his head. The Nawab adjusted the other, began to turn the dials. Then he picked up a small Grundig hand microphone.

'Ready to receive. Over to you - over,' he said, and pressed down the switch.

A voice began to speak into Love's ears, rising and falling, now slurred, but always just intelligible; a voice he had heard outside the station waiting-room in Villars. He could see the man with the scar down his face, see the sleigh-horses under their blankets, blowing out steamy breath above their nose-bags.

'Calling His Highness the Nawab of Shahnagar in clear,' the voice went on. 'A private message for the Nawab of Shahnagar. Are you receiving my signals? Over to you. Over.'

The Nawab cleared his throat, pressed the switch for speech. As he began to talk, Love could see that his face was wet with the sweat of fear.

Mr Chin flicked off the double switches, and the humming of the transmitter died instantly. He removed his earphones, unplugged them, shut the door of the cupboard marked 'European Holidays: Flight Times and Charges' that concealed the set.

'You did that very well,' he told the big man who sat with him, the scar on his face pulsing as though it had a life of its own, a faint dampness of nervous sweat on his forehead.

The man nodded, not agreeing, simply admitting that he had heard. He stretched his huge hands before him on Mr Chin's desk, flexing his fingers, as Chin disconnected the microphone, slipped it into the top drawer, locked the drawer.

The man saw that his fingernails were bitten and raw, and yet, oddly, he had no recollection of biting them. He stood up, looked at himself in a small wall mirror that carried an advertisement for air-sickness tablets. I could use those, he thought; I could use something to cure me, but am I really ill? His eyes stared back at him, empty of lustre or any expression, another man's eyes in his own face. Was he going mad, or was he already mad?

He sat down again, held his throbbing head between his hands, trying to solve a puzzle without a clue. Mr Chin watched him with distaste. He hated the body odour these Europeans so often carried with them, like a sour miasma. And yet hadn't he heard it said that they disliked Negroes, for the same reason? He hated their body hair, their reddish faces, their height and strength, almost everything about them. But he needed this man; he had to humour him.

When he had played his part, there could be an end to all this needless civility, just as the Gurkha prisoner in the house near the New Territories of Hong Kong had been eliminated after his usefulness as a translator was finished. They were transmitting in Tamil now; and the prisoner, an Indian captured on the Tibet border, was in his chair.

The Gurkha had died quickly; a cement sack pulled over his head and shoulders, a bullet fired up through the base of his skull from a silent .22 air pistol, and then the body flung into the bay for the sharks and the silver fish. Mr Chin wasn't sure how the big man would die when his time came. Personally, he liked to watch a man struggle, to see the beseeching message for mercy in eyes already dimmed by approaching death; to debase him, to promise freedom, and, as the thought of life uplifted his body again to deny it. With difficulty he brought his thoughts back to the present.

'You must be tired,' he said, not looking at the man directly in case any glimmer of his thoughts glowed in his eyes.

The big man nodded; he felt exhausted.

He had come in on the afternoon plane from Rawalpindi, travelling with the passport of a Colonel K. B. McKenzie. This had been stolen from the changing room of a swimming pool in Karachi. Mr Chin would destroy it now; it had served its purpose.

'Come and rest,' Mr Chin said, as pleasantly as he could.

He led the way to a small upper room. The floor was completely covered with a Turkestan carpet; the air felt thick with some heavy scent. The big man had smelt it before, but could not think where exactly. Could it be in a church? At a wedding, perhaps? He gave up trying to think; the effort hurt his head, brought on a pain behind his eyes.

A girl was sitting on a cushion in the corner, writing a letter with a ball-pen. She stood up as they entered, as though embarrassed at being discovered.

'This is Savitra,' Chin said. 'She is coming downstairs with me. You'll be alone here. I'll send you up some tea and sweetmeats, if you wish.'

The man shook his head; all he wanted was to be left alone.

Tea.

The word struck a gong in a long dim aisle of memory. Tea on a beach. A picnic in a field, with stones holding down the four corners of a tartan tablecloth. Egg sandwiches. A suitcase strapped on the luggage-carrier of a little car, one like that Ford Eight he had seen in Villars. South of the Border. Isolated, apparently disconnected, yet somehow connected thoughts fluttered in the lonely darkness of his mind like imitation snowflakes in the glass dome of a Christmas toy.

He bowed awkwardly to the girl. Savitra looked at him strangely, rather frightened by the cold emptiness in his eyes, the complete lack of expression on his face. She came down the stairs with Chin. He locked the door behind them.

'Who is that?' she asked in a whisper, afraid he might overhear. 'I don't like the look of him; there's something wrong with him.'

Chin smiled.

'There's something wrong with all of us,' he said gently. 'He'll be gone by tomorrow night.'

'He looks a killer,' said Savitra, glancing uneasily at the door.

Chin nodded.

'He is dangerous. And as strong as a bear. But he's all right so long as the trance lasts.'

'How long will it last?' she asked, fascinated yet repelled by the thought of this, massive man without a name in the room above. 'Where does he come from?'

'Never mind,' said Chin. 'It does not concern you. This does.'

He drew her down on the couch by the side of the desk; the room was warm from the afternoon sun, and its heat lingered, adding to the warmth growing in his loins. They heard no sound but their own breathing, and faintly, muted by distance, deadened by the thick walls, the cry of a sweetmeat seller outside, the hoot of a Jeep horn.

He put one arm around her shoulders, stroked her hair with the other. Presently Savitra slipped her sari from her. shoulders; Mr Chin unbuttoned the brocaded bodice she wore beneath, smoothed her breasts gently with his soft hands. The nipples grew, points, hardened; he touched them lightly with his fingers, passed the palms, across them. She slid down on the couch, slowly, so that, instead of being side by side, he lay half above her.

With a dancer's motion, she wriggled free of her sari; it floated, weightless, to the floor. Savitra wore nothing underneath. Chin looked at her, as though seeing her body for the first time; the firm, taut breasts, with the proud nipples, the flat stomach, the strong thighs that moved slightly, resisted, and then opened under his hand. Her body arched briefly, all muscles hard as he touched her; then she relaxed, released; her breath in a long, soft sigh.

Afterwards, they dozed briefly, lost together in the hinterland of love, halfway between wakefulness and sleep, in the peaceful foothills of the blind where hands speak with their own voices, where words are needless as a kiwi's wings.

Then, some time after, maybe a long time after, Mr Chin stood up, lit a cigarette. He grabbed some clothes to cover his nakedness. The room seemed suddenly colder, the sun had died long ago; a few mosquitoes whined in a far corner. He stood watching her through half-closed eyes; the conqueror and the conquered. Savitra felt his eyes on her; and covered her breasts with her sari; he saw her left hand flit down by the edge of a cushion. Why? What had she put there? Half in amusement, half from interest, he suddenly pounced across her, crushing her breasts with a lover's roughness, and pulled her hand away. She was holding a piece of blue notepaper, folded over three times. She must have concealed it somewhere, perhaps even in her hand, and then slipped it beneath the cushion.

'Please,' she said sharply. 'That's a personal letter. I was writing it upstairs.'

'Nothing's personal between us,' said Chin waggishly.

Savitra still held it tightly. Her face seemed tense, nervous. His interest grew. He lifted up her slim wrist in his left hand, slowly bent it back until the fingers with their lacquered nails fell open. The page fluttered to the carpet. He picked it up, began to read.

He had expected only to pretend to read, to be amused by a letter to a girl friend, to her mother, giving some flowery, feminine account of her job. But instead he read with amazement a document of an entirely different character; he read an hour-by-hour report of his activities.

The time at which he had gone in his Jeep to the airfield to meet an English stranger arriving from Rawalpindi; and when they returned. How they planned their journey the following morning. The wavelength on which he had just broadcast; even the words the Englishman had used.

He sat up, all warmth fled from his eyes.

'What's this?' he asked coldly.

There was no excuse. Savitra held up both her hands to protect her face from his anger, as though by not seeing it, it would cease to exist.

He hit her then with the back of his hand. His ring cut into the flesh of her cheek like a ripe peach. She touched the wound nervously with the tips of her fingers; they came away red.

'Who's it for?' he asked urgently, the need to know, anger, bewilderment, thickening his voice. 'Before I really hurt you.'

She hung her head. To confess would bring equal anger from those who had sent her. Yet not to speak could only mean instant pain. He hit her for the second time. She began to cry, her, shoulders shaking. Even as she cried he watched her delicious breasts bobble, and for a moment almost wanted her again. Then the thought of his own situation drove down the tide of rising lust.

Suddenly Savitra made up her mind. She said in a low, frightened voice: 'It's for your father. He wanted to know.'

'My father?' he repeated in amazement and disbelief.

'Yes. He's so proud of you. You know he is.'

He hit her again, not so hard this time, but hard enough to teach her that soft words did not always make an answer. His father.

All his life Chin had lived in the shadow of his father's achievements as a revolutionary; like a seedling planted in the shadow of a great tree, he had lacked the, chance to prove his own abilities, to grow up in his own way.

But after this assignment he would prove himself a man, able to stand with all the others, even the giants of his father's generation, whose names had supplanted the names of the old gods.

Mao, with his immense ruthlessness; the half-denigrated, half-admired, totally feared Stalin. Even with Ho Chi Minh, the most celebrated Communist leader in all Asia, senior survivor of the old guard leadership, the man he personally most admired.

They had met once in the gardener's cottage where Ho lived, behind the rococo palace in Hanoi, the former home of the old French governors. And, miraculously, although they had not been equal. Ho had treated Chin as though they were.

A little man with a long wispy beard - a man of many lives; a cook in the Carlton Hotel in London, a cabin-boy, a photographer's assistant in Paris; a man who had spent years in gaol, years on the run, who had always sought power and who at last had found it. A man who had been the impetus for driving out the French, who, like Mao, could still find time to write poetry. Mr Chin recalled one line Ho had written: 'I hear the autumn flute sounding coldly, a signal on the screened hillside.'

Now he heard cold signals himself where warmth had so shortly been. He had considered himself a man, but his father still considered him a youth. And this whore, this half-caste harlot had shattered the myth, had ruined the dream.

His father had not trusted him after all, but had to send this spy to watch him, to report on him, perhaps even to criticize him. Worse, he had to send a spy whom his father knew he would seduce. Perhaps she had also told him about that.

'Get up,' he said suddenly, his decision made.

'What are you going to do?' she asked. She held her hands crossways to protect her breasts in case he struck her there.

'Put on your, sari.'

He would teach this woman the lesson of treachery. Odd what thoughts could pass under their serene faces; their deceits left no mark on them at all; like an apple corrupt within, their skins could still glow with innocence, even love. Already he hated her; she was like a cake he had once eaten as a boy in Saigon, sweet on the tongue, sour in the stomach. All women were like that; every one. If the day had taught him nothing, it had taught him this.

He unlocked the door, held it open for her.

'I'm going to teach you a lesson, Savitra,' he said, his voice smooth as the hiss of a snake. 'You're afraid of that man upstairs, aren't you?'

She nodded, unable to find words, knowing already what was in his mind.

'Well, you are going to conquer your fear. You're not going to fear him, but to love him. Or die now.'

'No,' she said desperately. *'Please.* Anything but that. I'd do anything.' She put out her hand to touch him, but he brushed it away.

'Do you want to be hit again?' he asked her in a hard voice she had not heard before. 'Because I would like to hit you. And hurt you.'

He drew back his hand, bunching his fingers, turning the stone on his ring so that it would rip her flesh again.

She saw him do this and realized why.

'I'll go,' she said tonelessly, in a voice no louder than a sigh.

'I will be here,' said Chin.

He would have dearly liked to follow her up, to see them coupled together, the Englishman's huge body, with its strange blue tattoo-marks of serpents, a handclasp, a cross, pressed against hers, Savitra's long legs curled around him, his sex impaling her with the fierce red fury of rape.

He wanted to see her face then, a map of desire and fear, of pleasure torn from pain, a crucible of hatred, of him, of herself. He wanted to see all that, to savour the degradation, the bitterness of it; to enjoy her again at second-hand. But he feared the terrible anger of the Englishman.

Even for such a person, with his mind, moulded on the lathe of other men's will, sex would still be a private thing, an act alone, unseen, unheard. Mr Chin was afraid of his vengeance, his strength; so he waited, like a boy, on the stairs.

He heard their faint initial buzz of voices; the Englishman must have been sleeping. Then he could hear Savitra, speaking, urgency in her voice, but he was not near enough to hear what she was saying. Then he heard the noises. An exclamation of surprise, a movement of bodies, the long, laboured sound of, breathing; a murmur, a sigh, and silence.

And then Mr Chin heard the creak of a board, and the sound of sobbing; uncontrollable, and ultimate, seemingly without end.

He stepped down the stairs quietly and shut the door behind him.

*

Love was trying on the Nawab's boots in his room when he heard the door open softly behind him. He turned around; Mercedes stood with her back against the red curtains that trembled in the wind.

'Well?' he asked her. 'What news? Anything about the boy? You have given him that drug?'

'Yes,' she said. 'He's much easier.'

She took a step forward towards him, and he saw that she had been crying. They were barely a heartbeat apart; he could easily put out his hands and touch her and feel once more the warmth of her body through her shirt and the soft inviting firmness of her breasts. For a moment, he almost thought he would.

'Can I speak to you now, not just as a friend, but as a doctor who knows secrets - and keeps them?' she asked.

'This isn't a medical matter, Mercedes. It's a matter of blackmail and God knows what else.'

'Well, I must speak to someone and you're the only one who may remotely understand what I've got to say. I told you how my brother Cameron stayed behind in Korea with the Communists. Remember?'

'I remember.'

'I didn't tell you all the story then.'

'No? Does it matter now?'

'I think it does. Some months ago, in England, I received a letter from Cameron, smuggled over the border into Hong Kong and posted there. He said he wanted me to help him. He was unhappy and ill. They'd diagnosed cancer of the throat. He'd only a limited time to live.

'I knew he'd been wounded in Korea - I think he'd got something wrong with his jaw - maybe that wound had gone cancerous. I didn't know. All I knew was that he wanted to see me, and our mother. He said he was sorry for all the trouble he'd caused us.'

'Did he write the letter himself?'

'Yes, he said he'd got the use of a typewriter - he had some sort of job in an English-speaking library in Peking. Why?'

'Never mind. Go on.'

'He gave me an address in Hong Kong I could write to. Where a letter would somehow be smuggled over the border to him. But I wasn't to write to him direct. Ever. Of course, I wrote and said I'd do anything I could to help him, but what could I do, what did he want me to do?

'I didn't get a reply from him at all, but late one night I was waiting for the Tube in Covent Garden station - I'd been to see Fonteyn and Nureyev - and I'd just missed one train and the platform was empty.

'A Chinaman came down the stairs and approached me. I thought he was trying to pick me up, and I walked away, but he followed me. I was a bit frightened. Then he spoke to me. He showed me my own envelope, the actual one I had sent to my brother. He said that if I really wanted to, I could help my brother very much. But it, was all a bit irregular. It had to be, because of diplomatic relations and soon.'

Love nodded. He could imagine the scene easily enough. The girl's heels on the grey, empty platform echoing from the sooty advertisements for whisky and seaside holidays across the shining rails; the man following her past the automatic machines and the benches and the ugly orange tiles until she could escape no further.

The irony was that this must have taken place virtually beneath MacGillivray's office with its carefully cherished cover as a fruit wholesaler's. He doubted whether the girl knew of this; but possibly the Chinaman did. And what would MacGillivray say when he heard - if he heard?

'I was frightened,' Mercedes went on. 'Yet I hadn't seen my brother for fifteen years, so I agreed to do anything I could to help him. About a week later, I had a phone call at my office. I was told to apply for a job with someone I'd never heard of, the Nawab of Shahnagar, who was staying at the Connaught. He wanted to engage an English governess for his son. I was to get that job. I was even told the Nawab's room number.

'I wrote to him - I'd been quite good at English at school - and I put everything I had into that letter. I had an interview, was successful, and came out here.

'I thought the Chinaman had forgotten all about me until I had another phone call. And then I got lots more. Here. In 'Pindi. In Karachi. Even at Villars, telling me what to do.'

'And what did you have to do?' asked Love gently.

'Nothing ever against the Nawab, please believe me. You *must* believe me. Just little things. What was his private number at the Connaught? The flight he'd be on to Scotland. Who his guests were. That sort of thing.'

'Who would ring?'

'Always a man with a lisp. I couldn't hear him very well.'

'Did he ask for you by name? Did you ever see him?'

'No to both questions. He always asked for Josephine. I suppose if someone else had picked up the phone instead of me he'd just have rung off or said he was on a wrong number. That did happen once in London. The Nawab had a temporary secretary and she picked up the phone when it rang. She couldn't understand who Josephine was. I was in the room with her, and I couldn't tell her.'

'And your brother? What happened to him?'

'Nothing,' she said. 'That's the terrible thing. I never heard another word.'

'Do you think he's really alive - or was this all a trick?'

'I don't know,' said Mercedes wretchedly. 'I don't know what to think. You, see, I've never had any place where I could contact this man. He always calls me. I've no idea even what he looks like or where he is - but he must know where I am. Always.

'He could be up here with us now for all I know. I'm scared, terrified, in case something I did might harm my brother's chances. Or in case something happens to me.'

'As it happened to Iqbal?' asked Love gently.

'Oh, how could it? That's nothing to do with my trouble. That's something different altogether.'

'Have you ever heard of the International Committee for the Preservation of Big Game?' Love asked suddenly.

'No,' she said. 'Never in my life. Why?'

'I just wondered.'

'Well, what are you going to do, Jason? Are you going to tell the Nawab?' She spoke almost defensively, her eyes searching his face for some message of hope, comfort, encouragement.

Love shook his head.

'What's the use? It would only complicate the situation. It wouldn't help you in. any way. Or your brother. Or anyone. But when I get back, I think you should tell him. You owe that at least to him. Now, when did this character last ring you?'

'Yesterday.'

'Christ! The same man?'

'Yes. The Nawab was seeing one of his ministers. I took the call in his study.'

'What did he want to know?'

'About you.'

'Thank you very much. What about me?'

'Did we know whether you were coming up here? Who you were, and so on.'

'And what did you say?'

'I told him nothing. You must believe me. I said I didn't know.'

'You couldn't have sounded very convincing.'

'I tried.'

'Well, now do us all a favour, Mercedes, yourself included. Don't try so hard. No matter who rings, don't take the call. You already know we're going out across the river tonight, so there's no point in pretending we're not. But just in case you're still not telling me *all* the truth; I'm going to cover ourselves as best I can - and you, too.

'I'm going to write down what you've told me now, seal it in an envelope, and leave it in the palace to be opened if anything happens to us.'

'But something may happen to you, in any case,' Mercedes pointed out. 'You might have an accident.'

'Not me,' said Love. 'My mother was Scots and canny. As a result, I've a built-in survival mechanism. I'll live to be a thousand. Now, if you please, you go back to your charge, and I must get on with my packing.'

For a moment after she had left his room, he stood, her scent still in the air, the imprint of her mouth still on his, looking at his borrowed sweaters on the bed, at the revolver he had still to clean., He thought of the warning that had come over the radio to the Nawab; this was his last chance. If he did not pay the money over to the emissary, his son would be blinded. Both eyes were now affected; it would be a very simple matter, to make the blindness permanent. What a bloody awful mess, he thought; what a maze to be in without a map, without even a sign of a guide.

And if he hadn't been such a quixotic fool he could be starting the second week of his holiday in Villars; worse, here he was thinking too much about a girl he had only met a few days ago. He wondered what it would have been like to have known her for years: not always to be alone, the man on the outside looking in, seeing the glow in other people's lives, but only through a glass barrier, never feeling the warmth, never close in to the fire yourself. If only. The two saddest words in the English language.

Love caught sight of his face in the faded mirror above the mantelpiece and didn't like what he saw. He lit a Gitane and broke his revolver. The six small shells scattered across the carpet.

He was glad he had to go down on his hands and knees to find them; it gave him a chance to forget his thoughts.

CHAPTER SEVEN: SHAHNAGAR — THE KARAKORAM MOUNTAINS — LONDON, JANUARY 13-14

At five to eight that evening Love stood in the courtyard of the Nawab's palace, feeling the same inner conflict of emotions he had experienced so often in Burma twenty and more years earlier, before he set out on patrols with his platoon in the First Battalion, the Lincolnshire Regiment. Curious, contradictory sensations of relaxation and tension, which he thought he had completely forgotten and outgrown, now returned to haunt him. Come to think of it, he'd never been to Lincoln either before or since those days; he wondered whether he'd ever go now.

He flexed his legs and arms, hoping his muscles would be equal to the climb. A dread of slipping on ice-coated rocks, of breaking a leg and lying for hours in the freezing snow, hung like a dark cloud in the back of his mind. He had with him a little metal case he always carried on any journey. It contained two ampoules of morphia in needle-necked containers. In any accident the slender necks could be snapped and thrust into a vein, to bring relief from pain for an hour or more. He hoped he wouldn't have to jab them in one of his own veins; physicians dislike their own remedies.

The Nawab's whipcord trousers fitted him fairly well, and over two pairs of socks, his borrowed mountain boots, with their heavy rubber soles serrated like the tread of a tyre, felt as though they had been made for him.

Against the ferocious cold, for they would be high up in the thick snow of the upper slopes, Love wore three old khaki sweaters of the Nawab's, on top of a grey mazri shirt with a scarf at his throat. Ahnsullah had also lent him a balaclava helmet that he could pull well down over his ears, and he had provided him with a spare lanyard, a webbing belt and a holster. Love tied the lanyard to his borrowed Smith & Wesson and then knotted the other end round one of the buckles, as he used to do in the Lincolns. His passport, his travellers' cheques, his air ticket home, were all wrapped in a yellow oilskin pouch buttoned beneath his shirt where it would be hard for them to lose themselves.

The mountains, white under the fitful moonlight, filtered with shadows by huge, shifting clouds, looked empty of all life. Would they find anything up there that could lead them nearer the end of all the mystery? A creak on the wooden stairs broke into his thoughts; Ahnsullah was coming down. He wore a *kukri* with its two little sharpening knives in a wooden sheath at his belt balanced on the other side by a Webley .45. In two webbing pouches he had packed four phosphorus grenades, useful as floodlights, if nothing else.

Two dark shadows moved by the gate and became the Nawab's ADC, Hamid, and Abdul, one of his, orderlies; their eyes and teeth gleamed white in the gloom. Abdul relished the prospect of anything that made a break in an otherwise boring routine of polishing boots and cleaning the Jeep. He came from a fighting family; this adventure was entirely to his liking.

'Are you ready then?' asked Ahnsullah. 'I've suggested that the Nawab stays here. Four of us should be enough, and I don't like the idea of leaving the palace empty except for servants and the governess when the boy is ill. And especially not after that call.'

'That makes sense to me.'

'Good. I'll take command as I've often been part of the way before,' Ahhsullah continued. 'First, we'll speak in Urdu. You can follow?'

'If you don't speak too quickly,' said Love.

'I won't. Next, I've checked on the map where the place should be, but I'm leaving the map behind. I've got a bearing on it, anyhow. If we're intercepted by anyone hostile, we're simply stalking for this hunt the Nawab is laying on for the President.

'Now, I propose that you and I march together, Doctor, at

least until we're through the river. Then you go with Hamid to the right, east of the spot where Iqbal says the light came from. I'll take Abdul to the west.

'At a prearranged time, according to how tough we find the climb up the mountain, we'll move in together to the centre to the cave, or whatever it is. Thus we can cover all the ground systematically.'

'If we do meet anyone, what is our reaction?' asked Love.

'See who they are, and what they are. Appear friendly, if we get the chance to. We're not out to attack anyone, but simply to find out who or what is responsible for this light. And what the light is. I'll do the talking. In your, balaclava you don't look European. And there's no need to speak English. Don't let's complicate things. Any questions? No? Well, it's exactly eight o'clock. Synchronize watches.'

They put their wrists together; two sets of luminous hands pointed to eight.

'We'll go in single file. Abdul in front, Hamid behind, us in between. We'll march as in the army, for fifty minutes, and rest for ten. All right? Then let's go. And remember, Doctor, from now on, no talking in English.'

At first, the ground fell away to the river in a series of wide, terraced steps. A sharp smell of burning charcoal hung on the evening air; in the darkness some unseen stringed instrument stroked the night with music, scattering single notes like drops of water.

Love glanced behind him; here and there a tiny glimmer of light glowed through an open, unglazed window. The comforting beat of the diesel engine in the palace followed them down to the river. From that distance, the fluorescent strips of light around the walls flickered with a pale, ethereal luminosity, so that the whole building seemed to be suspended in the air, like a castle in a fairy-tale.

The dust underfoot was thicker and softer than he had imagined it would be; it welled up in choking fog around their boots, muffling their footsteps. Love tied his handkerchief over his mouth and nose to filter the air. When they reached the river, Abdul held his rifle, above his head to keep it out of the thundering, foaming stream, and led the way across a crude causeway of slippery, slime-smoothed boulders. They reached the shingle on the far side with their feet still dry, and began the long, slow climb up into the foothills.

At first they had turf under their feet, springy as if it had been planted in peat. There was no wind, and the poplar-trees stood so stiff and still that they might have been painted on a backcloth. As they climbed, the grass grew thinner, and finally fell away altogether. Love was grateful then for the Nawab's boots; the bald rocks were harsh and abrasive as a file.

Punctually, at ten to nine, they stopped. Love was sweating in his three pullovers, and sat down gratefully, his back against the base of a poplar, his feet stretched out, pointing up the hill so that the blood would flow away from them. At nine they were up again and on their way. They rested twice before they reached the line of the snow, where the air suddenly became sharp, so dry that their throats, already raw from silica in the dust, hurt each time they swallowed. Love pulled the handkerchief from his face, bent down and scooped up some snow to wipe his skin. He put a handful in his mouth, to melt on his tongue; disappointingly, it tasted of grit and chalk. He spat it out. They marched on.

As they marched, the snow grew thicker. They had to walk carefully on its thin, crisp crust, not sure how deep it might be underneath. Any effort at that altitude brought on its own inertia, and Love began to feel intensely weary. To lie down, to stretch his legs and fall asleep seemed a delight beyond all imagination. In an effort to fight the drowsiness, he tried to calculate how high above sea level they must be. They were probably nearly 18,000 feet up. He could understand now how people in hilly countries were generally content to lead placid lives; they simply had no surplus energy for discontent and strife. There might be a paper he could write on that one day. There might be a whole lot of things. One day.

As they halted at ten minutes to midnight, they were very nearly level with the estimated position of the light. Ahnsullah, who knew these hills from hunting expeditions, had followed his own landmarks; an outcrop of rock, grey against the snow, an isolated clump of poplars, a boulder that had once been part of a false peak. Beneath them, under the full moon, rolling mists filled the valley like enormous drifting puffs of cotton wool. They were now far above the roar of the river, in a world of silence. The shrouded quiet was only broken by an unexpected creak or crash, like a bough breaking, as some great piece of ice detached itself from a ledge above them, and swept away down into the freezing darkness in a long, slow slither of snow. The wind cut Love's face like a whip, making his eyes run with water. Then it froze the tears to his cheeks.

'According to my calculations, we're within two hundred yards of the spot now,' Ahnsullah told him. 'It should be almost exactly to the right from where we're standing.'

He pointed to a ravine cut into the mountainside. Under the moon the snow oh its slopes gleamed smooth and soft as white down on a pigeon's breast. But its appearance was totally deceptive; it might cover hidden holes by a few inches, or by as many feet.

'As soon as we start marching again, we'd better split up as agreed. How are you bearing up to the height?'

'I'll live the night'

'I hope we all do, my friend.'

'What if there's nothing?'

'If there's nothing, then we'll simply meet each other as we come in towards the same point,' said Ahnsullah. 'The exercise will be over, and it's back to bed at the double. Any other questions?'

'No.'

'Well, hasta la vista.'

'Watch where they settle,' said Love, momentarily lapsing into English. He watched Ahnsullah and Abdul go off to the left. Then he nodded to Hamid; they should be on their way.

Hamid stood up, shouldered his rifle, and followed Love off to the right, their heads bowed against the driving, angry wind that lifted loose, dry flakes of snow and flung them in their faces like frozen shrapnel. Love counted two hundred paces to give a rough estimate of two hundred yards, and added another fifty to carry them safely past the position where the light had been seen. Then they turned left, up towards the peak, and began to climb again.

The going was much steeper now, and snow had slid down from the more vertical slopes. Ice glittered in the moonlight like the sides of a glass mountain. They stopped once to listen, grateful for the chance of resting their aching muscles, and stood, bodies pressed against the freezing smoothness of the hillside, hearts thundering, ears popping with the exertion. There was no sound but the sough and shriek of the wind through crevices and holes in the frozen rock, the sudden creak and crack of breaking ice, as though the living mountain rebelled against the dead weight of such an infinity of frozen snow.

Under Hamid's woollen balaclava helmet. Love saw his face shine with sweat. His own vest and shirt were also soaking, and yet, when the wind penetrated these clammy layers of wool, he shivered. Slowly, they set off again towards the peak. The going grew, steadily more difficult; soon they would need climbing irons, and would have to turn back.

One moment they would be leaning against a shining almost vertical wall of ice; the next, the ledge on which they stood would crack, and they would go slithering down, grasping wildly at any lump of ice to stop themselves plunging on into the misty darkness of the hidden depths beneath. And the higher they went, the fiercer roared the wind. Frozen flakes of snow flurried about them like a demented fog, so that every few paces they had to stop and check their direction from the stars.

Suddenly, a promontory of snow moved ahead of them, white against white.

Its vague; moonlit shape resolved into a man wearing white

overalls and a white mask.

The movement was so quick, so entirely unexpected, that his curved knife flashed and fell in the moonlight before either Hamid or Love realized what was happening. And then it was all too late.

Hamid rolled forward slowly into the mist like a question-mark folding up. The snow ran red beneath him as he fell, his arms and legs extended, the four points of a cross, his rifle inextricably tangled on its sling., Very gently, like a sequence in slow motion, he slid away down the hill; the swirling wall of snow closed silently behind him.

Love's Smith & Wesson cracked.

The shot echoed thinly from the ice of the mountainside like the flick of an oiled whip. The man with the knife took a purposeful step forward, and then, as though moving in a dream, his step immediately lost all purpose, all impetus, and he also faded into the white background. As he fell, he dropped his knife; the blade shone, still edged with red, like a curved mirror under the moon.

'Christ!' said Love aloud and in English, because he didn't know the word in Urdu. His voice sounded strained and unfamiliar; his throat felt dry. What the hell was happening?

Two other shots cracked in the snow, snapping across his thoughts like bones breaking. But who was firing, friend or foe? There was no way to discover, and this was no time. Love dropped flat on his stomach to present as small a target as possible. The crust of snow broke beneath his weight and he sank, as though in a grave, to a depth of two feet.

Twenty yards across from him Ahnsullah pulled a phosphorus grenade from his pocket, ripped out the pin with his teeth, and threw it. Love ducked as the grenade erupted into a blaze of flame, turning the whole side of the hill to amber. Ahead, carved into the snow and ice, he could see the round black mouth of a tunnel, hidden from where they had been standing by a porch of snow. This must be the dark patch he had seen through the Nawab's glasses; they were right on target.

As the flare died away, leaving a sooty smell of smoke in the sharp air, the night seemed intensely dark; despite the moon, Love could see nothing at all. He lay trying to accustom himself to the darkness, feeling hopelessly vulnerable, as he had felt on the road from Villars to Bex; when crossing the ravine in Akbar's Jeep.

A crackle of staccato automatic fire exploded behind him. He spun around in the show towards it, as a group of figures in white leapt out from the tunnel. Two went down to Love's shots; the rest swept past him towards Ahnsullah and Abdul. Someone knocked Love's revolver out of his hand as he ran above him, and he rolled on his back kicking out uselessly with his feet.

Then a man was on top of him, his knees on his chest, his weight driving the breath from his body, blunt spatulate thumbs forced like wedges into his windpipe until he could hear nothing but the roar of blood in his ears, loud as the unheard thunder of the river far beneath. The sky turned to yellow and then to red; red for danger, red for death.

Suffocating, half buried in snow, imprisoned by the weight of his attacker. Love threshed about feebly. Then his consciousness began to fade, his efforts grew more faint. Desperately his fingers gouged in the snow; they touched his lanyard. He traced it out from his belt to the revolver, and then turned the butt inwards, upwards. He fired and fired again until the hammer rose and fell, clicking uselessly on the empty cartridge-cases.

The sounds of the shots were muffled by the body that now rolled heavily on him, its dead weight almost breaking his wrist. But at least the pressure was released from his throat. He sucked the cold, dry air greedily into his aching lungs, and the roar of his blood receded, the redness ebbed from the sky.

For the moment, he was free and still alive; it would be a good thing to stay that way. Sir Thomas Browne had once asked rhetorically: 'Who can speak of eternity without a solecism, or think thereof without an ecstasy?' But at that moment Love would have answered, 'Me.' To have postponed eternity successfully, if only indefinitely, seemed sufficient ecstasy. He rolled over on his stomach, feeling in his right-hand pocket for extra shells. Odd how such actions, once automatic, an essential part of living, and then forgotten for so long, instinctively returned to become a part of life again when danger reappeared.

He broke the revolver, reloaded, snapped it shut again and crouched up on his knees, wondering from which side the next attack would come. His eyes were growing more accustomed to the gloom. He could see three bodies in white overalls lying in the snow. Hamid must be dead, too. Then he saw Ahnsullah lying on his back, only a few yards away, half buried in snow. Love crawled towards him cautiously, on his hands and knees.

'Are you all right?' he whispered.

There was no answer. A thin trickle of blood and saliva oozed from Ahnsullah's mouth, and froze on his chin. His face glistened with the gloss of sweat that frequently precedes a violent death. Blood had seeped out through his shirt, his sweater, and reddened the snow.

'Who are they?' Ahnsullah asked weakly. 'What's happened?'

Love lifted his left eyelid; the pupil was dilated; he could see no light of reason or awareness in its gaze. There was no doubt that Ahnsullah was dying. As he looked down into Ahnsullah's drawn and uncomprehending face, flakes of snow began to fall, gently at first and then more quickly, until they whirled milkily about, blotting out all sense of direction.

He wiped the snow from Ahnsullah's face, felt for his pulse. The beat was feeble and irregular, growing weaker. Love, knelt beside him, unclipped his belt, rolled up the layers of sweaters and his shirt to examine the extent of his injuries. One bullet had pierced Ahnsullah's body between the third and fourth ribs on the left side. It must have passed through his lung; he was literally drowning in his own blood!

There was nothing Love could do to help him; he would die within minutes. Love pulled down the sweater's again and crouched, watching him, the falling snow like a white lace curtain between them; or a shroud.

'How bad is it?' Ahnsullah asked him, his voice so faint that Love could hardly hear the words.

'Are you in pain?' replied Love, ignoring the question. He had his morphia phials; he could smooth the last few moments; that was the least and also the most he could do.

'Only if I breathe deeply,' said Ahnsullah. 'What's happened? Where's everyone?'

'They're all right,' said Love. 'You'll be OK, too.'

Ahnsullah shook his head weakly.

'No,' he said. 'Not this time.'

He swallowed once or twice as though trying to speak, but the words remained prisoners in his throat. He closed his eyes again, and quite suddenly his pulse fluttered and stopped. Love had seen death come in too many disguises not to recognize its arrival. Even so, its sharpness and irrevocability always angered him. Poor Ahnsullah. Poor everyone.

He pulled the dead man's army identity discs, damp with blood, over his head on their string, felt in his pockets for any papers or letters that could identify him. But Ahnsullah was carrying nothing; even in death, he was a good soldier. Love undid his scarf, laid it over his face. There was nothing more he could do; his business, lay with the living, not the dead.

Love left Ahnsullah, rolled one of the men in overalls over on his back; ripped off his white mask. A smooth, olive-skinned face, hairless as an egg, stared with dead, uncomprehending eyes at the falling snow. So these people were Chinese. But where was the light and what had caused it? He was still no nearer any solution to the puzzle.

He pulled Ahnsullah's *kukri* from its sheath, cut away the dead man's smock. Underneath, he wore an olive green uniform; this was presumably some unit of the Chinese army. But what the hell were they doing up in the hills, and how many of them were there? The questions seemed endless, the answers as remote as the safe homeliness of Bishop's Combe and Somerset.

Love stood up uneasily, anxious to be away, but not knowing where to go, whether it was even safe to move. He bent over

Ahnsullah again, opened his ammunition pouches; three grenades still nestled inside, like the segmented iron eggs of some deadly bird. He slipped two in his trouser pockets, pulled out the pin from the third. Crouching, holding the grenade away from him so that he could throw it immediately should he be attacked, he began to creep towards the entrance to the cave. He paused for a moment to gauge the distance, and then lobbed the grenade into the dark mouth, dropping on his hands and knees to wait for the explosion.

Its boom echoed like a thunder-clap from peak to peak. Red flame, a black gout of smoke blew out angrily, as though from some gigantic backfire in the snow:

Love counted ten, as he remembered from his army days, and then moved closer to the entrance. It seemed unlikely that anyone could live after so large an explosion in such a confined space; but then could he live if anyone else hostile was left on the mountain? There was now no point in concealment; survival was now the only object. He had announced his presence; if he could not remain the hunter, he would instantly become the hunted. Of the two unsought roles, the former possessed slightly better hopes of survival.

Love moved inside the opening and found that it was. really a long tunnel; when he was sure he was not silhouetted against its mouth, he shone his pencil torch briefly around it. The tunnel seemed to be the bed of some underground channel that would carry melting ice in the spring, but which now was dry. Black walls, ribbed with ice, hung with stalactites, were plastered with splintered bones and shreds of cloth and bloodied flesh. It was impossible to tell from the shambles of chipped rock and ice how many people had been in the tunnel mouth. Only one thing seemed clear; no one could be left alive.

Love had no stomach to discover where the tunnel might lead; he wanted to be away while he was still alive to go. But first he must see if he could find any clues about the light; he had come too far not to force the mountain to yield its secret.

Crouched almost double to offer less of a target, he went on into the cave, moving cautiously, holding his torch out at arm's length to his left side. If anyone hostile still waited inside the mountain ready to fire at the moving light, their bullets should miss him, unless they were the hell of a bad shot. Love hoped that they weren't.

The roof sloped suddenly. He sniffed a faint staleness of cigarette smoke, an animal smell of urine and sweat; he was coming to living quarters of some kind. Then the tunnel swung sharply to the left, opening up into a small clearing, about twenty feet across, with a ceiling so low that it was impossible for him to stand upright. He flashed his torch briefly around the walls. Half a dozen groundsheets were spread out on the floor, covered with khaki blankets; little piles of clothes lay folded neatly near kitbags at their heads. Obviously troops slept here. But how many were still alive - worse, had they reinforcements?

In one corner, polished mess-tins and billy-cans reflected his torchlight; he saw an open sack of rice, an unlit Tilley lamp. It looked as though this was a fairly permanent base. Farther along, three rifles were piled together by their sling clips. He examined them; they were Russian Tokarev semiautomatic snipers' rifles. He slipped out the bolts, put them in his trouser pocket as an elementary precaution.

In the centre of the room stood a mule pannier. It contained a portable charging plant powered by a tiny American Clinton two-stroke engine. Three six-cell batteries were connected to it. A safe distance away was a grey Jerry-can. He opened it; the smell of petrol felt overpoweringly strong in the confined space; he closed it again.

The charger could not be simply for lighting, for he shone his torch at the roof and it was grey as slate, completely bare of any electric fitment. In any case, they had the Tilley lamp.

He moved the beam of the torch a few feet from the batteries. It lit up a small black box, a khaki pouch with some wires stuffed loosely under the lid. He opened this first.

Inside was an infra-red Sniperscope, stamped American Optical Co., an ingenious device to enable a sentry to spot any person or object moving in total darkness up to a distance of 125 yards at an angle of 45 degrees to the line of vision. Such an instrument could have enabled the Chinese to be aware of their presence long before they could see them.

He turned the equipment over in his hands. It consisted of an infra-red light source that gave out an invisible ray. This was reflected by any moving object, and converted into a visible image by a special telescope. The black box contained a power pack necessary to boost the low voltage of the batteries to something like the 20,000 volts needed to operate the mechanism.

Love wondered where they had found this; either in an American base overrun in Vietnam, or maybe even bought by a go-between at a government surplus sale. He cut the wires, removed the lenses, ripped off every connection he could see.

Next to the Sniperscope a white smock had been thrown over a triangular frame. He pulled away the smock. It had covered an ebonite tube, like a combination of a squat telescope and a surveyor's theodolite, built into an oblong black box, about eighteen inches from end to end, standing on a collapsible tripod.

He picked it up, removed the leather lens cap that covered one end; a circle of polished glass glittered bluely in the torchlight. Above the box was clipped a Bushnell Custom 7x35 telescopic sight with an ultra-violet filter for scanning against light reflected from the snow. Beneath the box were more coiled wires with crocodile clips. The box was stamped: 30 Joule Ruby Laser:

So this was the source of light that had dazzled Iqbal from a distance; the silent gun that fired no bullet, but a ray brighter than a thousand suns. This was the answer to the riddle, the twentieth-century basilisk that could strike and blind from a distance.

The laser was too heavy for him to move on his own. He guessed that one soldier would take each leg of the tripod when they had to carry it into position at the mouth of the tunnel.

Then the telescopic sight would enable the marksman to draw a bead on any target with remarkable accuracy. This would account for the fact that Iqbal had been dazzled deliberately in one eye and then in the other.

The laser gun was a precision instrument, and indeed the whole operation had the stamp of professionalism. This could not simply be a routine blackmail operation - but then what was it? How could unknown Chinese soldiers up in a tunnel of the Karakoram Mountains in the Himalayas have any contact with .an international charity, dedicated to preserving wild animals, with a headquarters in Switzerland?

He wished he could contact MacGillivray; he might know. But MacGillivray was on the other side of the earth, and Love was on his own. He had better be on his way.

Love snapped off his torch and stood in the darkness, listening. He could hear nothing except an occasional drip of water from some hidden part of the cave, a faint echo of the wind. The place seemed deserted; but it was impossible to say for how long. He tried to unscrew the laser from its tripod, but the bolts were wired and he had no pliers.

He twisted the big lens; it came away with a left-hand thread. He slipped it into his pocket, jabbed inside the box with his revolver until he heard a tinkle of broken glass. At least they wouldn't be able to use this again in a hurry.

He turned to leave, and then, on the impulse, ripped away one of the wires, wound the bare end around the positive terminal of the nearest battery, slipped the open jaws of the crocodile clip over the negative pole. The wire glowed red with the tremendous heat of a direct short; its rubber insulation smoked and melted. The Chinese would take some time to bring the cells up to standard now, especially if their plates had buckled under the enormous discharge. Then he ripped the plug lead from the Clinton engine, smashed the sparking plug with the butt of his revolver.

There was no more damage he could do here in the time. He tiptoed down the passage to the mouth of the tunnel and paused, listening, in case anyone lay in wait for him; but there was nobody and nothing. He went on and out into the darkness and the cold flurry of snow.

Behind him silence hung over the underground cavern, and then slowly, with infinite care and caution, a man came out from one of the passages. He wore thick, rubber-soled boots lined with fur, leather trousers, and, like Love, three sweaters over his shirt. His face was completely hairless, his eyes black beads in a ball of putty. He glanced around the cavern, listening at each of the entrances. Then he crossed the floor, pulled away a canvas sheet the colour of the wall that concealed another opening which Love had missed. Inside the opening was a folding canvas stool with bamboo legs. In front of him were two grey metal cases, a long-range vhf transmitter so designed that each part could be carried by one man.

He knew the plan. He was determined that nothing, no chance intervention by a European long-nosed barbarian, the stooge, of Imperialists, a lackey from a dead Empire, and some hired local mercenaries should interfere with the selected destiny of the Chinese People's Republic; or, on a personal level, his own freedom. For he was under no illusions about the anger that would follow the fracas of that night when the news reached his superiors.

He threw the switches, and sat waiting until the neon tube glowed to show that the valves were warm enough to transmit. Slowly, choosing his words as carefully as he had chosen his way from the other passage, he began to speak. His voice echoed thinly from the roof of the cave.

'Calling His Highness the Nawab. Calling the Nawab in clear. Are you receiving me? Report my signals. Over to you. Over.'

*

It was-half-past seven in the morning, GMT, and MacGillivray, who had been in his office since five, expecting a Most Immediate from Morocco, which had still not arrived, stood yawning by the double windows, watching the lorries of vegetables manoeuvre into position outside the wholesalers' shops in Covent Garden. A thin frost coated the pavement with white rime; it was very cold outside; but the air in his room felt stale, used up.

He felt a bit like that himself, and leaned against the wall radiator, thankful for the dual blessing of its warmth through his trousers and the fact that it took some of the weight off his legs. He thought, not for the first time, how great a proportion of his working life had been spent in waiting; for suspects to move; for agents to report, for someone to crack. They also serve, etc.

Miss Jenkins entered with a tray of coffee and a circular tin of the shortbread he liked. He examined the tin with its unlikely red and green tartan wrapping, the picture of the stag for ever at bay against unknown enemies. He knew how the stag felt.

'Anything in?' he asked automatically, not because he thought there would be, apart from the Morocco thing, for it was early yet, but because there was always the hope, the chance, that some message of interest or significance might have been received from the decoding room beneath Storey's Gate. The question had become almost an automatic reaction to seeing her, a mild joke between them.

His secretary shook her head.

'Nothing yet, sir. But the DR is due any minute now.'

MacGillivray nodded, went back to his thoughts. The coffee tasted bitter on his early-morning tongue; even the shortbread had lost some of its sweetness. He lit a cheroot instead, and was about to throw the match into the empty fireplace, when the buzzer sounded twice on his desk. He pressed down the key, thankful for any interruption. The voice of Superintendent Mason of the Special Branch filled the room.

'Bit of news for you, Mac,' he said. 'Couple of our fellows had a word with that chap Rafferty. We got on to him first on a technical thing about selling a car without its five-year test, and then swung the conversation.'

'Good,' said MacGillivray, chewing at his cheroot. What did he say?'

He didn't really care what he said; in fact, he didn't greatly care what any of them said, but you had to show enthusiasm to your colleagues or their interest withered, too. Christ, he felt tired.

'He said this,' said Mason. 'I'm going to paraphrase his statement. It goes on a bit.'

'Ah,' said MacGillivray, coming in on his cue. 'So he signed a statement?'

'In the end. He'd been with Ryan in the Glosters in Korea. They were captured in the first Chinese push in 1950, and didn't get out of the bag for a couple of years.

'Both of them were brainwashed, and indoctrinated, of course. Ryan decided to stay on in China, but Rafferty came home to be a sleeper. He'd been trained like Blake and the others for this, and he certainly foxed all our people who interrogated him.

'Anyway, he stayed quiet until about six months ago, when this hairdresser fellow MacLeod - who's also known as McCasey and O'Rourke, with passports in all three names, by the way - came on the scene. He's a pro agent. His job was to put Rafferty back in business. We picked him up, too, but we'll probably have to let him go. Lack of enough direct evidence to convince a jury of grocers. It's all circumstantial. But at least the fact we're on to him means he's lost his value to the other side. That's something.'

'Of course,' MacGillivray agreed dutifully.

'Rafferty's task was to cultivate Ryan's sister, Mercedes. She's got herself a job as a governess or something to the son of this Nawab fellow. I don't know whether this was organized as well, but I wouldn't be surprised! These people are thorough. You've got to hand it to them. No doubt they'll be keeping tabs on her, too.'

'No doubt,' agreed MacGillivray. This fell into the copybook Communist pattern of breaking a complicated case into its individual components, then selecting the weakest link and subjecting this to stress. It also became the pattern for blackmail and threats and fear; and the further a person was drawn into this labyrinth of deceit, the harder it was to find any way out. Often death opened the only door. His adjutant came in carrying one of the familiar folders stamped with the red star of secrecy, and tied with pink tape. MacGillivray waved at him irritably to open it. The adjutant picked out a decoded message. MacGillivray glanced at the prefix; it was from his man in Hong Kong. He read it without surprise; that emotion was a luxury which only the young, the inexperienced and naive in his business could afford. He would never be any of these things again; nothing could ever surprise him now.

Mason went on speaking. 'Anything on this character Ryan? You've had your fellows check him, I take it? What's he up to?'

'A message about him's just come in,' said MacGillivray. 'Can't say exactly what he's up to. Last heard of in Peking, working in an English library, of all things.'

'You think they've been blackmailing his sister through him? Maybe telling her he'd get out if she plays ball?'

'Could be,' agreed MacGillivray for something to say. This was all very admirable, but he still was no nearer any solution to his basic problem: why should an apparently honourable society like the International Committee for the Preservation of Big Game be involved in a scheme to blackmail an Eastern ruler for £2,000,000? He was beginning to wonder whether there was any connection, whether he had imagined the whole thing.

'Well, I don't know where this kid is now,' Mason was saying, 'but she must be on a pretty hot seat. And if they get away with the money they're after - whoever they are - she'll almost certainly end up dead, just in case she ever had the idea of talking.'

'And if they don't, if something goes wrong, they'll need a scapegoat, and she's tailor-made for the part. Have you anyone who can pass the warning along to her?'

'Not a pro,' said MacGillivray carefully. 'But I've got one, fellow who seems to be coming along fairly well for an amateur.'

'Ah, amateurs,' groaned Mason. 'Remember all the bloody trouble you had with that Dr Love fellow in Teheran? We don't want all *that* again.'

'I'm sure he doesn't, either,' MacGillivray agreed suavely. 'As a matter of fact, he's the chap we're relying on at this moment in Shahnagar. 'Bye for now.'

He flicked down the switch, and pressed the button for his secretary.

*

The snow was easing slightly, but a milky fog had rolled from the valley up the sides of the mountains, making descent impossible. Love could never find his way down in such conditions. Worse, he could hear a distant chatter of voices. As he climbed down, slithering and sliding, now upright, now on all fours, panting with the exertion at such a high altitude, fearful lest he should miss his footing and plunge into the opaque unknown beneath, they grew louder. They were coming up the hill towards him.

Love lay back against the smooth, ice-covered rock, eyes closed, trying to gauge their direction, but it was impossible.

One moment, they seemed to come from the left; the next, from the right. They were probably being deflected by echoes. He began to retrace his steps, slipping, floundering in the snow as he climbed up the mountain again. The voices seemed now to come from a wide arc, and grew louder all the time; they must be closing in from several directions.

Love looked at his watch; it was nearly half-past three. He felt tired and cold, with only a vague idea of the direction in which Shahnagar lay. Safety was at least four hours away, if he made no mistakes at all. And how could he find Shahnagar in fog without a guide, a map or compass? The question answered itself; he couldn't.

He had no idea what lay to the right or to the left of the cave; the only other possibility was to hide up inside the tunnel somewhere until sunrise, when the fog should lift. He groped his way again, along the dark, dripping passage. A few feet in from the opening, he paused. He might as well leave his pursuers something positive to remember him by; he would not pass that way again, therefore anything that he could do, etc.

He ripped off a length of double flex from the charging engine and tied one strand round one of Ahnsullah's grenades, then to a rock. He looped the second wire round the handle, tied the other end to another rock across the passageway. Then he took out a box of matches, replaced the firing-pin with a match. It would be strong enough to hold the handle against the spring, but if anyone touched the stretched wire, the jerk would snap the match and the grenade would explode.

Now, goodbye to all that. He went on into the centre space, and shone his torch around the walls; to the right, its beam revealed a dark opening; he would have to risk where this led. The floor sloped steeply almost immediately and grew slippery with ice. Love fell once with a clatter of boots, and went ahead more cautiously.

He could only use his torch sparingly because the battery was minute, and even this pinprick of light could give him away. He crept on, feeling his way against the slimy walls, now and then crouching on his hands and knees as the slope grew more acute. Effort and reaction had dried his mouth; he would have given all his travellers' cheques for one drink of cold water. Once he reached up and pulled away a finger of ice to suck, but it tasted bitter as acid, rusty with pyrites. He spat it out.

Suddenly, he stopped. He had heard a noise, a voice, a cough. Since these sounds could not be coming from behind him, they must be in front. The full irony of his situation rushed in on him as he stood transfixed, his back against one wall of the tunnel, eyes closed in his weariness. He was not going away from his pursuers, as he had imagined; he was walking towards them.

Love listened, almost mesmerized by the indistinct voices, trying desperately to work out what he should do, what he could do. But his mind seemed too numb, too tired to produce any solution; the long climb, the ambush, the cold, rarefied air, the reaction from violence and death had drained him of energy, of his declension of will. He kept repeating to himself: 'I must get out, I must get out.' But how? Jesus Christ, but how? He could only go forwards or back; and in both directions unknown enemies waited for him.

He started to, go on again slowly, because if he stayed where he was, discovery would be inevitable. After about five minutes by his watch, the tunnel swung sharply round to the right and the slope became much steeper. The air grew colder. A few paces more, and he was looking out at the rolling mists of dawn, while the wind chilled the sweat on his forehead. He had reached the end of the tunnel.

He could hear the voices now quite plainly; four or five different people speaking in a language he did not recognize. They made no attempt to whisper; either they did not know he was there, or they didn't care. Neither possibility provided much comfort for him. His only hope of escape was to bring them into the tunnel where the walls could confine them, and make a dash for freedom.

He moved back until he could just see the round rim of the opening. Then he tapped with his knuckles on the wall of the cave. The talking continued. He gave a low animal moan, as though wounded and in pain, and tapped again. Then he waited, his heart pounding, little trickles of sweat running down his back. Still they went on talking. What was the matter with the bastards - were they deaf? He gripped his revolver by its barrel and beat the stock against the wall. This time, the talking stopped.

He gave another moan in case they were listening. Never disappoint an audience.

The mouth of the cave grew dark; someone was coming inside towards him. Love waited, his revolver raised. The man called something over his shoulder to his companions; there was a general scrabble of feet on the rocks as they came in behind him. He counted four men, all briefly silhouetted against the round opening of the tunnel mouth. The first man crawled in to within twenty feet of Love; possibly the slope was too great for them to walk upright; he would remember this on the way out.

Love counted three to himself, raised his Smith & Wesson, took first pressure.

The report boomed like a cannon in the confined space. He fired again and again and again. His ears rang like bells with the echoes; the smell of cordite filled the air. He did not know who or how many he had, hit, and he did not care. He reloaded and began to run towards the entrance, slithering as he went; it was like running on a sloping ice rink. At the tunnel mouth he paused again. The sun was rising, touching the pale sky with gold; after the gloom of the tunnel, the early morning air seemed almost unbearably sharp and sweet. He went forward cautiously into the mists of day, crouched up in the way men walk under the prospect of attack. As he reached the opening, he jumped to the left in the snow in case anyone had the tunnel mouth covered; but there were no shots, no sounds. He was alone on the mountainside; the sun was already burning through the mist. He had no clear idea where he was heading, or how far he had walked inside the hill, or where the others were, but so long as he kept going down, he must eventually reach the river that bisected Shahnagar.

Love climbed down until the snow grew thinner, then grudgingly gave way to rock; and then the rock to loose stones, and the loose stones to springy peat and grass. And finally he was standing at the edge of the river where the air was damp with its spray, and its roar drowned every other sound. The sky was quite light now, the fog and mist had gone. The poplars stood tall and still, each leaf glossed with dew; there was no wind. The river looked shallower than where he had crossed it with Ahnsullah and the rest, with a bed of round, smooth pebbles. He bent down and scooped up a handful of water to dash over his face and rinse out his dry mouth. Then he waded into the stream.

When the icy water reached his knees, numbing them, the strength of the current almost overwhelmed him; he struggled on slowly, crawled out on the other side, and lay for a moment on the damp rocks, sodden with spray. He must have slept, because suddenly the sky seemed much lighter and the sun drew steam from his damp clothes. He stood up, aching with cold and fatigue, his sodden trousers sticking to his raw flesh. Wearily, he began to climb the cultivated terraces on the other side of the river. Men hoeing the dusty ground shaded their eyes against the sun and watched his slow and painful ascent.

He could see no sign of the Nawab's palace, no rest house, no landmark he recognized. Where the hell was he? He shielded his eyes with his hand and scanned the distance. A handful of flat-roofed square houses clustered together about two miles ahead of him, and, as he turned, a flash of sunlight caught the windscreen of a Jeep going north.

He reached the rudimentary stone wall by the edge of the road, and sat down on it thankfully. Behind him, the mountains soared, white, remote and majestic, as unreal as painted scenery on a stage. In the warm, friendly sunshine of a Himalayan morning, the events of the previous night had the same quality of make-believe. He thought of Ahnsullah, Hamid, of the other, unknown warriors. Would he ever be able to find his way back to the life he had known in Somerset, to the country doctor he had once been? Even as he asked himself the question, he knew the inescapable answer.

He stood up, began to walk towards the nearest building; it had a wooden veranda under an ornamental frieze; a red tin postbox was nailed to one of the wooden roof pillars. Three old men squatted in the sunshine on the scrubbed boards, passing the stained ivory mouthpiece of a hubble-bubble from one to the other, with all the essential ceremonial of old age and empty lives. They had watched this sahib since he had crossed the river; now they stared in silence as he stood at the bottom of the wooden steps.

'Kya bat hai, sahib?' the oldest man asked him. 'What is the matter?'

His face had sunk in over his toothless gums; the skin hung wrinkled and loose, his red-tinted beard was trimmed and pointed, like a sharp spade. In his ancient, faded face, a map. of forgotten experience, his old eyes glittered, bright with curiosity, like the predatory eyes of a snake.

'Is there a telephone here?' Love asked him.

The old men looked at each other as though they had to agree silently on a reply. Then the man who had spoken made up his mind.

'Inside, sahib. With the clerk.'

Love went into the room behind the veranda. On one wall was pinned a five-colour portrait of Field Marshal Ayub Khan, the President of Pakistan. Beneath this a young man in horn-rimmed spectacles sat at a wooden table, jigging up and down in the Eastern way as though in a primary stage of St Vitus' dance. The table in front of him held an International Post Office Guide, a feather fly swat, the inevitable paperweight of iron pyrites. Behind him, to one side, the curved horn mouthpiece of an ancient brass telephone sprouted from the wall.

'Can you give me a direct line to the palace?' Love asked him.

'Yes, sahib.'

'Then please put me on to the Nawab at once.'

The clerk picked up the receiver, started to wind the handle. At the open window behind the post office, Love could see the faces of the old men; they had moved round, eager to eavesdrop. The clerk handed the separate ear-piece to Love. A voice spoke thinly into his ear against a shower of static.

'Ji? Yes?'

'I must speak to the Nawab,' Love said. 'It's most urgent.'

'The Nawab is not accepting any calls, sahib,' the voice told him in English.

'But this is imperative. I am Dr Love.'

'Dr Love is not just now here, sahib.'

'I know. I am Dr Love.'

'Not just now speaking, sahib,' the voice interrupted again. 'Please ring later. All gone out.'

The line went dead. It would be useless to ring again; he remembered too many other Eastern telephone conversations at cross-purposes. He would have to go to the palace as fast as he could.

Love turned to the clerk.

'Have you a vehicle of any sort - a Jeep, a car, a truck - I can borrow or hire to reach the palace?' he asked. 'I'm a doctor. It's important. Vitally important.'

'I'm sorry, sahib. We have nothing.'

'How far is it?'

'About two miles.'

'Right,' said Love, glancing at his watch. Thanks for the use of the phone.'

If he hurried, he should reach the palace by eleven; that would give him an hour to carry through his plan before the man from Gilgit was due. He walked down the steps and along the road. A coolie came towards him carrying a basket of sweet Hunza apples. Love picked one out, tossed the man an eight-anna piece, the only-coin he had on him. Only as he bit into the apple did he realize how hungry and tired he was.

The morning sunshine touched the dust with gold, and the road climbed reluctantly but steadily all the way. The only people he passed were a string of men carrying leafy branches on their backs at the half-trot, half-run of the coolie. For the last half-mile he cut across country to save a few hundred yards. When he was in the middle of a ridged field, a Jeep went by on the road behind him, going south slowly, half obscured by the trees, trailing a long plume of dust that swallowed it up.

It was five minutes past eleven by Love's wrist-watch when he finally climbed the wooden steps of the Nawab's palace. The hall was empty; a smell of wood-smoke and polish lingered in the air; a grandfather clock portentously measured out seconds as though they were all-important.

'Koi hai?' called Love. 'Anyone about?'

A door opened cautiously upstairs; the Nawab leaned over the banisters, his face wrinkled with amazement, disbelief.

'Jason!' His voice cracked with his surprise. 'But I don't understand. I was told you were dead. And yet you're here, thank God! What happened? Where's Ahnsullah?'

'I'm sorry, Shagger,' said Love, sitting down wearily on the nearest chair. 'But Ahnsullah is dead. Shot. And so is Hamid. I'm not sure about Abdul. We ran into an ambush and lost each other. I tried to ring your palace from a post office up the road, but the man who took the call here couldn't understand what the hell I wanted. So I came on, and here I am.'

'But I had a radio call at about three this morning,' the Nawab said, coming, down the stairs. 'A man - not the usual fellow who calls - said you'd all been killed. And Iqbal would also be killed - not just blinded - unless we paid over the money. I've had him under guard ever since in an upper room.'

Love crossed to the window. He looked out across the sunlit valley, over the terraced fields, the angry river, at the frozen hills beyond. So they still kept some secrets.

'I didn't find that radio;' he said, almost thinking aloud. 'In fact, I didn't even think of looking for it.'

What an idiot amateur he had been. Maybe MacGillivray was right in his denunciations of non-professionals. Maybe anything, maybe nothing.

'But at least I found the laser.' So he hadn't been entirely wrong; about most things, maybe, but not about everything; not about this.

He pulled the lens out of his pocket, laid it on the table.

'They'll not be using that for a while, anyway.' He felt in another pocket, produced the three bolts from the rifles in the cave. Then he remembered something else.

'Let's borrow your glasses a minute.' The Nawab handed him his field-glasses. Love raised them, and once more the side of the mountain filled the room; stalactites hung like sharp ice teeth in the jaws of the tunnel.

As Love watched, a stocky figure in boots, sweater, and leather trousers came out cautiously and stood for a moment, field-glasses raised to his eyes, looking towards the palace. Love wondered whether they were powerful enough to pick him up at the window. Maybe he should wave to him.

'Have a look,' he said. As Love handed the glasses to the Nawab, the whiteness of the mountain erupted in an orange flash of light. Seconds later, because of the distance, delayed thunder of the explosion rattled the glass panes in the window frames. The Nawab lowered his glasses, and turned to Love in perplexity.

'A trip wire to one of Ahnsullah's grenades,' explained Love laconically. 'Something to remember us by.'

He took the Nawab's glasses again, focused them on the mountainside. The explosion had completely blocked the tunnel; the dead had buried the dead. He looked at his watch; the time was twenty minutes past eleven.

'At least I'm back in time to help you with a suitable welcome for this character who's coming from Gilgit for your, money,' he said. 'We've nearly three-quarters of an hour until he's due.'

'What do you mean?' asked the Nawab. 'He's already been and gone.'

'Gone? But he was due here at noon, wasn't he?'

'He was,' agreed the Nawab. 'But this fellow who came on the radio this morning said the time had been put forward.'

Then Love remembered the Jeep he'd seen on the way to the palace, going north and south again. The room suddenly filled with silence. Somewhere, in a shady part of the veranda a lizard croaked throatily. The wind veered, bringing with it a smell of wood-smoke and dried apricots; the wooden structure of the palace creaked slightly.

'So you've paid the money?' It was more a statement of fact than a question. He already guessed the answer.

'I've given them a draft,' admitted the Nawab, shamefacedly. 'For God's sake, don't look at me like that. What else could I do in the circumstances? I was told on the radio you were all dead. I thought we'd lost.'

Christ, thought Love bitterly. All these efforts, all these deaths and then - this. Resentment burst like bile within him. But surely there was one shot left in the locker, one last chance to redeem this folly of inertia, to even up the score?

'Who came up here?'

'Two men.'

'Chinese?'

The man who collected the money was. A very fat man. The other man seemed European. He spoke English, anyway. With a lisp.'

'Did he now,' said Love slowly, hearing again the tick of the bomb in the neck of the petrol tank on the road to Bex, remembering the voice outside the station waiting-room.

'Well, all's not quite lost,' he said. 'You can phone ahead to Gilgit. Have them stopped. Cable the bank not to honour the draft.'

'I can't. I've already tried. They've cut the line to Gilgit.'

'To hell with the telephone line. Send a radio message to Gilgit or 'Pindi even with that damn radio set you've got!'

'They've smashed the valves, Jason. The thing's useless.'

'Well, your Jeep? We can phone from a post office along the road, and still get them held in Gilgit before they can catch a plane. Once they're away from Gilgit we've lost them. We must stop them now. Don't you see?'

'Of course I see. But it's impossible, Jason. The Chinaman took the rotor arms from both the Jeeps - Ahnsullah's and mine - before they left. We've nothing mobile here except horses.'

Horses. The power of a horse, the power of a hundred and seventy horses. The Cord.

'What about the Cord?' Love said quietly. 'I bet they didn't know you even have that damn thing?'

'The Cord. My God, Jason, you're right! The Cord!'

He struck a bell with his fist. A bearer materialized in the doorway, a genie in a long white coat.

'Tell the Keeper of the Cord to have the car out immediately,' the Nawab told him. 'Check the petrol, and bring me my .303 and fifty rounds. At once!'

'In the meantime,' said Love gently, 'if you've got such a thing as a Bacardi and lime. And a sandwich...'

He glanced round the room.

'Where's Mercedes?'

'Mercedes,' repeated the Nawab. 'But they took her to Gilgit with them. Didn't I tell you?'

'You're joking,' said Love:

'I wish I were,' the Nawab retorted.

'But what do you mean, they took her to Gilgit? As a hostage - or as an accomplice?'

Had he been wrong about her? Instead of Mercedes being a naive girl, anxious to help her brother, had he been the one who was naive?

'I don't know, Jason. She locked herself in her room when they arrived. She certainly didn't even want to see them, let alone go with them; she was frightened of something, that was obvious. But the Chinaman went up and called through the door. She came down at once.'

'What did he tell her?'

'I couldn't hear it all - I was worried about the money and my son. But it was something about a man called Cameron.'

'Cameron? But that's her brother's name.'

For a moment, nothing made any sense at all, and then the pieces of the jigsaw suddenly meshed together in his mind; the picture was complete.

CHAPTER EIGHT: SHAHNAGAR — LONDON, JANUARY 15-22

The Keeper of the Cord came into the room, salaamed the Nawab gravely.

'The Cord is full of petrol, sahib. I have had the engine running for half an hour earlier this morning as usual.'

'Right,' said Love. 'Then let's go. We're going to give this beast a road-test after twenty-eight years. It's the great awakening. Resurrection morning.'

'They've, far too much start,' said the Nawab pessimistically. 'We'll never catch them.'

'We'll have a bloody good go.'

Through the window Love could see the huge blue car being manhandled into the yard.

'You've got no means of signalling here?' he asked. 'Flares from the mountain tops, beacons, fires? That sort of thing?'

'I'm sorry, no,' said the Nawab. 'Up to now the telephone has been sufficient.'

'Well, make a note of it for the next time. It's always best to have a second line of defence.'

Tiredness had drained from Love, leaving him feeling curiously elated. The altitude, the alcohol, the prospect of adventure once more had sent a rush of adrenalin into his blood. Exhaustion would come later with reaction, but now the present was what mattered, the present and the future.

'Ready?' he asked the Nawab.

'Ready. You drive, Doctor. You're the expert.'

Love climbed in behind the wheel, blipped the throttle and watched the red rev-counter needle fly round the dial. The oil pressure climbed to sixty and then dropped by ten pounds; the engine was perfect, the mains must be like new. He kicked down the clutch and accelerated. The familiar growl of the four-inch exhaust boomed back from the hills.

At first he had to hold the car in second gear, because the surface was so rough that above thirty the car rocked so violently from side to side that he feared it might turn over. Just out of Shahnagar they met a mule train on its way in from Gilgit. The drivers threw themselves against the sides of their terrified beasts to hold them against the rock wall of the cliff until the car had passed. Then the road stretched ahead, empty as the sockets in a skull. Thankfully Love flicked the little gear-change lever through third, into top. Gilgit, here we come.

*

Ahead of them in the Jeep, Mr Chin was also driving as fast as he dared, but with three aboard, plus their luggage, the Jeep dipped and rolled heavily on each corner. He did not relish this; like all professionals in his business, he distrusted any risks, and abhorred those he considered unnecessary.

Certainly all other foreseeable difficulties had been minimized in advance. The telephone wires to Gilgit were cut in several places; the two Jeeps at the palace were immobilized and in the name of his travel agency he had chartered one of the PIA Fokker. Friendships at Gilgit to fly them out to Rawalpindi.

There were a few loose ends, of course, but nothing important. That ludicrous English doctor must be dealt with, for instance, if he survived his experiences in the hills, but this could easily be arranged, either in Gilgit or elsewhere; he could see no complications there. Was he an agent or just a genuine doctor? The question, once so important, now did not even deserve an answer. He was an amateur and this was the age of the pro, of the team, the organized many against the individualistic few.

Mr Chin thought of the other Chinese moving back across the mountains, cutting steps in the solid ice of the higher peaks until they reached their advance post fifty miles away, fifty miles nearer home, where the helicopters could pick them up.

He thought of his father, lying in his familiar cane chair, the rice wine at his elbow, full of wise saws, and memories of pioneering days with Mao, cultivating his tobacco plants, writing poetry, like Ho Chi Minh.

Once, he had told him, Mao had changed places with a rickshaw coolie and let him ride in the chair while he pulled the shafts. Mr Chin had appeared greatly impressed, but privately he thought the gesture futile and ridiculous; he would never do a thing like that himself. He would never change places with anyone; not now. He might hate his father, fear him, resent him, but now he had proved himself a man to rank with him. He could hate him as an equal, not from inferiority.

He drove in a glow of self-congratulation. He had succeeded; the Nawab's letter of intent to withdraw £2,000,000 from his sterling balance was in the inner pocket of his jacket, the safety flap buttoned down over it. Now his task was all but over. He would abandon the Jeep in Gilgit, catch the plane to Rawalpindi, and then simply disappear.

Friends in the Chinese Embassy would meet every plane at Chaklala airport until he arrived; although he had already told them of his plan, they were more experienced in these matters; they knew that fog in the Gilgit valley could cancel all flying, that pilots might fall ill, that an engine could stall.

They played things the safe way, and as soon as he reached Chaklala they would provide him with one of a dozen identities on which they had already decided. He might be a traveller on a Tibetan passport, a merchant from Inner Mongolia, a diplomat on his way to Europe. Within a couple of days he would be back in Peking, having proved himself worthy of those pioneers, his father among them, who had endured and survived that heroic Long March from thirty-odd years before.

As a special mark of favour his father had arranged a personal interview for him with Mao in the capital, either at his office in the old gold-roofed Imperial Palace, or at his house behind Thinking of Kindness Hall.

But Chin wasn't thinking of kindness now; he was thinking of success, of the fruits of triumph. He glanced sideways at Mercedes, wondering at her thoughts. She sat holding her brother's hand. He was perched up among the bags in the back. Now and then the girl would make a remark to him, shouting against the wind and the roar of the engine. She kept referring to times long past, a school outing, a holiday at Southport when they were still children.

The big man's trance was wearing thin now; splinters from her memory were pricking the veneer that had overlaid his mind so heavily. A record in the Alp Fleurie in Villars; a disc beginning to turn, an arm dipping, the stylus slipping into its groove. A memory of a beach and striped canvas chairs, and laughter; always laughter, when there had been none for so long. The inside and the outside. A face at a half-forgotten window in a row of houses, each the same, but this one different because of a mother's smile; this was not a house, but home. Faces he saw in his mind and yet could not quite recognize, like reflections in the ripples of a pond, blurred, changing, a likeness, but not quite a likeness. The words of a song swam to the surface of his consciousness.

And then Mercedes voiced his thoughts.

'What was that thing we used to sing there on the beach, and in the boarding house? Something about going down Mexico way? Remember?'

He remembered it immediately; the two of, them at the piano, in the stuffy front parlour; the smell of cabbage from the kitchen, the gramophone at the picnic, the portable on the beach; the record at the Alp Fleurie. South of the Border. The lock-gates of memory were almost ready to open fully; the bolts were all but shot, the trickle that precedes disaster at the dam had begun.

Sometimes they talked, but mostly they sat in silence, holding hands, braced against the bumping of the Jeep; both smiling. The lost were found again, the lonely would be alone no more.

Mr Chin changed down for a bad hairpin. A crowd of coolies holding rock-hammers in their hands scattered to let him by, then stared resentfully after the choking cloud of dust that the

Jeep swirled around them.

He wondered what would happen to the girl and her brother. His orders were to bring them both back to Rawalpindi. After that, their future would be decided by others. They knew too much to live. Probably there would be two needles of dope, and then a long, cold flight back to Peking in trunks labelled 'Diplomatic Radio Spares', fitted with slings and Sorbo cushions and the rest. Or maybe a meal to celebrate their safe arrival, then the sudden gripe, the instant, unspeakable pain, the swift burial. He would leave the means to his colleagues; they were all practised in such matters, and such details, like the future of Dr Love, were of no great importance. They were simply another item on a profit-and-loss account, an entry in the balance sheet of life or death. It was no concern of his. He glanced briefly in the driving mirror. There was nothing behind him but his own dust; and there would be nothing, for they had lost and he had won, and one victory would lead to another, just as one defeat would lead to another.

This was the lesson that history had taught and his race had learned; and this was only the first step in his own Long March. Who knew where the road would lead him?

*

Love shouted against the hammering of the wheels on the road, the growl of the exhaust.

'You were right. We'll never catch him. The most we can do is 40 on a few stretches, and he's probably doing that, too. In the army we had a saying - "Sweat saves blood, and brains saves both." Remember? Can't we fox him somehow? Don't you know *any* short cuts?'

The Nawab shook his head, his body pressed against the back of his seat, his left hand gripping the top of the windscreen, as the car bucked and dipped.

'None!' he shouted back. There's only this one road, except where it branches across the suspension bridge.'

'You think he's taking that?'

'No. There's no need to, anyway. There are no landslides. The road's open.'

'Could you close it somehow?' asked Love.

'How?'

How, indeed; a fair question. Then Love remembered the detonators that Ahnsullah had left with the army unit on the way north. He turned to the Nawab.

'On the way from Gilgit, Ahnsullah dumped some detonators with the Sappers and Miners. Why not get on to them and tell them to blow the road? They've got enough explosive.'

'Bloody good idea,' shouted the Nawab. 'But it depends whether they've a field telephone, and we can get through. The post office line's cut. There's a sub-post office further on. I'll try there. Can't you beat some more speed out of this thing?'

Love accelerated, dropped the little gear lever back into third; the huge car leapt on the rutted road like a stallion. At each corner he blew his horns, trusting that any road-makers hearing the triple blast of the Stenors would leap for their lives. If they didn't, they might not have another chance.

They roared between a blur of paddy fields, past a row of scattered square houses, a wooden plough pulled by two oxen. A long wooden building with green painted shutters faded by too many summers loomed on their right.

'Stop!' shouted the Nawab. 'There it is.'

Love kept the engine running while the Nawab bounded up the steps and into the post office.

'I want to speak to the Sappers and Miners unit who are somewhere between here and Gilgit,' he told the clerk. 'Urgently. Have you a line?'

'Yes, Your Highness. We've a link-up with their field telephone. I can get you through straight away. All other calls to Gilgit are impossible, though. The line's been cut. I've reported the fault, but...'

He shrugged, began to crank the handle of the ancient telephone. The Nawab picked up the instrument. A faint voice, dimmed by miles of wire, spoke in his ear.

'Hello, yes?'

'This is the Nawab of Shahnagar speaking,' he said. 'I want to speak to your Commanding Officer urgently.'

A pause; the click of a connection,

'Captain Jahjid here, sir,' another voice informed him. 'Can I help you?'

'Yes,' said the Nawab. 'Listen carefully, Captain. This is a matter of the highest priority. A Jeep is on its way past you. It's driven by a Chinaman, with a European and a European girl. All three are to be treated as enemies of the State. They haven't reached you yet, I suppose?'

'No, sir. We've seen no vehicles at all except the ration truck.'

'I understand that my nephew. Captain Mogul Ahnsullah, brought a supply of detonators up to you from Gilgit the other day?'

'Yes, sir.'

'Then get your chaps to blow a hole in the road big enough to take that Jeep. Stop them in any way and at any cost. But *stop them!* I'll take full responsibility. These people may slip through an ordinary road block. Blow a damn big hole in the road so that *nothing* can get by. *Now!*'

The Captain paused. Either the Nawab was mad or this wasn't the Nawab speaking, or he was mad himself; none of the alternatives gave him much comfort: He cleared his throat nervously; there was nothing about such eventualities in Army Regulations.

'Could we have these orders in writing, sir?' he asked cautiously. This was his first command; he didn't want it also to be his last. After all, his job was to supervise the repair of the road, not its destruction. Still, the Nawab was the Regiment's Colonel-in-Chief. If this was the Nawab.

'If we ever reach you, you can have them in vellum, Captain. But for God's sake blow that road! *Now!* It's absolutely essential that they don't get through.'

'It will be done. Your Highness.'

The telephone went dead. The Nawab hurried down the stairs again and jumped into the Cord.

'I've spoken to the Captain,' he said as they shot away, with spinning tyres and a roar from the open exhaust. 'I've told him to blow the road. He's assured me he will.'

'Is there any way round for their Jeep if he does?'

'No. They'll have to turn back.'

'Then we'll meet them?'

'Not necessarily. They'll try to cross over on the wires at the ravine.'

'What if they take to the hills on foot and abandon the Jeep? Could they do that?'

The Nawab shook his head. 'Where could they go? They'd never get away like that. Gilgit's their only escape route.'

They drove on in silence for a few minutes.

Then: 'Can we reach the bridge before them?' Love asked.

The Nawab shrugged.

'It's doubtful. Depends how far they are ahead already. They've got a good start, you know.'

'I do know. Is there any other way over the river we could take to meet them on the other bank?'

'Yes. There is one, but it'll nearly kill the old car.'

'So long as it doesn't nearly kill us,' said Love. 'With £2,000,000 you can resurrect a lot of old cars. Where is this way?'

'About four miles ahead, there's a ford. If, you keep the revs high so the water doesn't get up into the exhaust, we should just make it. The river's not in full flood.'

Milestones came and went; two men shaped a rock wheel; a woman led her child for a walk. Then the river gleamed on their left across the fields.

'Look out!' cried the Nawab, pointing. 'There's the turning!'

They were almost past a gap in the low wall that had run along the left of the road to meet a village of the familiar square houses. Love wrenched the cream steering-wheel; the nose of the big car dipped like a ship and then swung over. They left the road, bumped over dry paddy fields, rough with huge corrugations as a giant's washboard.

A herd of cows grazing on the scrubby grass threw back their heads and bolted at the sight of them, kicking up their back heels in frantic anxiety to escape from the path of this roaring, blue monster.

A row of wooden stakes, peeled of all bark, smooth as bones, marked a cough track to the river. Along this footpath a line of men jogged through the dust towards them, wooden yokes slung across their shoulders. From each side hung a square, rusty tin of water. The Nawab shouted to them as they passed, waved for them to turn and follow. They set down their tins obediently, began to run after the Cord.

Ahead lay the river, brown and fast-flowing, both wider and shallower than Love had imagined it. Judging from the rocks that stood out from the stream, smooth as pigeons' eggs and slippery with spray, the depth seemed possibly only eighteen inches. He hoped he could avoid these rocks: just one blow on the vulnerable sump or front differential would end their chase immediately.

The track through the paddy fields sloped down gently towards the water; the dust was now matted with dried cow-pats, and the dark droppings of other animals. This was obviously a drinking place for the cattle before they were driven up into the fields. Love stopped the Cord; the cloud of dust that had trailed behind them blew over their heads like a private sirocco.

'It's going to be touch and go,' said Love unhappily. 'These rocks look pretty dangerous to me. And if it's sandy underneath, we'll not get anything like enough traction.'

'That's why I called these fellows,' said the Nawab, opening his door. 'You drive on. If the engine fails, we'll pull you across somehow.'

By now the runners had caught up with the car and stood in a breathless ring around it, awed at being in the presence of their ruler, a little perplexed by what he was going to attempt. It was one thing helping to pull a four-wheel-drive Jeep through the river, but quite another to attempt it with this enormous car. They had all heard about the Cord for nearly thirty years; some of their fathers had helped to carry it in pieces over the passes from Gilgit in the days of the old Nawab, before they were born. But this was the first time they had actually seen the vehicle; it lost nothing in its vast and glittering reality.

Love engaged bottom gear; the car moved forward slowly as he slipped his clutch and revved the engine to keep water out of the exhaust pipe.

Half a dozen men followed on either side, hands on the wings, the bumpers, the doors. The Nawab waded out into the river, and standing up to his knees in the swirling water, began to guide Love across the worst of the rocks. The front wheels sank down to their hubs, then spun round furiously on the muddy river bed, churning the water into a flood of yellow ochre.

With a great shout from the men, the back wheels dipped from the bank into the river, and the bellow of the exhaust turned to a gurgling, strangulated bubble as the end of the pipe went under the surface. Steam blew out and hung above the river, like mist.

The current was far stronger than Love had imagined. He had to hold the steering-wheel hard down to the left to prevent the car from yielding to its force and swinging downstream. If this happened, they would never be able to turn it back to be at right angles to the bank. They would simply be swamped, and founder, half-submerged, in the middle of the river.

Already the windscreen was drenched with spray, and the floor awash; his trousers and shoes were soaked. Now men from the far bank, who had heard the shouts, began to run out towards the car, splashing through the water, paying out a long rope behind them as they came.

The Nawab tied one end around the front bumpers; the far end was already made fast to the trunk of a chinar tree on the bank. Then the Nawab, waving his arms like the conductor of an orchestra, shouted: 'Ek! Doh! Tin! *Char!* One! Two! Three! *Four!*'

At the last number the men on the rope, bent almost double against the strain and the current, heaved like a tug-of-war team; those splashing and stumbling on either side of the car added their strength. Inch by reluctant inch, foot by foot, the Cord moved on.

The front wheels were now spinning on a strip of sand that lined the centre of the river bed. The red needle on the speedometer registered a wild seventy miles an hour, but they were barely making two. If the wheels kept slipping at this rate, Love feared he would rip the tread off the front tyres, and yet he dare not take his foot from the accelerator, or the silencer would fill with water, the engine would stall, the race would be lost.

He slipped the clutch brutally; great clouds of steam blew out underneath the car. Then it rocked on its springs, and the long horizontal louvres on the sides of the bonnet dipped forward at a dangerous angle. Another few inches deeper in the water, and the plugs would be soaked. Fortunately, the distributor was high up above the banks of cylinders and should stay dry. The Nawab and his helpers streamed with water. Their clothes stuck steaming to their shining bodies, but at least the car was halfway across, and other men were now wading towards them from both banks, winding their turbans more firmly round their heads as they came. Soon, at least twenty were pulling or pushing the car.

They were over the worst now. Love could feel the strength of the current weaken on the front driving-wheels, but grow stronger on the rear. The sand underneath changed to gravel again; the whirling tyres gripped, and the Cord surged forward, almost running into one man who was pulling too close to the front.

One more heave, another, and the spinning front wheels began to churn yellow mud on the far bank, throwing streams of the stuff far behind them into the river. One last pull and the wheels were biting the grass, throwing up a flurry of silica dust and small stones as they turned. Steam blew but from the ventilation louvres, but no matter; they had crossed the river successfully, they were on land again. The car crawled slowly up the bank like some glistening, blue amphibious monster from the past.

The villagers, delighted at this break in their normal routine, cheered and clapped their hands above their heads like boxers after victory. The Nawab climbed out on to the bank, held up his hands for silence.

'Tell the head man of your village to report to my minister this evening,' he shouted. 'I will give you a present of fifty rupees to every man who has helped us now!'

Fifty rupees! It was a fortune; two months' money for half an hour's work. They began to beat each other on the back with delight, grinning at their good fortune, almost unable to believe the generosity of Allah, and Mahomed, his one true prophet, who had moved their ruler to reward them in so princely a fashion. Truly, this was a day to remember in time to come; to speak about over hubble-bubble pipes; such a day would not quickly come again.

The Nawab untied the rope from the Cord's front bumper, threw it on one side. Then he jumped in beside Love. They shot forward through the paddy fields, along a track marked by peeled stakes as on the other bank, and turned right onto an unmade road. The Nawab wiped his soaking face with his handkerchief.

'We've made it!' he shouted triumphantly. 'And in that current, Jason, I tell you, I never thought we would.'

'You're not the only one,' Love snouted back. 'How far is the bridge?'

'Several miles yet. But now we're almost certain to be there first.'

They swept along the dusty track, a replica of the road they had left; then they began to climb, and suddenly, far beneath them, and ahead, Love saw the familiar round towers of the old suspension bridge. A. Jeep was being winched across, and for a moment his heart missed a beat in case they were too late; but no; it was going the other way.

The Nawab focused his glasses on it.

'Forestry Jeep,' he said. 'No panic'

The road dipped sharply towards the towers. Love swung the Cord into the clearing that faced them, and then backed up behind a cluster of bushes that would screen it from the other bank. Half a dozen coolies appeared from a bend in the road, brought out by the beat of the exhaust. They laid down their axes and rock-hammers in a line and came running forward to turn the winch. Then they saw the Nawab, and paused awkwardly to salaam him.

Love recognized several of the men who had refused to give him their names. How long ago had that been - only two days, or a lifetime of experience away? They shuffled their feet uneasily, also recognizing him.

Love beckoned to the tallest of the coolies; he stepped forward reluctantly. His eyes, bright as a bird's, flickered from Love to the Nawab to Love again. Love handed him a five-rupee note. His hand closed over it like the grab of a crane.

'I want to borrow your coat and your head-dress,' Love told him in Urdu. 'Only for a few minutes. Then you'll have them back.'

The coolie looked across anxiously at the Nawab for advice. The Nawab nodded. 'Do as the sahib says,' he told him.

The man took off his coat reluctantly, unwound his long turban. Love pulled on the coat over his own sweater, wound the turban round his head. It felt damp and gritty to his scalp.

'What's this for?' asked the Nawab. 'Why the disguise?'

'I might pass for an albino coolie at this distance if I keep my back to them,' Love replied. 'We can't have this going off at half cock. They won't be expecting either of us here. But if they've got glasses, we've had it.'

The Nawab trained his own glasses on an open bend in the road across the river, about a couple of miles south from the swaying ropes.

'Here's a Jeep,' he said suddenly. 'Three people in it. Two men and a woman. Quick. What are you going to do?'

'First, you get all these coolies out of it so they can't give any warning. Half of them were here when I was ambushed. They'd taken money then, so they may now.'

The Nawab shouted to the coolies, waving his hand towards, the bend of the road. Reluctantly, they slunk away, looking back over their shoulders, chattering among themselves.

'Now,' said Love. 'Here's what I propose. When the Jeep arrives and they ring the bell to be winched over, they'll take us for coolies. You wave back to them, and then we'll both turn the winch. I'll keep my back to them.

'Halfway across, we stop. You shout that the winch has jammed or something. Say I'm coming out to make some adjustment. Then get under cover with your rifle and draw a bead on them. I'll go out in the little chair-lift towards them, as though something has gone wrong.'

'What if something goes wrong - as it will when they see your face?'

'I'll still keep my back to them. We'll have to take it from there. You can keep me covered with your rifle.'

'Why go out on your own? Why not let them land here and then hold them up?'

'Because they'll recognize us when they're near enough. Then they'll start firing. That can only have one end. Either we're all shot, or they are. Also, with these coolies, we're hopelessly outnumbered.

'The only other way - apart from my suggestion - is to pick them off in cold blood when they're hanging from the ropes - as Ismail Beg tried to do with me. That way we'll learn nothing, either. My way, we may not, too but at least we've a sporting chance.'

'It's risky,' said the Nawab unhappily.

'Life's risky,' pointed out Love.

'I still don't like it.'

'Nor do I. But at least we both know how your ancestor the Ra felt when he galloped out to start the final of that polo match you told us about! Remember?'

'I remember.'

The Nawab held out his hand.

'Good luck, Jason,' he said. It sounded pathetically inadequate; ten to make and the last man in; and Love was the last man.

Love pushed his revolver into the inside pocket of his borrowed jacket, bent down in readiness over the winch. Danger had sharpened his senses; he savoured the thick, cloying scent of some yellow blossoms, saw a tiny insect creep across the metal base of the winch, meet another, pause and then go on; felt the shining brass handle warm through his palms.

The Jeep had stopped between the pillars across the ravine. Love, still bent over the handle, had an inverted view of a fat man in a light linen suit brushing the creases and dust from his trousers. The man walked across to the bell, smoothing back his hair with one hand. He did not appear to be in a hurry. Love recognized him, even at that distance, as Mr Chin.

The boom of the brass bell rang out seconds after he struck the metal. A flight of birds flew screaming from the tree-tops, turned their wings against the cobalt sky. The river roared on. There was no other sound.

The Nawab slipped forward the safety catch on his rifle, laid it down carefully in some bushes near the winch facing the ravine, and came running out, waving towards the distant Jeep.

'Ata, sahib,' he cried. 'Coming, sir.'

He gave an exaggerated wave to Love and the two of them, feeling like amateur actors in a play, threw their weight against the handle. It threw their weight right back at them and didn't move a cog.

'The ratchet,' panted Love. 'The damn thing's locked.'

The Nawab lifted the ratchet sprag and slowly, jerkily, the big cog wheel began to turn. The hawser, creaking, polished with age, wound itself painfully on to the capstan like a long silver serpent.

Love kept his back against the ravine.

'Let me know when they're in the middle,' he grunted between his teeth. 'I can't see anything from where I'm standing.'

It was far more difficult to turn the handle than either had imagined; the bearings were dry; the friction, immense. He could understand now why the coolies worked in a group. Only the strength of the ratchet stopped the capstan from unwinding and the Jeep from sliding back to the far bank.

'They're about halfway,' said the Nawab, sweat streaming down his face.

'OK,' said Love. 'This is where we leave them for a bit. And where I leave you. Once more unto the breach, dear friend.'

The Nawab locked the ratchet, stood up and turned to the driver of the Jeep. He cupped his hands and began to shout, half in Urdu, half in English.

'I am sorry, sahib, but it is a breakdown. One of the cog wheels. It will take some time.' He waved his arms apologetically, shrugged his shoulders as though he could only do his best. Above his head the birds wheeled warily, black crosses against the sun.

'Hurry up!' shouted Mr Chin from behind the wheel. His voice, thinned by distance and the wind, sounded impatient. 'We're on Government business. Most urgent. Ten rupees to each of you if you can get us across quickly.'

'It's the winch, sahib,' the Nawab shouted back. 'We must wait to repair it. We may need your help. My friend will come out and bring one of you over. Please be patient.'

He turned to Love.

'Over to you,' he said. He stood for a moment by the winch, shading his eyes against the sun as he looked at the Jeep, and then bent low over the winch as though searching for the fault. He pulled his rifle along the ground closer to him where he could pick it up more easily.

The Jeep horn sounded again angrily. Love took a deep breath, and ran, head bent down, to the pillar, climbed into the swaying wooden box, crouched down with his back to the Jeep. He began to pay out the rope that would pull him out alongside it.

The box turned and swung to and fro in half-circles with each fevered tug he gave on the rope. The rope itself was far rougher than he had anticipated and rubbed his palms raw. He shut his eyes not to see the thundering river pouring over the rocks so far beneath. He prayed that the supporting ropes were not as rotten and frayed as they seemed from where he squatted. Christ, what an idiot he was to become involved in all this when he could so easily have avoided it. Never, never again; this was positively the last time. On this or any other stage.

Clenching his teeth, he forced himself to pull more vigorously; the sooner he was over, the less chance of a rope parting, of being discovered. Then he felt the box hit something solid with a blow. He opened his eyes. The box was bumping against, the Jeep trolley. Now came the most dangerous moment; his success, possibly his life, depended on the speed with which he was recognized and who reacted first.

Love turned round towards the Jeep. Three pairs of eyes looked down at him.

From over the steering-wheel Mr Chin stared at him in disbelief, his eyes mere slits. He had pushed his sunglasses up on his forehead; his face, darkened with dust, had two large sallow circles where the glasses had been. He looked like an ancient, evil owl.

Next to him, Mercedes' face registered equal amazement, and incredulity. 'You,' she said softly.

In the back, perched up on bedding rolls, his face floury with dust, sat the big man whom Love had last seen in Villars. He watched Love with a curiously dead face, empty of all expression, his eyes like blank windows in a house when everyone was away.

Love seized one of the vertical ropes that held the Jeep's trolley to the overhead hawser and leapt up on the trolley, then on to the bonnet. The little box he had left swung out into the air and banged back against the trolley.

Love held on to the mudguard with his left hand, whipped out his Smith & Wesson with his right.

There was a crack, like a dry branch breaking. His hand jerked back as though on a spring; the revolver spun uselessly away, and down into the river. A Lüger had grown in the big man's hand, as though it was part of him, an extension of his arm. The muzzle pointed at Love's head.

'So,' he said gently. 'You must be the English doctor.'

'The same,' said Love. He feinted to the left to throw his aim, ducked to the right, and jumped!

The windscreen had been folded forward; he leapt over it, landed on the gunman's lap. The speed of his movement and the sudden sway of the Jeep as it rocked under his arrival, surprised them both. The man fired again, but the shot went wide. Love almost overbalanced as the Jeep lurched; for a second he thought he would fall as one bundle pitched out from the back and dropped. He flung out his right hand to steady himself. The big man brought down his Lüger sideways against Love's face, laying bare the white and shining bone.

Love reeled dizzily under the blow, sagged back against Mr Chin, pinning him behind the wheel. Dimly, from far away, he heard Mercedes scream: 'No! No!'

He pivoted on his back against Chin, kicked out at the gunman with both feet, then jumped at him. He gave a right hook to his jaw but the man rode the punch, brought up his Lüger for the second time. Love seized, his wrist, held it, bent it up, up and back. Veins stood but in their foreheads like knotted blue cords as they struggled for mastery. The gunman pressed the trigger once, twice, but the bullets went wide, singing harmlessly into the sun. Then the man's hand opened, the gun dropped out. Love instinctively eased the pressure; the man ducked his head, brought it up under Love's jaw, momentarily stunning him. He reeled back weakly, falling between Mercedes and Mr Chin, his head striking the gear-levers. The big man leapt on him, his huge flat thumbs pressed into his throat, throttling him.

Love had no weapon, no revolver on a lanyard, none of MacGillivray's gadgets. As the Jeep rocked and swayed, he could see now a background of blue sky, now rocks and the angry river, and all the while the huge face of his opponent grew and grew, red, contorted with hate, streaming with sweat, until it filled all the world and there was nothing else, nothing at all.

Love tore feebly at the man's, wrists, drove his own arms up and outwards as he so, often had taught his British Legion judo class at Bishop's Combe was the way to break a stranglehold. But nothing could budge or break the stranglehold of this man. He was too strong, the leverage was too great, he was here to kill.

Love felt consciousness ebb away; the red face merged into the red of the sky, of the river. His ears rang with unseen chimes; he was ready to begin the long fall into the red fog, the red nothingness. The big man shifted his position slightly; one knee was wedged against the corner of a case. In moving he eased his hold briefly on Love's throat for a fraction of a second, just long enough for Love to suck a little air into his tortured lungs, just long enough for the red mist to thin, for a memory to flash from his brain to his voice.

He shouted, as he had been taught to shout in The Buffs, in Chaucer Barracks, Canterbury, in the Officers' Training School at Belgaum, in Southern India; as he had forgotten he could shout, as every nerve told him he had to shout now or die.

'Drop *that, Private Ryan!*'

For an instant, the huge fingers faltered, their iron grip slackened, loosened, fell away. Love sucked in great draughts of air, sweeter than any honey, richer than retsina, the wine of the gods.

The name, forgotten for years, shamed, denigrated, buried under other identities beneath woolly layers of deep hypnosis, cut like a lance to the quick of the big man's memory. The past rushed in through the open wound, widening it, overwhelming him. Number, rank and name. 01743284 Pte Ryan, C. The Glosters. Who was he now, then? What war was he fighting? Whose side was he on? Who was this Chinaman, this English doctor? Why was he in this Jeep with his sister? The questions beat hammer-blows at his brain. He was hoarse with other voices.

He tried to stand, dredging for words to question, to explain, to find a way out of the maze. At that moment the Jeep rocked, he threw put his hands to keep his balance, and in moving lost it.

Arms outstretched like the thin wings of some strange, unwieldy bird, he fell. For a moment he seemed to hang at an angle, not moving, crystallized in time, a frozen frame from an antique film; and then he was gone, turning over and over in the clear, bright air, his jacket billowing out behind him, his trousers plump funnels of pale cloth.

Love struggled to his feet as the Jeep swung wildly. Mr Chin brought up the heavy ring spanner he kept beneath his seat and hit him with it on the side of the head. Love collapsed at the same moment as the Nawab's rifle cracked. Chin fell forward, stunned; the bullet had grazed his left temple, nicking the top of his ear. His chest caught the horn button in the centre of the steering wheel and the strident, off-key bleat of the Autolite horn brayed out across the echoing ravine like a demented sheep.

Mercedes half sat, half crouched in her seat, holding on to the swaying dashboard, mesmerized by the sudden, fearful mass that sprawled across a rock in the centre of the river. She had found her brother after years of life without him; and within hours of the reunion with the strange, remote, aloof person he had become, she had lost him again; this time for ever.

She turned and looked at Love.

All her pent-up feelings, unchannelled, unexpressed, the amalgam of fear past, guilt and anguish, found their focus and exploded. Here was the man whose meddling had unleashed this train of tragedy. But for him Cameron would still be alive. Suddenly she found her voice;

'You killed him, you stupid, interfering bastard!' she screamed. 'You killed my brother! Jesus God! I hate you, hate you, hate you! Murderer!'

She struck him wildly, clawing at his face with her fingernails, tearing his hair, screaming into his ears as he lay senseless.

She was still hysterical, sobbing, shrieking, cursing, choking for breath to express her hate when the Nawab and the coolies winched in the Jeep and seized her.

*

The buzzer sounded twice on MacGillivray's desk to show that his callers had arrived. He pressed the button to release the electric locks, lit a cheroot, smoothed down his jacket, stood up.

His adjutant showed in two visitors.

The Nawab wore a dark blue city suit with a cutaway stiff collar, a Sandhurst tie. With him stood Love, in a tweed suit and casual, checked shirt. A square piece of sticking plaster down the side of his cheek gave his face a lop-sided appearance; he looked pale and tired, more like a patient than a doctor.

'Please take a seat,' said MacGillivray easily.

'About the only nice thing you've ever offered me,' said Love; they both sat down in the shabby, leather arm-chairs.

It was a week since the Nawab had shouted to the coolies, and together they had wound in the Jeep with Love and Mercedes and Mr Chin. From that moment events had happened so swiftly that Love found it difficult to remember them all, let alone the order in which they had occurred.

He dimly remembered a nightmare journey in the Cord, with the Nawab driving but almost as though it had happened to someone else. Then the familiar smell of ether, but this time he was on the wrong side of the mask; the thirteen stitches in his face still ached when he tried to smile, and why should he try? He had little enough to smile about.

Captain Janjid, of the Sappers and Miners, cautious as ever and anxious to make sure that the Nawab was who he said he was, had arrived with half a dozen men in a lorry at the edge of the ravine in time to take charge of Mr Chin and Mercedes and had brought them down to Gilgit.

Then Love saw how far the lines reached from MacGillivray's office in Covent Garden. Four men suddenly arrived from Rawalpindi on the morning plane. Two were Pakistanis, one Chinese from Singapore, the fourth a Canadian. The man from Singapore explained that he was a distant cousin of Mr Chin; the others promised to help take care of him. The Canadian also brought a cable from Mercedes' mother to her which no-one else saw.

They all flew out on the afternoon plane with Mercedes and Mr Chin, who was under heavy sedation, wrapped in blankets on a stretcher. A minibus at Chaklala took them to a house on the road to Abbottabad. It was leased to an English company, Ruskin Holdings, with an office in Covent Garden.

There was a minor incident at Chaklala. Mr Chin, who, the Canadian explained, had a severe head injury and so could not move, but had in fact to be strapped to the stretcher for his own safety, began to behave in a quite extraordinary way. He started to struggle, to writhe under his blankets (which also concealed the straps that held him), to shout that he was Chinese, that he was being kidnapped.

A group of Chinese businessmen, who were waiting at the airport for some reason of their own, apparently to meet some passengers from Gilgit who hadn't arrived, watched this outburst with interest, and for a moment it seemed as though they would come over and speak to Mr Chin, whose face was almost completely concealed by bandages, but the man from Singapore spoke to them instead. It was a terrible thing, he said, when your own cousin, a man as close as your brother, lost his reason; they agreed entirely, life was often terrible.

They watched the minibus out of sight and waited about for a bit longer because someone was sure there was another plane that day, but he was wrong; this had been the last one. Then they went back to their car - a station-wagon with curtains drawn over the rear windows - and drove, thoughtfully back towards Rawalpindi.

None of them said very, much on the way; they were all thinking about a radio call they had to make that night, about an old man who lay in a cane chair, a glass of rice wine at his elbow, a man on whose whim their lives could depend.

Love heard about this later; at the time all he wanted was to be away. He and the Nawab spent two days at the Nawab's winter palace in Lahore, then flew back to London; their tickets had been booked for them by the local representatives of a London firm, the Belvedere Trading Co., also with offices in Covent Garden, in the names of Mr. Pickard and Mr Mahomed.

Now, back in MacGillivray's office, all this seemed so remote, so unreal that Love wondered whether any of it had ever happened.

'Never thought I'd come to see *you* here again,' he told MacGillivray, not entirely joking. 'Not after what I've been through. It's against my religious principles.'

He grinned; MacGillivray handed round his box of cheroots.

'Well,' said Love expectantly, looking from one to the other. 'I've heard bits and pieces so far, but not the whole thing.'

'Life is all bits and pieces,' said MacGillivray pontifically. 'You never hear the whole thing. Ever.

'I won't bore you with the politics of it, Doctor,' he went on. 'But the Chinese, as you may know, still follow the Stalin line of Communism, simply because Mao Tse-tung learned all he knows from Stalin. Like Albania, they just don't jell with the present rulers in Russia, who have got over this phase of Communism and who tend to something a little more liberal. Maybe the Chinese will, too, in ten or twenty years, but right now, so far as they are concerned, life is real, life is earnest and the more earnest they can make it, the better.

'What they need most of all as an independent Communist country - if you ever could have such a contradiction - is their own Intelligence system, that can feed their rulers with the information they ask for - and not just what the Russians will let them have or think they need.

'But you can't have an international spy network nowadays unless you've got a great deal of negotiable currency in all sorts of countries. You have to pay for information, and sometimes the price comes high. Now the Chinese have very little foreign exchange, and what they have is being used. There is nothing to spare for an enterprise on this scale with permanent agents and cover organizations and so forth. Also, because they are Chinese, they're very easily identifiable, they are remembered, remarked on, so anything they've tried of this kind before has been run by intermediaries - Westerners who do the actual spying, the copying of documents and formulae and orders of battle and so forth, and then sell them. This is the most expensive way of gathering information for you've got to pay for *every* scrap - useful or not - or else you risk losing your contact.

'Then someone - one of Mao's own contemporaries, an old, ailing character, a descendant of some Chinese poet, hit on the idea of blackmailing a number of very rich men in the East, to raise money to finance a proper Intelligence scheme.

'They would threaten these rich men that unless they paid over a minimum sum of £500,000 or more - in the Nawab's case it was £2,000,000 - and he was the last on their list - their children's sight would be affected. They set up a cover to accept the money in Switzerland - the International Committee for the Preservation of Big Game.

'They decided they could carry out their threats at long range and with very little risk by using portable lasers. They needed no direct contact for this. There would be no link to involve them, and consequently, a minimal chance of discovery. And having this cover in Geneva meant that any money they collected would be negotiable anywhere in the world.'

'But if they'd got away with this scheme, as apparently they very nearly did - how would it work?' asked Love. 'Surely it would still be difficult for Chinese agents to appear to be anything but Chinese? Apart from having a lot more money, wouldn't they be conspicuous and suspect right away?'

'Yes and no, Doctor. What's the biggest change in all provincial towns in Britain now? Not only the skyscrapers and the supermarkets, but - Chinese restaurants! You're so used to them that if you see a Chinaman, you at once think he's a waiter off-duty - if you think anything about it at all. They're part of the accepted scene. There couldn't be a better cover for Chinese spies over the whole country - and in America and Canada and Australia - than an international chain of Chinese restaurants, all doing legitimate trade, but each with one or more trained agents attached to the staff.

'Say you sited one near an underwater weapons base, another near an experimental radar station, a third near the germ warfare labs, and so on. It would be as valuable as if we were allowed to run a chain of Olde Worlde Tea Shoppes right across China, and packed them with agents dressed as distressed gentlewomen waitresses. See what I'm getting at?'

'Perfectly,' said Love. But he didn't really. He only saw a part of the picture, perhaps not even the most important part. He saw Mercedes again, cold, hostile, bitter. The girl he had known and loved briefly in the rest house at Shahnagar had disappeared; this girl was not the same, would never be the same.

But then was he the same person, either? All these deaths: Ibrahim Khan, Bahadur, Ismail Beg, Cameron Ryan, plus others unknown, unseen, even unmet - and what had been achieved? A plan had been thwarted, changed, made to turn its course. But the delay was only temporary. There would be other plans, other people eager to mount them, equally careless of danger and death, believing they served a cause greater than the sum of all their lives. Twelve disciples had also believed that, long ago. But these people?

No one had won decisively, no one had lost; all that both sides, all anyone had gained, was time; to fight again, to live, to die another day.

Love drew his hand across his forehead, touched his wound; it still ached. He had known in Shahnagar that the elation would not last, for nothing lasts, nothing at all; after summer, winter always comes, but somehow he had told himself that this would be different; this wasn't like the others. Now he knew that it was. Now a part of the cold of the mountains had followed him here, would follow him everywhere, an icicle at his heart.

And what had he learned beyond the knowledge that he

knew so pitifully little? He had learned something he should have known years ago; that you couldn't live for ever in the clouds. Eventually you had to climb down to reality and leave the dream behind. And as you lost one more illusion, you realized with immeasurable sadness there were so very few left to lose.

A discreet knock on the door scattered his thoughts. MacGillivray's secretary came in carrying a tray. The cups, Love noted inconsequentially, were thick, white Ministry of Works issue; even the spoons had been stamped with the official crown. It all seemed so unbelievably official and drab and orthodox, like a visit to a local income tax office; the dusty furniture, the fawn walls, the brown-painted doors, now these cups. Had this impersonal room really any connection with what had happened in the Himalayas?

'How about Mercedes and her brother?' he asked for something to say, anything to break the depression of his thoughts.

'Very clever little scheme,' said MacGillivray admiringly; as a professional, he liked to praise the arrangements of other pros. The Communists played one against the other - and neither guessed what was happening.

'They told the girl she'd be helping her brother to escape if she played ball with them. And then they hypnotized the poor devil Ryan and sent him off to keep tabs on the Nawab. He had to report what information she gave him over the phone. They probably told him that if he went over to the West his sister would suffer. The irony was that they spoke to each other several times a week. He was so heavily hypnotized that he didn't recognize her voice. He hadn't spoken to her for sixteen years in any case, and she had not spoken to him at all since he was wounded, and didn't know how badly his voice had been affected.'

'And if they'd got away with this, what would have happened to them?'

MacGillivray shrugged; these were very naive questions. How easily one could tell the amateurs from the pros, the gentlemen from the players.

'I'd say an overdose of something. An air bubble in a vein. Something of that kind. They knew too much to be allowed to live, you see. They were expendable.'

'I see,' said Love again, but still he didn't see. He saw only one episode that had ended, one part of an iceberg, immense, and infinitely frightening; but an even greater, more dangerous part still lay submerged, hidden, unseen; but there.

'Of course, the Nawab's been very decent,' said MacGillivray approvingly. 'He's not taking it out on the girl. After all, she was only trying to help her brother. There wasn't any deceit in her - not as we term it, I mean. He's not keeping her on as a governess, naturally, but she'll get over it.

'She'll settle down somewhere. Canada or Australia, I think. Somewhere faraway. She's young.'

'Yes,' Love agreed, as though they were discussing someone he had never met; had never loved. 'You're quite right. She's young.

'All this money they must have collected. Who gets it now? What happens to it?'

'I'll tell you,' said MacGillivray, pouring the tea through a tarnished strainer, speaking like a lecturer who says 'That's a good question,' when someone in his audience queries what surely should be obvious. 'I'll tell you. Doctor. We can't break up the Committee, apparently - for legal reasons, of all things. It's a trust, or some such thing. And the people who've given money are so glad to be off the hook that they don't seem to miss it all that much, anyhow. They're all immensely rich. It's almost small change to them. So we're going to keep on with the Committee - only we'll see that it's run properly.

'We're using some of the money in Nairobi this month, as a matter of fact, to start a game reserve. Then we've plans for another in Natal. So you see it's going for a purpose the original big game preservation committee never imagined - actually to preserve big game!'

'I see,' said Love flatly. 'Is that all?'

'Not quite,' said the Nawab, leaning towards him. 'You remember my old Cord?'

Love nodded. He remembered it perfectly, could still see its blue, blunt coffin-nose, spattered with mud, sticking out through the trees by the edge of the bridge. Yes, he remembered it well.

The Nawab stroked his chin with one hand as though a little embarrassed about what he had to say.

'You told me how you'd lost your own Cord at Villars. I know what that meant to you. I'm not a car lover like you, and I felt it might be a good thing to give mine a change of place - after all, it's been in the same room for twenty-eight years!

'So, to cut a long story short, I've had it flown out to 'Pindi and put three good fitters on it. They're reconditioning it after our run; then I'm having it shipped over here.

'I'd like you to accept it with my best wishes - and my thanks. After all, you may have gone about curing my son in a round-about way, but you certainly succeeded. I had a cable this afternoon to say both eyes are vastly improved. No pain now at all.'

Suddenly they were both smiling, MacGillivray and the Nawab; and Love grinned with them. Everything was not always black, not all the time; nothing lasted for ever. And after the darkest night the sun would shine eventually. Maybe it was beginning to shine now. Maybe a whole lot of things.

'Now,' said MacGillivray briskly, 'what'll it be, Doctor? One lump or two?'

Stogumber, Somerset, England; Gilgit and Rawalpindi, Pakistan

ABOUT THE AUTHOR

James Leasor

James Leasor was one of the bestselling British authors of the second half of the 20th Century. He wrote over 50 books including a rich variety of thrillers, historical novels and biographies.

His works included the critically acclaimed The Red Fort, the story of the Indian Mutiny of 1957, The Marine from Mandalay, Boarding Party (made into the film The Sea Wolves starring Gregory Peck, David Niven and Roger Moore), The Plague and the Fire, and The One that Got Away (made into a film starring Hardy Kruger). He also wrote Passport to Oblivion (which sold over 4 million copies around the World and was filmed as Where the Spies Are, starring David Niven), the first of nine novels featuring Dr Jason Love, a Cord car owning Somerset GP called to aid Her Majesty's Secret Service in foreign countries, and another bestselling series about the Far Eastern merchant Robert Gunn in the 19th century. There were also sagas set in Africa and Asia, written under the pseudonym Andrew MacAllan, and tales narrated by an unnamed vintage car dealer in Belgravia, who drives a Jaguar SS100.

www.jamesleasor.com Follow on Twitter: @jamesleasor

BOOKS IN THIS SERIES

Dr Jason Love
The West Country doctor, vintage car expert - particularly the pre-War American classic, the Cord - and part time secret agent.

One of the best-selling thriller series from the 1960s through to the 1990s. Published in 19 languages.

Described by the Sunday Times as the "Heir Apparent to the golden throne of Bond"

Passport To Oblivion

Passport to Oblivion is the first case book of Dr. Jason Love ... country doctor turned secret agent. Multi-million selling, published in 19 languages around the world and filmed as Where the Spies Are starring David Niven.

'As K pushed his way through the glass doors of the Park Hotel, he realized instinctively why the two stumpy men were waiting by the reception desk. They had come to kill him. ...'

Who was K - and why should anyone kill him? Who was the bruised girl in Rome? Why did a refugee strangle his mistress in an hotel on the edge of the Arctic Circle? And why, in a small office above a wholesale fruiterers in Covent Garden, did a red-haired Scot sift through filing cabinets for the name of a man he knew in Burma twenty years ago? None of these questions might seem to concern Dr Jason Love, a country practitioner of Bishop's Combe, Somerset. But, in the end, they all do. Apart from his patients, Dr Love has apparently only two outside interests: his supercharged Cord roadster, and the occasional Judo lessons he gives to the local branch of the British Legion. But out of the past, to which all forgotten things should belong, a man comes to see him - and his simple, everyday country-life world is shattered like a mirror by a .38 bullet.

"Heir Apparent to the golden throne of Bond" The Sunday Times

Passport In Suspense

West German submarine 'Seehund' is hijacked during N.A.T.O. manoeuvres in the North Sea. Neo-Nazis want it for a daring operation; seeking out pockets of escaped war criminals in South America, they promise the elderly men free trips home under new identities if they will detonate three atomic devices at carefully positioned points on the sea bed. The subsequent chain reaction will then drastically affect the world's climate, turning both Britain and America into arctic wastelands.

Holidaying in the Bahamas, Dr. Jason Love witnesses at close range the shooting of a beautiful brunette in a speedboat. She had been mistaken for Israeli spy Shamara, assigned to investigate millionaire Paul V. Steyr. Blind and insane, Steyr is the mastermind behind the terrible neo-Nazi plot. Only Love, teamed with Shamara, can stop him...

'The action is supersonic throughout.'
The Guardian

'A superb example of modern thriller writing at its best'
Sunday Express

'Third of Dr Love's supercharged adventures... It starts in the sunshine of the Bahamas, swings rapidly by way of a brunette corpse into Mexico, and winds up in the yacht of a megalomaniac ex-Nazi... Action: non-stop: Tension: nail-biting'

Daily Express
'His ingenuity and daring are as marked as ever'
Birmingham Post

Passport For A Pilgrim

Dr Love's fourth supersonic adventure.

'Super suspense and, as usual, Love finds a way.'
Daily Express

'Bullets buzz like a beehive kicked by Bobby Charlton'
Sunday Mirror

'Action is driven along at a furious pace from the moment the doctor sets foot in Damascus.. a quite ferocious climax. Unputdownable.'
Sheffield Morning Telegraph

'Thriller rating: High'
The Sun

Love-All

Dr Jason Love's sixth case history of suspense. Attempted political assassination in the cauldron of Beirut, sees the doctor cum secret agent in a cliff-hanging mission to the Middle Eastern drug belt.

'Fans of Dr Jason Love will take special delight in this cliffhanger'

Daily Express

'Not only the best story about Jason Love but one of the most superbly action-crammed tales of the year'
Birmingham Evening Mail

Love And The Land Beyond

On vacation in the Algarve, with his precious Cord car, the country doctor, and occasional spy, Jason Love, accepts an invitation from a rich friend of a friend. This leads to a web of double-cross, murder and mystery, connecting deaths in Oregon and Portugal, in a race to secure smuggled vital secret formulas, against East Germans and the Mob.

Frozen Assets

Dr Jason Love, a West Country physician, is regarded as one of the world's experts on the pre-World War II American Cord car. With its long, coffin-nosed bonnet with two stainless steel exhaust pipes protruding on either side, its steeply raked split windscreen, front wheel drive, retractable headlights and integral construction, it is not so much a car as a personal statement. When an insurance company is asked to insure for 10 million pounds a Cord Roadster in Pakistan, it asks Dr Love to fly out and check why the car is worth so much.

What appears to be a routine trip becomes a nightmare.

The discovery of the body of an early traveller - preserved for centuries in an Afghanistan glacier — leads to a hunt to uncover deposits of rhodium, one of the world's rarest minerals. Its discovery could revolutionize Afghanistan's economic future — but can Love get there before the Russians?

'Splendid sit-up-all-night-to-finish fun' Sunday Telegraph

'The urbane man's James Bond makes a welcome return' Daily Express

Love Down Under

https://www.amazon.co.uk/dp/B08D7ST2MS/ref=as_sl_pc_qf_sp_asin_til?tag=jameleas-21&linkCode=w00&linkId=f45b2644f26d347355c802a4b27fb36d&creativeASIN=B08D7ST2MS

Before Jason Love - the West Country doctor with a passion for the 1930s American Cord car flies out to visit Charles Robinson, a fellow Cord enthusiast, in Cairns, Australia, someone in his Wiltshire village entrusts him with a straightforward mission: to find the Before Jason Love - the West Country doctor with a passion for the 1930s American truth behind a relation's mysterious drowning accident off Cairns.

But when he arrives down under, the simple enquiry rapidly leads to other, more disturbing questions: what is the fearful secret hidden in Robinson's past that has terrified him for years, and who are the shadowy figures he dreads will find him? Who is the man with metal hands who can see as well in darkness as by day, and why should a total stranger attempt to murder Dr Love on the top of Ayers Rock?

Jason Love, in his latest and most baffling case, must battle to find the answers to these and other questions as the wheels of suspense and surprise spin as fast as the tyres on his supercharged Cord.

'A mixture of Ambler, a touch of Graham Greene, mixed well with the elixir of Bond and Walter Mitty'
Los Angeles Times

Host Of Extras

The bawdy, wise-cracking owner of Aristo Autos is offered two immaculate vintage Rolls straight out of a collector's dream: one is a tourer, the other an Alpine. The cars, and Aristo, get in on a shady film deal which leads to a trip to Corsica with the imperturbable Dr Jason Love and the infinitely desirable Victoria - and to the cut and thrust of violent international skulduggery.

'... an entertaining and fast-moving adventure.' Daily Express

'It's all great fun and games, with plenty of revs.' Evening Standard

'... a clutch of thrills and sparks of wit.' The Yorkshire Post

BOOKS BY THIS AUTHOR

They Don't Make Them Like That Any More

They don't make them like that any more. Cars, that is. They don't, and they never will again. Which accounts for the enormous world-wide interest in old motors of every description, and the fantastic prices that they fetch. Behind this latest manifestation of the international antique trade, lies a strange and secret world, where dealers offer for sale cars they do not own, where rich collectors willingly pay thousands for some mechanical abortion that can barely drag itself up a hill without a following wind, simply because it's rare. Usually, hazards in this old-car business - as in any other - are run by the buyer. But there are also risks for those who sell – as the proprietor of Aristo Autos discovers. He deals exclusively in motoring exotica, and when he's unexpectedly offered one of the rarest cars of all, a supercharged Mercedes two-seater 540K, he buys it immediately. There's a clear two-and-a-half thousand quid profit for him in the deal. But soon he realises there's also a clear danger of death, for someone else desperately wants this car for some very special, private reason. Someone who will kill to get it. But who, and why? The only thing to do is to find out, and he does - travelling a sinister trail, blazed by old cars and young girls, that leads from London to Spain to Switzerland.

'Number one thriller on my list ...sexy and racy'
Sunday Mirror

'Devoured at a sitting... racy, pungent and swift'
The Sunday Times

'A racy tale ... the hero spends most of his time trying to get into beds and out of trouble ... plenty of action, anecdotes, and inside dope on exotic old cars'
Sunday Express

Mandarin-Gold

It was the year of 1833 when Robert Gunn arrived on the China coast. Only the feeblest of defenses now protected the vast and proud Chinese Empire from the ravenous greed of Western traders, and their opening wedge for conquest was the sale of forbidden opium to the native masses.
This was the path that Robert Gunn chose to follow... a path that led him through a maze of violence and intrigue, lust and treachery, to a height of power beyond most men's dreams — and to the ultimate depths of personal corruption.
Here is a magnificent novel of an age of plunder — and of a fearless freebooter who raped an empire.

'Highly absorbing account of the corruption of an individual during a particularly sordid era of British imperial history,' The Sunday Times

'James Leasor switches to the China Sea more than a century ago, and with pace and ingenuity tells, in novel form, how the China coast was forced to open up its riches to Englishmen, in face of the Emperor's justified hostility' Evening Standard

'In the nasty story of opium - European and American traders made fortunes taking the forbidden dope into nineteenth century China, and this novel tells the story of their deadly arrangements and of the Emperor's vain attempts to stop them. Mr. Leasor has researched the background carefully and the detail

of the Emperor's lavish court but weak administration is fascinating. The white traders are equally interesting characters, especially those two real-life merchants, Jardine and Matheson.'
Manchester Evening News

Most books by James Leasor are now available as ebook and in paperbacks. Please visit www.jamesleasor.com for details on all these books or contact info@jamesleasor.com for more information on availability.

Follow on Twitter: @jamesleasor for details on new releases.

Jason Love novels
Passport to Oblivion (filmed, and republished in paperback, as Where the Spies Are)
Passport to Peril (Published in the U.S. as Spylight)
Passport in Suspense (Published in the U.S. as The Yang Meridian)
Passport for a Pilgrim
A Week of Love
Love-all
Love and the Land Beyond
Frozen Assets
Love Down Under

Jason Love and Aristo Autos novel
Host of Extras

Aristo Autos novels
They Don't Make Them Like That Any More
Never Had A Spanner On Her

Robert Gunn Trilogy
Mandarin-Gold
The Chinese Widow
Jade Gate

Other novels
Not Such a Bad Day

The Strong Delusion
NTR: Nothing to Report
Follow the Drum
Ship of Gold
Tank of Serpents

Non-fiction
The Monday Story
Author by Profession
Wheels to Fortune
The Serjeant-Major; a biography of R.S.M. Ronald Brittain, M.B.E., Coldstream Guards
The Red Fort
The One That Got Away
The Millionth Chance: The Story of The R.101
War at the Top (published in the U.S. as The Clock With Four Hands)
Conspiracy of Silence
The Plague and the Fire
Rudolf Hess: The Uninvited Envoy
Singapore: the Battle that Changed the World
Green Beach
Boarding Party (filmed, and republished in paperback, as The Sea Wolves)
The Unknown Warrior (republished in paperback as X-Troop)
The Marine from Mandalay
Rhodes & Barnato: the Premier and the Prancer

As Andrew MacAllan (novels)
Succession
Generation
Diamond Hard
Fanfare
Speculator
Traders

As Max Halstock
Rats – The Story of a Dog Soldier

Printed in Great Britain
by Amazon